AN AMISH
SCHOOLROOM

AN AMISH SCHOOLROOM

THREE STORIES

AMY CLIPSTON
KATHLEEN FULLER
SHELLEY SHEPARD GRAY

ZONDERVAN

An Amish Schoolroom

A Class for Laurel Copyright © 2021 by Amy Clipston
A Lesson on Love Copyright © 2021 by Kathleen Fuller
Wendy's Twenty Reasons Copyright © 2021 by Shelley Shepard Gray

Requests for information should be addressed to:
Zondervan, *3900 Sparks Dr. SE, Grand Rapids, Michigan 49546*

ISBN 978-0-310-36584-6 (downloadable audio)

Library of Congress Cataloging-in-Publication Data
Names: Clipston, Amy. Class for Laurel. | Fuller, Kathleen. Lesson on love. | Gray, Shelley
 Shepard. Wendy's twenty reasons.
Title: An Amish schoolroom : three stories / Amy Clipston, Kathleen Fuller, Shelley
 Shepard Gray.
Description: Grand Rapids, Michigan : Zondervan, [2021] | Summary: "From three
 bestselling authors of Amish fiction come three charming stories of new school years
 and new romance"-- Provided by publisher.
Identifiers: LCCN 2021011899 (print) | LCCN 2021011900 (ebook) | ISBN
 9780310365822 (paperback) | ISBN 9780310365839 (epub) | ISBN 9780310365846
Subjects: LCSH: Amish--Fiction. | Christian fiction, American. | Romance fiction,
 American.
Classification: LCC PS648.A45 A55 2021 (print) | LCC PS648.A45 (ebook) | DDC
 813/.01083823--dc23
LC record available at https://lccn.loc.gov/2021011899
LC ebook record available at https://lccn.loc.gov/2021011900

Scripture quotations are taken from the *Holy Bible*, New Living Translation, copyright ©
1996, 2004, 2015 by Tyndale House Foundation. Used by permission of Tyndale House
Ministires, Carol Stream, Illinois 60188. All rights reserved.

Zondervan titles may be purchased in bulk for educational, business, fundraising, or sales
promotional use. For information, please email SpecialMarkets@Zondervan.com.

Printed in the United States of America

HB 10.03.2021

CONTENTS

A CLASS FOR LAUREL
BY AMY CLIPSTON

A LESSON ON LOVE
BY KATHLEEN FULLER

WENDY'S TWENTY REASONS
BY SHELLEY SHEPARD GRAY

CONTENTS

GLOSSARY

ach/ack: oh
appeditlich: delicious
Ausbund: Amish hymnal
bedauerlich: sad
bobbli/boppli: baby
bruder: brother
bruders: brothers
bruderskinner: nieces/nephews
bu: boy
Budget, The: Amish newspaper
buwe: boys
daadi: grandfather
daadihaus: small house provided for retired parents
daed/dat: dad

danke/danki: thank you

dawdi: grandfather

dochder: daughter

dochdern: daughters

doktah: doctor

dumm: dumb

Dummle!: Hurry!

Englisher/Englisch: non-Amish person

familye: family

frau: woman/wife

freind: friend

freinden: friends

froh: happy

gegisch: silly

geh: go

gern gschehne: you're welcome

grosskinner: grandchildren

Gude mariye: Good morning

gut: good

Gut nacht/naut: Good night

haus: house

Ich liebe dich: I love you

ja/jah: yes

kaffee/kaffi: coffee

kapp: prayer covering or cap

kinn: child

kinner: children

kocha: cook

kumm: come

liewe: love, a term of endearment

maed: young women, girls

maedel: young woman

mamm/mutter: mom

mammi: grandmother

mann: man/husband

matin: morning

mei: my

naerfich: nervous

naut: night

nee: no

nix: nothing

onkel: uncle

Ordnung, The: the written and unwritten rules of the Amish; the understood behavior by which the Amish are expected to live, passed down from generation to generation. Most Amish know the rules by heart.

schee: pretty

schmaert: smart

schoolhaus: schoolhouse

schtupp: family room

schweschder/schwester: sister

schweschdere: sisters

sehr: very

sohn: son

Was iss letz?: What's wrong?

Wie geht's: How do you do? or Good day!

GLOSSARY

wunderbaar: wonderful
ya: yes
yer: your
yung: young
zwillingbopplin: twins

A CLASS FOR LAUREL

AMY CLIPSTON

With love and appreciation for Maggie.
Your friendship is a blessing!

FEATURED CHARACTERS

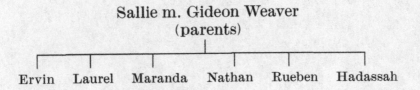

Sallie m. Gideon Weaver
(parents)

Ervin   Laurel   Maranda   Nathan   Rueben   Hadassah

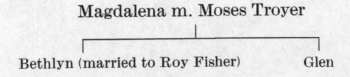

Magdalena m. Moses Troyer

Bethlyn (married to Roy Fisher)   Glen

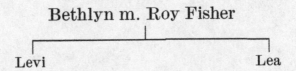

Bethlyn m. Roy Fisher

Levi   Lea

CHAPTER 1

LAUREL WEAVER FELT NERVOUS flutters in her stomach as the van bumped along the rock driveway. She rode past a sign announcing Troyers' Furniture and toward a large, brick building with solar panels angled on the roof. Behind it sat two log cabins, a barn, and two other buildings. One looked like a shed and the other a *daadihaus*.

She fingered the hem of her black apron as she took in her new home, and her mouth dried. Oh, how she hoped the Troyer family would approve of her and that the rest of the community would accept her.

Please, God, let me represent my home well and make the school board grateful they hired me as their teacher.

The driver, Rob, brought the van to a stop by the front porch. "Here we are," he said. "I'll get your suitcases for you."

"Thank you." Laurel climbed out of the passenger seat and brushed her hands down her apron before making sure her prayer covering was positioned just right on her head.

She took in the gorgeous purple mountain range topped with snow in the distance. Monte Vista, Colorado, was beautiful and so different from her home in Bird-in-Hand, Pennsylvania.

The mid-August, late afternoon sun warmed her cheeks as she turned toward the house. Just then, the storm door opened, and a petite woman who looked to be in her early- to mid-fifties came down the steps toward her. Her light-brown hair peeked out from under her prayer covering, which was more cone-shaped than Laurel's traditional Pennsylvania heart-shaped one. Also, she wore a blue dress and an apron that tied at her waist instead of one like Laurel's full-body apron.

"You must be Magdalena." Laurel rushed over and shook her hand. "I'm Laurel Weaver. I've never been out West. The mountains are so *schee*." Laurel gestured toward the horizon. "I'm so grateful to be here."

Magdalena smiled. "And we're *froh* to have you here." She looked past Laurel to Rob. "Hi, Rob. Thank you for picking up Laurel from the train station."

"You're welcome." Rob glanced at Laurel. "I'll carry the bags if you lead the way."

"Lovely." Magdalena turned to Laurel. "Would you like to see your *haus*?"

"*Ya*. Please." Laurel followed Magdalena behind the

main house with Rob in tow. "How far is the schoolhouse from here?"

"Just up the road. It's a quick walk."

"Oh *gut*. So I'm guessing your husband makes furniture?" She pointed to the large building with the sign on it.

"*Ya*, he works with our *sohn* and our son-in-law. They make bedroom suites, dining room tables, china cabinets, end tables, and the like." Magdalena pointed toward the building. "That's the showroom and the workshop."

"I've never seen solar panels on an Amish building before. How do the men use them?"

"Oh, the panels power the air compressors, which, in turn, power their tools."

"How interesting!"

Then Magdalena pointed to another large building. "That's a supply shed." She pointed toward the barn. "And the barn and stable." She indicated the other log cabin and said, "*Mei dochder* and her family live there."

"I love your log cabins. I've never seen one before."

"*Danki*." Magdalena nodded her head toward the small, one-level brick house. "And here is the *daadihaus*. My mother-in-law decided to move in with *mei dochder*, Bethlyn, to help her with the *kinner* after my father-in-law died, so it's been empty for a few years. We cleaned it for you."

Laurel followed her up the steps, where two rocking chairs sat side by side on the porch. Cheerful flowers smiled over from a nearby garden. "It's lovely."

Magdalena unlocked the front door and pushed it open.

Rob set the two suitcases down right inside the door. "Is there anything else you need?"

"No, thank you," Magdalena said.

Rob turned to Laurel. "I hope you enjoy your time here."

"I'm sure I will."

As Rob headed back toward his van, Laurel stepped into the small living room and glanced around at the little kitchen area with one counter, a few cabinets, a stove, and a refrigerator.

Magdalena opened the refrigerator. "I bought you some groceries. There's milk, eggs, bread, cereal, pasta, and some meat. There are spices in the cabinet there too."

"*Danki.* That's so generous."

"*Gern gschehne.* You can use our driver to go to town for more groceries. There's also a store within walking distance if you want to go on a nice day." Magdalena moved toward a doorway. "In here's a small utility room with cleaning supplies and a wringer washer." She pointed to another door. "And there's a line out back to hang your laundry."

Laurel took it all in. "Just wonderful," she said.

"The bedroom and bathroom are back here." Magdalena led her through the small family room to the bedroom, which included one little closet, two dressers, and a double bed. "The bathroom is right here."

Laurel peeked into the small bathroom.

"I'm making supper now. Why don't you get settled and then come over around six?"

"*Danki*. I look forward to meeting the rest of your family. You mentioned that you have a *sohn* and a *dochder*, right?" Laurel asked.

"*Ya*."

"I have five siblings. I'm the second oldest." Laurel thought of her family, and her heart clenched. "May I use your phone to let my parents know I arrived?"

"Of course. The phone is in the workshop." Magdalena steered Laurel back toward the large building with the signage on the front.

They walked in the side door, and the smell of wood and stain filled Laurel's senses as they moved past toolboxes, workbenches, piles of wood, and furniture. A hammer banged and an air compressor hummed, and she spotted two men working on furniture. One had his back to her, and she could only see his sandy, light-brown hair.

The other man turned and gave her a smile and nod. He had dark-brown, wavy hair and a dark-brown beard. His eyes were dark blue, and he was fit with a trim waist. Laurel guessed he was shorter than her older brother, Ervin.

Magdalena led her into an office, where a man sat at a desk, which was peppered with papers, books, and catalogs. The room also included a few chairs and filing cabinets.

The man gazed up at her and stood. With his light-brown hair and matching beard sprinkled with gray, he looked to be in his mid-fifties. He had a wide smile, hazel eyes, a prominent nose, and a rotund middle. "You must be Laurel. I'm Moses. Welcome!"

11

Laurel reached over and shook his hand. "It's so nice to meet you."

"How was your trip?"

"*Gut. Danki.* It was just long. I'd never been on a train before."

"We're glad you're here," Moses said.

Magdalena pointed to the phone. "Laurel wanted to use the phone to call her family."

"Oh, of course." Moses came around the desk. "Take your time."

"*Danki.*"

Moses and Magdalena walked out to the shop while Laurel sat down at the desk and dialed the number for her family's farm. As the phone rang, she envisioned her mother and father rushing toward the large, red dairy barn to answer it. She closed her eyes and imagined their large, white farmhouse with the wraparound porch and the vast, green pasture. Her chest constricted once again.

"Hello?" Her father's voice sounded through the line.

"*Dat!*" Laurel nearly yelled into the phone.

"Laurel, I've been waiting for your call. How are you?"

"I'm fine. I just got here." She sank back into the desk chair.

"How was the trip?"

"*Gut.* Long." She cupped her hand to her mouth to cover a yawn. "I'm just really tired. It was difficult trying to sleep sitting up in the seat."

"Have you met the family?"

"Just the *mamm* and *dat* so far—Magdalena and Moses. Their *dochder* and her family live here too. The men make furniture, like bedroom suites and curio cabinets. And the *daadihaus* where I'll be living is so lovely. How is everyone?" Laurel's heart twisted as she thought of how much she already missed her family.

"Everyone is fine. They told me to tell you that they send their love."

"Oh." She frowned. "I was hoping to talk to *Mamm* and everyone."

"It's after dinner here. Your *mamm* has Hadassah in the bath getting her ready for bed.

"Right." She rubbed her forehead. "I forgot the time difference."

"Maybe you can call earlier next time?"

"Of course." She sat up straight. "Well, tell everyone I love them."

"I will. *Ich liebe dich.*"

"I love you too, *Dat. Gut nacht.*"

"*Gut nacht,*" he said before the line went dead.

Laurel hung up the phone and then pushed herself up from the chair. She walked out to the shop where Magdalena and Moses stood. The other two men had left.

"*Danki* for letting me use the phone," Laurel told Moses.

"You're welcome to use it any time. I'll see you at supper," Moses said.

"Come in at six," Magdalena reminded her before they walked out of the shop together.

"I'll go unpack and freshen up," Laurel told Magdalena.

Laurel made her way back to the *daadihaus*. She glanced around the little space as the silence crept in, and she rubbed her hands together. Having a place she could call her own was a new thrill, and she couldn't wait to see more of this new community as well as her new schoolhouse.

She unpacked her clothes, hanging her dresses and aprons in the closet and stashing her undergarments and stockings in the dresser. Then she washed her face and changed into a fresh dress and apron.

Soon it was a few minutes to six, and she couldn't wait any longer to meet the rest of the Troyer family. She ambled past the row of barns to the back of the main house, where she hurried up the back porch steps and then knocked on the door.

She heard female voices in the kitchen, and then the back door opened, revealing a petite woman with light-brown hair and the same sky-blue eyes as Magdalena. She looked to be in her late twenties or early thirties.

"Hi, I'm Laurel. You must be Magdalena's *dochder*."

"I'm Bethlyn." She pushed the door open. "It's nice to meet you."

"*Danki.*" Laurel followed her into the kitchen, where the smell of meatloaf made her stomach gurgle, reminding her that she hadn't eaten for more than six hours.

Magdalena worked at the counter mixing together a salad while an elderly woman with gray hair, hazel eyes, a wide smile, and wire-rimmed glasses gathered up drinking glasses and carried them to the table.

Laurel walked over to her and held out her hand. "Hello, I'm Laurel."

"We've been looking forward to your arrival," the elderly woman said as she gave Laurel's hand a gentle squeeze. "I'm Dorothea."

"This is my mother-in-law," Magdalena explained as she set the bowl of salad onto the long oak table.

"How nice that you live here," Laurel said. "Both of my grandparents live nearly an hour away from my family, so I never got to see them much." She turned to where Bethlyn had started setting the table. "May I help you?"

"*Ya*, please." Bethlyn handed her a stack of plates.

Laurel took the dishes and set the table for nine. She looked over at Bethlyn, who was gathering utensils. "Magdalena mentioned that you have *kinner*. Do they go to school?"

"They'll be in first grade. They're in the *schtupp* reading books." Bethlyn stuck her head in the doorway. "Levi! Lea! Come meet Teacher Laurel."

"*Zwillingbopplin!*" Laurel grinned as they scampered into the kitchen. With their light-brown hair and blue eyes, the children resembled their mother.

"I made you a present." Lea grinned up at her, and with her missing front tooth, she had an adorable smile. She handed Laurel a piece of paper with a picture drawn in colorful crayons. "That's you, me, and Levi at the school." She pointed out the schoolhouse and the three figures standing by it.

Laurel clucked her tongue as warmth filtered through her. "Oh my goodness, Lea. This is so *schee. Danki!*"

Lea's smile widened.

"She likes to draw all the time," Levi said.

"And what do you like to do?" Laurel asked.

Levi scrunched his nose and looked up at the ceiling. "I like to go fishing with *mei onkel* Glen."

"That sounds fun."

"Maybe you can go with us sometime," Levi said.

"I would love that." Laurel turned toward the counter. "I'm going to put your drawing up here so it doesn't get ruined, Lea."

"Wash up, *kinner*. Your *daadi*, *dat*, and *onkel* will be coming in very soon." Bethlyn set out the utensils.

Laurel found a pitcher of water in the refrigerator and filled the glasses while Bethlyn set out napkins and bowls for the salad, and Dorothea brought a bottle of homemade dressing to the table. Magdalena pulled a large pan of meatloaf and a dish of baked potatoes out of the oven while Bethlyn spooned green beans from a pot on the stove into the serving bowl.

They had the meal served just as Moses and the man she'd seen earlier walked into the kitchen.

Magdalena turned toward the men. "You met Moses earlier, and you saw my son-in-law, Roy."

Both men turned toward Laurel and nodded their hellos.

"Where's Glen?" Magdalena asked.

"He was finishing a project," Moses said as he dried his hands. "He'll be in shortly."

The men finished cleaning themselves up and then moved

toward the table. Moses sat at one end while Roy took a seat beside him.

"Let's go ahead and eat. Glen can join us later," Moses announced.

"Teacher Laurel! Sit by me." Lea patted a seat next to her.

"I'd love to." Laurel took a spot between the twins while Magdalena sat at the other end of the table, and Bethlyn sat between her husband and the end seat.

After a silent prayer, they began to pass around the meatloaf, baked potatoes, salad, and green beans. Soon their utensils were scraping the dishes as they ate.

"Oh, Magdalena, this meatloaf is *appeditlich*," Laurel told her.

Magdalena nodded. *"Danki."*

"You have to give me the recipe. *Mei mammi* has a recipe with barbecue sauce. Have you ever had barbecued meatloaf?"

Magdalena shook her head.

"It's so *gut*. I brought her cookbook with me. I'll have to write down the recipe for you."

Magdalena gave a slight nod. *"Danki."*

The back door opened, and footsteps sounded from the mudroom before a young man with sandy light-brown hair hurried into the kitchen and crossed to the sink.

"I'm sorry I'm late. I was just trying to finish up a dresser," he said as he scrubbed his hands. He craned his neck over his shoulder, and his gaze landed on Laurel. "Hi. I'm Glen."

Laurel was so struck by his handsome face she could barely manage a reply. "Hi," she finally spluttered.

He was the most attractive man she'd ever seen with his perfectly proportioned nose, high cheek bones, and warm smile. His face was tan as if he had spent a lot of time out in the sun, and his green eyes reminded her of her father's lush pasture in the spring.

"This is our *sohn*," Magdalena announced.

Glen dried his hands and then walked over and took a seat beside his sister.

"We had a rush order of a bedroom suite, and I had to get the dresser stained." He bowed his head in silent prayer.

Laurel ate a few more bites of meatloaf and tried not to stare at Glen.

"How was your trip, Laurel?" Roy asked.

"*Gut.*" Laurel forked more meatloaf. "It was exciting to see so many states, and I had never been on a train before. That was an adventure." She divided a look between Roy and Bethlyn. "I appreciate that you and the other parents on the school board agreed to offer me the job. I promise I'll work hard and do my best not to let you down."

Roy swallowed some green beans and then wiped his dark beard with a napkin. "We were grateful that you applied. Not many *maed* responded."

"I was thrilled at the opportunity to come out and see another community. It's so different from back home in Pennsylvania. Have you ever been to Lancaster County?"

They all shook their heads.

"Oh, it's mostly farmland. *Mei dat* is a dairy farmer. You don't have any dairy farmers around here, do you?" she asked.

"No," Moses said.

"A farm is so much work, but I'm sure making furniture is a lot of work as well." Laurel glanced around the table and found everyone watching her with something that resembled curiosity. She smiled as heat crawled up her neck.

"You're right, Laurel. We work very hard." Glen's expression was friendly. "But we love what we do, right, *Dat*? Right, Roy?"

"*Ya*, we do," Moses agreed.

Laurel ate more meatloaf. "I can't wait to see the schoolhouse. Also, do you know if I will have an assistant?"

Bethlyn lifted her glass of water. "*Ya*, her name is Rena Ebersol, and she's eighteen. She's a brand-new teacher."

For the remainder of the meal, Laurel and Bethlyn discussed the school. When Laurel found Glen watching her, she hoped she wasn't blushing.

After supper, they enjoyed a chocolate pie before Laurel helped the women clean up the kitchen. Afterward, the women walked out to the porch, where the men and the twins sat.

"*Danki* so much for the *appeditlich* meal." Laurel shook Magdalena's hand.

"Oh, I almost forgot." Bethlyn reached into her apron pocket and pulled out a key ring containing one key. "This is for the schoolhouse. I thought you might want to go there tomorrow and start setting up."

"That would be perfect." Excitement coursed through Laurel as she slipped the key into her apron pocket next to the picture Lea had drawn for her.

"I can take you first thing tomorrow morning before I start work."

Laurel pivoted to face Glen as he smiled over at her from the porch swing. *"Danki."*

"Gern gschehne. I'll be there bright and early," he promised. "How about eight?"

"Okay." Laurel turned back to Magdalena. *"Danki* again for supper."

"Gern gschehne," Magdalena said.

Lea rushed over and hugged Laurel's waist. "I'll see you tomorrow."

"I look forward to it." Laurel touched Lea's nose, waved to the rest of the Troyer family, and then pulled her small flashlight out of her pocket before heading to the *daadihaus*.

Once inside, she set the flashlight on the kitchen counter and placed the picture Lea had drawn beside it, along with the key.

After taking a shower, she pulled on her nightgown and brushed out her waist-length blond hair before climbing into the double bed. Then she stared up through the darkness toward the ceiling as visions of her family flickered through her mind. She tried to ignore the loneliness that crept in, and instead, she opened her heart to God.

"Lord," she whispered, *"danki* for bringing me to

Colorado safely. Help me be the best teacher I can for the community. Please help me find *freinden* and a place here. And let my family know I love and miss them."

Then she closed her eyes and waited for sleep to find her.

CHAPTER 2

THE SMELL OF PANCAKES, sausage, and coffee permeated Glen's nostrils as he jogged down the stairs and into the kitchen the following morning.

"*Gude mariye*," he said as he sat down at the kitchen table and took in the appetizing meal set out in the center.

His parents repeated the greeting before they bowed their heads in silent prayer. Then they began to fill their plates with the delicious food.

Glen drenched his pancakes in butter and syrup before digging in. "Everything looks fantastic, *Mamm*."

"*Danki*," she said.

"It is." *Dat* picked up his mug of coffee. "We have a busy day ahead of us, Glen. That bedroom suite will be picked up this afternoon."

"I'm almost done with the dressers and nightstands. Then

I'll start on that curio." Glen ate a bite of sausage and picked up his mug of coffee.

"You need to take Laurel to the schoolhouse before you get started," *Mamm* reminded him.

"I know." Glen worked to keep his smile at bay.

The truth was that he couldn't wait to see Laurel and walk to the schoolhouse with her. He'd spent the evening thinking of her. With her hair the color of sunshine, intelligent blue-green eyes, pink lips, and high cheekbones, she was beautiful, but she also had a sweet way about her that intrigued him.

"That *maedel* is a chatterbox," *Mamm* continued with a dramatic wave of her hand. "She's very excited to be here."

"I think she's nice." Glen set his mug on the table. In fact, he loved how she wasn't afraid to talk. So many of the young women in his youth group were shy, but Laurel was the opposite, which fascinated him. He wanted to hear what she had to say.

Mamm nodded. "She seems very sweet."

"*Ya*, she is." *Dat* cut up his pancakes. "It must be difficult for her to have left her family. You heard her say that she's never been outside of Pennsylvania, and she's so young."

"How old is she?" Glen asked.

"Twenty."

He nodded. So, she was three years younger than he was.

"Make it quick when you take her to the schoolhouse," *Dat* said. "We have a lot to do today." His father continued to discuss work while they finished breakfast.

23

After carrying his dish to the counter and then running upstairs to brush his teeth, Glen hurried down the short path to the *daadihaus* and knocked on the door.

"Just a minute!" Laurel's voice sounded from somewhere inside.

Glen glanced out toward his sister's house and imagined Bethlyn and her family enjoying their breakfast.

The door swung open, revealing Laurel in a turquoise dress that complemented her eyes, along with a black apron.

She looked up at him and gave an embarrassed smile. "I'm so sorry. I was so exhausted last night that I overslept. Come in."

He followed her into the family room, and the aroma of coffee wafted over him as she walked to the table in the small kitchen, where a half-eaten scrambled egg sat on the plate.

She picked up the plate and carried it toward the sink. "I thought I had set my alarm, but I guess I didn't."

"You can finish eating, if you like," he told her.

Her light eyebrows lifted. "You sure?"

"Of course."

"*Danki.*" She sat down and scooted her chair closer to the table. "I guess the *haus* was too quiet. *Mei haus* in Pennsylvania is always noisy, but I'm sure I'll get used to it."

He sat down across from her and rested his elbows on the hardwood. "The time change probably affected you too."

"*Ya.*" She swallowed some egg and then pointed her fork at him. "I hadn't thought of that."

"So, you have five siblings?"

She nodded as she sipped her coffee. "*Ya*. Ervin is twenty-two. I'm twenty. Maranda is eighteen, Nathan is fifteen, Rueben is twelve, and Hadassah is eight."

"I'm sure your *haus* is much louder than mine."

"Meals are always an adventure with everyone talking over everyone else." She finished the egg and then gathered up her plate, utensils, and mug. "How old are you?" she asked over her shoulder while she washed them at the sink.

"Twenty-three."

"I thought you were older than I am."

He walked over to the counter and leaned against it. She was a few inches shorter than he was but taller than his mother and sister. "So, your *dat* is a dairy farmer?"

"That's right." She graced him with another pretty smile as she set her dish on the drying rack. "And you're a carpenter."

"*Ya*, I am. *Mei daadi* passed the business down to *mei dat*. Roy's *bruder* inherited his *dat*'s bulk food store, so Roy decided to join our company. He had learned some carpentry skills from his *daadi*, so we just trained him on what we build."

"*Mei onkel* Ivan is a carpenter, but he makes outdoor furniture. He sells things like picnic tables, windmills, light-houses, benches, gliders, and rocking chairs. I have five cousins who work for him." She continued talking as she dried and stowed the dish, utensils, and mug. "They're all really *gut* carpenters. You are too. I saw the furniture when

I used the phone. I'd love for you to show me what you've made."

"I'll have to give you a tour."

"I can't wait." She jammed her thumb toward the bathroom. "I need to brush my teeth. Is that all right?"

"Take your time." He walked over to the front windows and glanced outside just as Roy walked from his house to the workshop. He imagined Roy listening while *Dat* gave him his instructions for the day, even though Roy already knew what needed to be done. *Dat* liked to be in charge, which Glen understood. After all, it was his business, and their reputation was on the line with every piece of furniture they created.

He heard footsteps behind him, and Laurel appeared with a large, overstuffed tote balanced on her slight shoulder.

He held his hand out. "Let me carry that for you."

"*Danki.* It's so heavy." She handed him the tote and then continued on to the kitchen and picked up a lunch bag. "I'm bringing all of my supplies so I can get organized." She walked to where he stood by the door. Then they started out together and down the porch steps.

"Did you teach in Pennsylvania?" he asked as they continued down the path, past the workshop and his parents' house.

"*Ya,* I've been teaching since I was eighteen. I just love it. It's so fun to get to know the *kinner* and watch them learn. There's nothing more satisfying than when a scholar figures out how to read or how to do a math problem after struggling."

He smiled at her, impressed by her passion for teaching. "That must be a sight to behold."

"Oh, it is. I had a *bu* in class last year who really struggled with reading, but he never gave up. I remember the day when he read his first word. Oh, the joy in his eyes." She beamed. "It was just so *wunderbaar*. I could see God working with him."

He nodded as they turned onto the road and started up the hill toward the school.

"What do you like to do for fun, Glen?"

"I like spending time outdoors, mostly. I like to hike, fish, and hunt."

"That must be why you're so tan."

He chuckled. "*Ya*, I suppose so."

"Levi told me that you take him fishing."

"*Ya*. Do you like to fish?"

She shrugged. "I haven't been in a few years, but it sounds fun."

"What do you do with your youth group?"

"We play a lot of volleyball."

"We do too."

They chatted easily until Glen pointed to the small brick building that sat beyond a fence, along with a swing set and a large field where he recalled playing softball during recess. "And there's your schoolhouse, Laurel."

Her smile widened. "I can't wait to get started. Bethlyn mentioned while we were doing dishes last night that I have a meeting with the school board tomorrow. I have so much to do."

They walked up the front steps, and she unlocked the door. He followed her into the large, open room with the rows of desks that brought back memories of his time in school. A blackboard that spanned the front of the room hung behind the long desk where his teacher had once sat.

"I was going to make a giant tree and then decorate it with all of the students' names on the leaves for fall. I'll have them all find their names." She pointed to a section of the wall. "I think I'll hang it over there. Bethlyn said she'll give me a list of names tonight, but I can get started without them."

She set her lunch box on the desk and then began looking through shelves stocked with supplies.

"You like to draw?" Glen asked, unable to take his eyes off her.

"Oh, very much. I love to draw nature scenes."

"How nice. I look forward to seeing your drawings. Here's your bag." He set the tote bag on the desk. "And I guess I'll leave you to it. Have a *gut* day." He nodded and then ambled toward the door.

"Glen?"

He spun to face her. "*Ya?*"

"Is there a church service this Sunday?"

"*Ya*, there is. Would you like to ride with me?"

"I'd love to."

"Great. See you later, Laurel." He waved and then hurried out the door and down the steps toward the road. He looked over at the playground and imagined Laurel standing there surrounded by children during recess. Surely the children would adore her sweet personality. She seemed to have the perfect temperament for teaching.

He shook his head and recalled how she had talked about her family and her life back home in Pennsylvania. Although he'd just met her, he couldn't remember the last time he'd met a *maedel* that he wanted to get to know so quickly.

Thoughts of Laurel continued to swirl through his mind as he continued down the road toward home. He walked into the shop and through the showroom, past the bedroom suites, dining tables with matching chairs, curio cabinets, china cabinets, and end tables.

Glen stepped into the workshop, where hammers banged, saw blades whirred, and air compressors hummed. The familiar and comforting scent of wood and stain hung in the air.

Dat walked over to Glen's work area. "How did it go at the schoolhouse?"

"It went well. Laurel is excited to start teaching."

"I'm glad to hear it."

Glen pointed to the nightstands in his work area. "Should I get started on the second coat of stain for these?"

"*Gut* plan. Call me if you need me." *Dat* turned and headed back to his work area.

As Glen turned his attention to his work, thoughts of Laurel lingered in the back of his mind. He couldn't wait to see her again.

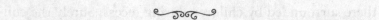

Laurel climbed into Glen's buggy Sunday morning. "*Gude mariye.* I never had a chance to talk to you yesterday. How was your day?"

"*Gut.*" He looked so handsome in his Sunday black-and-white suit as he guided the horse down the driveway. "I finished up a project at the shop and then helped *mei dat* with some chores. How about you?"

"I went grocery shopping and got the *haus* organized. Then I worked in the schoolroom all afternoon. Rena Ebersol, my assistant, came too. We hit it off right away. She loved my idea of putting all of the *kinner's* names on leaves and putting them on the tree. I'm also going to draw a farm scene and tell the scholars about my home in Pennsylvania. You should come by and see it."

He smiled over at her. "I will."

"I'm so glad I met Rena because now I have someone to sit with at church. Sitting with strangers can be intimidating."

"Really?" He gave her a sideways glance. "I have a feeling you've never met a stranger."

She angled her body toward him. "What do you mean?"

"You're so outgoing that I assumed you make *freinden* wherever you go."

"Well, I do get *naerfich* when I meet new people."

He scoffed. "You're kidding, right? You seem completely at ease."

"I'm glad it seems that way to you."

"Did you get to talk to your family?"

"I called yesterday, and I talked to my parents and almost all of my siblings. Ervin was out on a supply run, but I got to talk to everyone else, including my baby *schweschder*. She's excited to start school next week." Laurel's heart turned over as she recalled Hadassah's little voice. "Your niece reminds me of her."

"Really?"

"*Ya*, she's so sweet and outgoing, and she loves to draw. Hadassah likes to draw pictures too."

"Did she get that from you?"

"Maybe." She studied his handsome profile. "What's your favorite piece of furniture to make?"

He tilted his head. "I haven't really thought about it, but I guess maybe it's dressers. I like making triple dressers with the shelves and mirror on top."

"Why's that?"

"I don't know." He looked sheepish. "It's just fun to create the little patterns in the wood and the shelves."

"What is your least favorite piece to make?"

"I really don't dislike any pieces, but end tables aren't very exciting. At least the ones that are plain."

"So you like being artistic and adding patterns in the wood."

"Right."

They continued talking about his work, and she silently marveled at how comfortably conversation flowed between them. She'd never met a man who was as outgoing and easy to talk to—and he seemed to appreciate the same quality in her as well.

Her hands began to tremble when they arrived at the Zook family's farm where the service was being held today. Now she would meet the members of her new community. She hoped and prayed they would accept her.

Glen halted the horse and then faced her. "Are you ready?"

She plastered a smile on her face. "As ready as I'll ever be. Rena said she'd look for me, so I'll be fine."

"*Gut.* I'll see you after the service."

She climbed out of his buggy and headed toward a group of young women standing next to a large red barn. When she spotted Rena among the women, Laurel quickened her steps.

At eighteen, Rena had dark hair and dark eyes, and she was tall and thin with a long nose and sweet smile.

"Laurel!" Rena called, walking toward her. "Come meet *mei freinden.*" She took Laurel by the elbow and brought her into the center of the group. "Everyone, this is Laurel, the new teacher." Rena introduced Laurel to the half-dozen young women one at a time.

Soon it was nine o'clock, and Laurel walked with Rena and her friends into the barn. They took their seats in the unmarried women's section of the congregation.

Laurel picked up her copy of the *Ausbund* and turned to the opening hymn. She scanned the sea of unfamiliar faces, and a twinge of longing moved through her. Though she was thrilled for this new adventure in her life, she missed her family, her home congregation, and her friends. But teaching in Monte Vista was the opportunity of a lifetime, and Laurel resolved not to allow her homesickness to ruin it.

She sat up straight and looked across the barn to where Glen spoke to a man Laurel hadn't met. He looked to be about Glen's age with reddish-brown hair and a round face. Glen grinned at something the man said, then turned his head and found Laurel's gaze.

When their eyes met, Laurel's heart did a little flip. He nodded at her, and she bobbed her head in recognition before turning her attention back to the hymnal.

The song leader began singing the first part of the verse, and Laurel and the congregation joined in. While she sang, she considered her budding friendships with Glen and Rena. As long as she had a friend or two, she could make it in this new community.

"So, that's Laurel." Jerome Esch, Glen's best friend since first grade, sat across from him at lunch after the service. "She's *schee*."

"She is, and she's sweet and funny." Glen lifted his cup of coffee.

Jerome raised his eyebrows. "You like her."

"Sure I do. She's different from the *maed* here."

"How so?"

"She's not shy and she likes to talk. *Mei mamm* called her a chatterbox, but I find it endearing." Glen looked over to where Laurel talked to an elderly man while filling his coffee cup. She looked pretty today in a pink dress with a white apron that was the length of the dress, unlike the aprons the women wore in his community that tied at the waist.

"You should invite her to come with us this afternoon when we get together to play volleyball."

"I was already planning to do that. I think she'll enjoy meeting some more folks in the community, and it will give me a chance to get to know her better." Glen tilted his head as he looked at his best friend. "What about you and Faith? Have you talked to her *dat* yet?"

Jerome shook his head. "Not yet, but I'll get around to it."

"By the time you get around to it, she may have moved on to someone else."

He grimaced. "I'm just not ready."

"What are you waiting for? You've known her since we all started first grade together."

"But this is different. Becoming more than *freinden* is a process. We're still getting to know each other."

Glen rolled his eyes. "For months now you've been talking about asking her *dat* for permission to date her."

"I'll do it when the time is right."

Glen shook his head. "If you wait too long . . . ."

"I know." Jerome nodded behind Glen. "Look at that. Laurel and Faith are talking."

Glen peeked behind him and spotted Faith, a petite redhead with a smattering of freckles across her little nose, smiling and nodding as Laurel talked to her. He imagined Laurel sharing stories about her community back in Pennsylvania. Faith looked interested as she smiled and laughed at something Laurel said.

"Wouldn't it be nice if they became close *freinden* like we are and then we could go on double dates?" Jerome asked.

"Slow down there," Glen told him as he faced his best friend once again. "First of all, you need to muster up the courage to talk to Faith's *dat*. And second, I don't know Laurel well enough to even guess if she'd be interested in me."

Jerome pointed at him. "How about this? I'll work on asking Faith out, and you work on getting to know Laurel better."

Glen shook Jerome's hand. "You have a deal."

Glen waited outside the barn for the women to finish lunch. When he spotted Laurel walking out with Faith, he hurried over to her. "How are you?"

"*Gut*. I just need to make sure the ladies have all of the help they need in the kitchen and then I'll be ready to go home." Laurel gave a little laugh. "It feels so funny to call this place home, but I suppose it is. Well, at least it is for now." She started toward the kitchen.

Jerome walked over to him. "Is she going to join us?"

"I haven't had a chance to ask yet. She's checking in the kitchen to see if they need any help." Glen looked toward the porch.

After a few minutes, the back door opened, and Laurel and Faith walked out together. Excitement overtook Glen as the two women walked over to where he stood with Jerome.

A smile turned up Laurel's lips as she held her hand out to Jerome. "Hi, I'm Laurel."

"It's nice to meet you." Jerome shook her hand and then grinned at Glen before turning his attention back to the young women. "I've heard a lot about you."

Laurel blushed. "Oh dear. I hope it was all *gut*."

"Of course it was," Glen said. "Would you like to join us for volleyball and singing this afternoon?"

Faith gave Laurel a hopeful smile. "You must come with us."

To Glen's surprise, Laurel's smile faded. "Oh, I don't know."

"Why not?" Faith asked.

"Tomorrow is my first day of school, and I need to be well rested. I thought I would spend the afternoon reading and praying."

"But you need to meet some more people," Glen offered. "And Sunday afternoon youth events are the best place to do that."

"*Ya*," Faith said. "It will start to feel like home here once you've made some *freinden*."

"Exactly," Jerome chimed in.

Laurel looked over at Glen as she worried her lower lip. "Okay, but I can't stay out too late."

"I promise we'll be home at suppertime," Glen said.

"I need to go home to change out of my church clothes before we go."

"I do too," Glen said.

Laurel's smile was back. "Great! Then let's go."

"Will you ride with me, Faith?" Jerome asked.

Faith gave him a sweet smile. "Of course."

Glen and Laurel headed toward his buggy, and after hitching up the horse, they climbed in and headed toward home.

"So, how did you like the service?" he asked as he guided the horse toward the road.

"It was very nice, and everyone seems so friendly. I was grateful to meet Faith." Laurel turned toward him. "Is she dating Jerome?"

"No."

"I think she wants to."

"You do?" He glanced over at her.

Laurel chuckled. "It's very obvious. When we were pouring *kaffi*, she kept looking over at him. And she was in a hurry to get over to him after we ate lunch. Does he like her too? It seems like he does . . ."

"You're very intuitive."

"So, they *do* like each other! Is he planning to ask permission to date her?"

"I've been telling him to ask, but he hasn't found the courage yet."

"Will her *dat* say no?"

"I doubt it. We've all known each other since we started school."

"He's just *naerfich. Mei bruder*, Ervin, was *naerfich* when he asked his girlfriend's *dat* for permission, even though they'd known each other all their lives too. He finally summoned the courage, and they've been dating for three years. I think he's going to propose to her soon."

"Will they build a *haus* on your *dat*'s farm?"

"*Ya*, I think so. I think Rachel Ann will be a wonderful *schweschder*. I look forward to when they marry."

"That's nice." He was overwhelmed by her sweet heart. Laurel was a special *maedel*.

"How far do we need to go for the youth gathering?"

"It's not far from home. We'll stop there to get changed and then continue on," he said. "Do you like playing volleyball with your youth group?"

"*Ya*. I always enjoyed hosting, too, even though it's a lot of work to get ready."

He felt himself relax as she chatted about her experiences back home. He could listen to her talk all day, and he was grateful she was going to give him the chance to do just that.

CHAPTER 3

LAUREL COULDN'T STOP SMILING as she stood beside Glen while they played volleyball later that afternoon. She had more fun than she'd ever imagined.

Not only had she met more young people her age but she'd laughed so much that her belly ached. She was grateful Glen had convinced her to come today. He was right—she needed to meet more people in order to start to feel at home. And she had also enjoyed spending more time with Glen. He was so friendly and outgoing, and she had a feeling that they would become close friends.

A young man on the opposing team served the ball, and Glen leapt up with ease and spiked it back to them. When a young woman on the other team missed, Laurel and her teammates cheered.

"That means we won," Laurel announced. "You're an amazing player, Glen."

"It wasn't just me. It was the team." He pointed toward the house. "Why don't we get some lemonade?"

Laurel walked beside him toward the house and noticed that many of the youth group members looked over at her as they walked by. She stood out since she dressed like a member of a Pennsylvania settlement, but she didn't mind the stares.

She nodded at the strangers as she continued toward a table set up with bowls of potato chips and pretzels, along with plates, cups, and a jug of lemonade.

"Are you having a *gut* time?" Glen asked.

"I am." She picked up a plate and piled snacks on it before pouring a cup of lemonade. "It's a *schee* day." She looked up at the cloudless azure sky and the gorgeous purple mountains topped with snow in the distance. "It's so lovely here."

He looked out toward the mountains. "I guess I take it for granted since I've lived here my whole life."

"I bet you do." She popped a chip into her mouth.

"Laurel!" Faith called as she rushed over and grabbed her arm. "There you are. I want you meet *mei freinden. Kumm!*" She turned to Glen. "I'm sorry, but I need to borrow her."

Laurel looked at Glen and shrugged.

"We'll talk later," he said.

Laurel's heart lifted as she allowed Faith to steer her toward a group of young women. It was turning out to be an absolutely wonderful day.

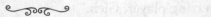

"Looks like you and Faith got along well," Glen said to Laurel as he guided his horse toward home later that evening.

He had been pleasantly surprised when Laurel wanted to join the youth group for supper instead of going home earlier. He had been a little envious that Faith had pulled Laurel away from him and kept her preoccupied with her friends for most of the afternoon, but Glen kept reminding himself he would be able to talk to Laurel during their ride home. Besides, Laurel needed some female companions since she certainly would miss her friends back home. Still, he was grateful for the one-on-one time with her.

"We did. Her *freinden* are so nice. They took me in right away."

He gave her a sideways glance. "Why wouldn't they?"

"Isn't it natural to wonder and worry about new people?"

He shook his head. "I knew they would like you."

"I appreciate that." She smoothed her hands over her black apron. "*Danki* for inviting me today."

"You don't have to thank me." He peeked over and found her looking out the window toward the mountains in the distance, and he suddenly wanted to know everything about her. "Did you leave a boyfriend back home?" he asked. The words leapt from his lips with little forethought.

She chuckled as she turned toward him. "No, and I doubt I would have come if I'd had one."

He felt relieved at her response. "How did you decide to apply for the job?"

"I saw the ad in the *Busy Beaver*, and I thought now was

the perfect time to see more of the country before I fall in love, settle down, and start a family."

"You're the bravest person I know."

Her cute little nose scrunched. "You think so?"

"*Ya*, I do."

She shrugged. "I just don't want to regret never taking a chance."

"Tell me more about your family."

She settled back in the seat and then shared funny stories about her siblings' antics during the remainder of the ride home.

When they finally reached the house, she waited outside the barn while he took care of the horse and buggy.

"Would you like to come inside and visit with my parents and me?" he asked when he met her outside the barn.

"Oh, no, *danki*." She pointed toward the *daadihaus*. "I really do need to rest for tomorrow. I bet I'll struggle to fall asleep as it is."

"I'll walk you home." He walked beside her to her door, and then she turned toward him and gave him a shy smile.

"I really had a nice time today."

"I did too." When he shook her hand, a tiny spark shimmied up his arm. "Have a restful evening."

"You too." She gave him a winsome smile before disappearing into the house.

Glen felt a spring in his step as he ambled back toward home, then headed inside and found his parents sitting in the family room reading.

Dat looked up from the Amish newspaper, *The Budget*. "How was your afternoon?"

"*Gut*. We played volleyball over at the Yoder place." Glen sat on the sofa across from their wing chairs. "Laurel came with me, and Faith introduced her to the other *maed*."

Mamm peered over her reading glasses at him. "Oh, how nice. How did everyone like her?"

"I think she and Faith will be close *freinden*."

"That's nice," *Mamm* said.

"*Ya*, she fit in like she'd grown up with the rest of us." Glen grinned. "I've never met anyone like her. She never runs out of words, and she's just open and honest. At least, she seems honest. She's not afraid to be who she is. And she's so brave. I can't imagine just up and leaving my family for a 'new adventure' as she put it. She's just amazing."

Mamm seemed pensive. "Huh."

"What?" Glen asked.

Mamm's expression was almost accusatory. "You like her."

"Of course I do." Glen studied his mother. "Don't you?"

Mamm studied him. "You realize she's not going to stay here. She just came to spend a few years here for the job. You shouldn't get attached. If you do, then you'll wind up with a broken heart."

"I'll be careful." But deep down, he could already feel himself growing closer to Laurel than he wanted to admit. For the first time, he seriously considered what it would be like to get attached, fall in love, get married, and have a family with a special woman. And he liked imagining all of those things with Laurel. He just needed to find out if Laurel thought about him the same way.

Excitement overtook Laurel as she glanced around the schoolroom early Monday morning. She'd arrived at the schoolhouse shortly after six to make sure the room was in order. She looked over at the tall brown tree she'd created out of construction paper with its colorful red, yellow, and orange leaves, each one featuring the name of one of the students she would teach.

Beside the tree she had created a farm scene with drawings of barns, a farmhouse, cows, and a rolling patchwork of green fields, reminding her of home.

As she looked at the sea of wooden desks, her heart turned over in her chest. She was certain she'd be blessed by each of the students in the classroom.

"I think we're ready." Laurel rubbed her hands together and turned to Rena. "Did I forget anything?"

Rena laughed. "No. You've thought of everything, and your murals are gorgeous. All of the worksheets are ready for each grade, and you have all of the songs ready too. I think you're set for the entire week."

"I like to stay organized." Laurel looked at the clock on the wall. "They should be here any minute."

Rena walked out toward the door and opened it. "We have scholars."

Laurel stood at the front of the room, happiness bubbling through her as the children began filing into the schoolroom. "Good morning!"

Boys and girls from first to seventh grade walked in and greeted her before putting away their lunch bags and taking a seat in the row corresponding with their grade.

Lea walked into the schoolhouse beside her twin brother and ran to Laurel. "Teacher Laurel!"

"Hi, Lea." Laurel grinned as the little girl hugged her.

Lea looked up at her. "I'll be your helper if you need one."

"I would love that. But for now, please put your lunch bag in your cubby and find a seat." Laurel touched her head.

Lea hurried away with her long braids bouncing behind her, and she stowed her lunch at the back of the classroom.

More students arrived and conversations swirled around as the children put away their lunch boxes and then took their seats.

"Good morning, everyone!" Laurel announced, and the murmur of conversations ceased. "I'm Teacher Laurel, and this is Teacher Rena." She pointed to Rena at the back of the room as she waved.

"We're so excited to be here with you this year. My name is Laurel Weaver, and I'm from Pennsylvania. Does anyone know where Pennsylvania is?"

One of the boys in seventh grade raised his hand.

"Yes." Laurel pointed at him. "What's your name?"

"I'm Aaron Zook," he said. "Pennsylvania is on the East Coast near New Jersey and Maryland."

"Very *gut*!" Laurel pointed to the mural she drew. "*Mei dat* owns a dairy farm like that one there. There are many dairy farms in Lancaster County where I'm from." She looked around the room. "Now, I'd like to know your name, your favorite color, and how many siblings you have. Let's start with our first graders."

As the small children in the first row began their introductions, Laurel felt herself relax. She was going to love her new job in her new community, and she was grateful God had brought her here.

Laurel yawned as she locked the schoolhouse door later that evening. After a long first day, she had stayed late to grade papers and prepare for tomorrow.

Now she had to go home and find something for supper, but first she had to find the strength to walk back to the house. She yawned again as she hefted her heavy tote bag up on her shoulder. Then she pulled the little flashlight out of the small zipper compartment in her bag and started down the hill toward the house.

Above her, the bright hues of the red, orange, and pink sunset were starting to dim as a loud chorus of cicadas sang the day into night. Laurel's shoulder started to ache, and she felt the weight of her exhaustion bogging down her steps.

By the time she reached the Troyers' home, she was certain she might fall over. She headed up the rock driveway, past the main house and shop, moving toward the *daadihaus*. When she glanced over toward Bethlyn's house, she spotted a lantern burning on the porch and a figure sitting in the rocking chair. Laurel lifted her hand in a wave as she kept moving.

"Laurel!" Dorothea's voice sounded out over the loud cicadas. "Come tell me about your day."

Surprised, Laurel stopped moving. "I'd love to." She smiled at the idea of talking to Dorothea. After all, she missed her *mammi* so much! She strode over to Bethlyn's house and up the porch steps.

Dorothea patted the empty rocking chair beside hers. "Sit, *mei liewe*, and tell me everything."

"*Danki.*" Laurel set her overstuffed tote bag on the porch floor and then sank down into the chair. "Well, I was very organized and prepared, but I'm still concerned about doing a *gut* job. I'd love for you to come and see how I decorated the schoolhouse. I love to draw, so I drew a giant tree and leaves that have each child's name on them. I also drew a dairy farm and told the class about my home in Pennsylvania. We did some drawings this afternoon.

"I tried to make the day fun. We sang and we had recess. But we also did our math and spelling. And I had so many papers to grade. Rena offered to stay and help, but I feel it's really my job, you know?"

Dorothea grinned at her as she spoke.

"The *kinner* seemed to like me," Laurel continued. "They were all well-behaved, except for one *bu* in the third grade."

Dorothea's hazel eyes lit up with excitement. "Was that

the *bu* who brought a lizard into the schoolhouse? Levi and Lea shared a bit of the story at supper."

Laurel laughed. "*Ya*, that's right. He thought it was a *gut* idea to show the lizard to a *maedel*, and she started screaming. Then the younger *kinner* started yelling, and next thing you knew, we had total chaos."

"*Ach* no!" Dorothea hooted. "How did you manage it?"

Laurel cupped her hand to her forehead. "I nearly lost control of the classroom, but I got it back again. I had him stay after and sweep as his punishment. I don't think he'll do it again."

Dorothea patted Laurel's hand. "You look worn out. Why did you work so late?"

"I wanted to make sure I'm ready for tomorrow." She looked out toward the mountains, which were shrouded in darkness. "I want to do my best so the scholars like and respect me and the school board doesn't regret hiring me."

"Why would they regret hiring you?"

Laurel shrugged. "I don't know."

"Well, you don't need to get everything done in one day. I have a feeling you're a perfectionist."

Laurel felt her cheeks heat. "You've already figured that out?"

"*Ya*, I have. You need to remember we all fall short of the glory of God, and you're doing your best, which is all we can ask."

"That's true." Warmth swirled in Laurel's chest as she smiled at Dorothea.

"How do you like it here?"

"I like it." Laurel hesitated as she thought of her family.

Dorothea's bright, intelligent eyes sparkled in the light of the lantern. "Is something else on your mind?"

Laurel looked down at her lap and brushed a piece of lint off her black apron. "I miss my family."

"I'm sure you do, but you'll feel at home here soon. I promise you that."

"*Danki.*" Laurel covered her mouth with her hand to hide another yawn. "Well, thank you for the visit. I need to go find something to eat and then get some rest."

"You have a *gut nacht*," Dorothea said.

"You too." Laurel stood and lifted her heavy tote bag. Then she stilled as Glen walked toward the porch.

He rested one foot on the bottom step and leaned on the railing as he smiled up at her. "There you are."

"Hi, Glen," she said. Her heart did a funny little flip as she took in his handsome face. She'd missed him today. Could he have missed her too?

CHAPTER 4

"I'VE BEEN WATCHING FOR you to get home." Glen looked up at Laurel and took in her surprised smile.

"You were watching for me?"

"Of course I was. I've been thinking about you and praying for you all day." He inwardly cringed when he realized how much he'd confessed. Surely, she'd think he was obsessed with her, but the truth was that he cared—and he hoped she cared for him too. "How was your first day?"

She set her bag down on the porch floor and shielded her mouth with her hand as she yawned. "Excuse me. It was *gut* but also very long."

Mammi looked over at Laurel. "I think this young *maedel* is a perfectionist, and I told her we all just do the best we can."

"Have you had supper?" Glen asked.

Laurel yawned again. "No, not yet."

He stood up straight. "I can help with that. I'm sure *mei mamm* has leftovers."

"Oh no." Laurel waved him off. "I could never impose. I can make a sandwich at home."

"Don't be *gegisch*," *Mammi* said. "You're our community's new teacher, and you traveled so far to come and bless us with your talents. The least we can do is feed you."

"Exactly." Glen climbed the stairs and lifted her bulging tote bag onto his shoulder.

Laurel hesitated. "I don't want to bother your *mamm*. She's probably getting ready for bed."

"Glen knows how to warm up food, right?" *Mammi* gave him a pointed look.

"Of course I do." He started down the stairs. "Let's go."

He glanced over his shoulder to where Laurel stood looking uncertain.

Mammi shooed her down the stairs. "Go on!"

Laurel shook Glen's grandmother's hand. "*Gut nacht*, Dorothea. I enjoyed talking with you."

"Not as much I as enjoyed talking with you. Now, you go have a hearty supper after working hard all day." *Mammi* beamed up at Laurel.

Gratefulness swamped Glen. He could see the admiration in his grandmother's eyes for Laurel, and he was certain *Mammi* saw how special Laurel was.

Laurel sidled up to him, and they walked down the path that led to his parents' house.

"Do you like grilled chicken and noodles?" He looked over at her as they approached his parents' porch steps.

"I do."

"Perfect." He motioned for her to ascend the steps first.

She climbed up on the porch, and he followed her before opening the back door. Then they walked into the kitchen.

He set her bag down on an empty chair and then nodded toward the one beside it. "You have a seat, and I'll warm up the food for you."

"I can do it."

"Nope. You're my guest. Just sit, and I'll be right back." Glen entered the family room, where his mother sat reading a book. "Laurel just got home, and I invited her to come and have some leftovers."

Mamm's eyes widened as she set her book and reading glasses on the end table. "You invited her to eat?" Her whisper was laced with surprise.

"I can warm up the food. I just wanted to let you know." He lowered his voice.

She pursed her lips and stood. "I'll do it."

"No. Sit."

Mamm frowned. "I can help." Then she crossed to the kitchen. "Hello, Laurel." Her voice sounded too happy. "Glen told me he invited you for supper."

Glen suppressed a sigh as he followed her.

Laurel looked embarrassed as she stood and crossed to the stove. "Oh, I don't want to cause you any trouble, Magdalena. I'll warm up the food."

"It's no trouble at all." *Mamm* retrieved the container of chicken and noodles and then turned on the oven before setting the food in a pan. "I'll just stick this in the oven for a few minutes."

Laurel found a dish and utensils and set a place for herself while Glen poured her a glass of water from the pitcher in the refrigerator.

"Tell me more about your first day." Glen set the water on the table by her place setting.

"It was *gut*. I felt prepared." Laurel moved to the sink and washed her hands before leaning back against the counter. She described the murals she'd made, the songs the students sang, and the story of the boy who brought the lizard into the schoolroom after recess.

Glen grinned as she talked on about her day while *Mamm* stood by the stove, keeping her back to them.

After several minutes, *Mamm* pulled the pan from the oven and emptied the contents onto Laurel's plate. "Here you go."

"I really appreciate this, Magdalena," Laurel said as she sat down at the table. "I'm so worn out after today, and the thought of cooking made me want to just curl up in bed. But I'll happily clean up the kitchen."

"I'll help clean up too," Glen added.

"*Danki*. Enjoy." *Mamm* disappeared into the family room once again.

Glen sat down across from Laurel as she bowed her head in silent prayer.

When she looked up, she smiled. "Now, why don't you tell me about your day?"

"It was not as exciting as yours. We didn't have any lizards in our shop—that I'm aware of, that is."

She laughed as she forked a piece of chicken.

"I'm working on a curio cabinet now." He shared stories of his work while she ate her supper.

When she was done, he located two pieces of chocolate pie in the refrigerator and brought them to the table.

"I feel bad eating your family's food," she told him.

"You're our guest." He took a bite of pie and swallowed it. "Did you want to call your family and tell them about your first day?"

She nodded as her smile wobbled. "*Ya*, please. I'm afraid my family is already in bed, but I'd like to leave *mei mamm* a message. My instinct is still to share everything with her even though it's harder to reach her now."

"I'm sorry you miss them so much." His chest squeezed. "Do you regret coming here?"

"No, I don't, but it's an adjustment. That's why I'm so worried about doing a *gut* job. I'm trying my best to focus on the Lord and my work. Still, I can't stop thinking about my family."

When they were done eating, Laurel called and left a message for her mom, then helped Glen clean up the kitchen before they walked together to her house. She unlocked the front door, and he set her tote bag just inside.

"*Danki* for supper," she said.

"*Gern gschehne.* Sleep well." He shook her hand and enjoyed the brief moment passing between them.

She gave him a little wave. "You too. *Gut nacht.*"

Glen looked up at the stars shimmering in the clear night sky. They seemed to smile down as if they felt the happiness soaring through him. How he had enjoyed his time with Laurel tonight! When he was with her, he felt his heart come alive!

Worry nipped at him as he recalled her homesickness. While he understood how much she missed her family, he also prayed she would fall in love with Colorado and choose to stay. If so, then he might have the opportunity to date her—with her father's permission, of course. But only time would tell.

Glen's head was still buzzing with thoughts of Laurel when he walked into the family room, where his parents sat reading in their favorite wing chairs. They looked up as he sat down on the worn, brown sofa across from them.

He looked at his mother. "*Danki* for allowing me to share our supper with Laurel."

"I was shocked you invited her," *Mamm* said.

"I saw her on the porch talking with *Mammi* and decided to invite her in to eat. She was so tired, and I thought she might appreciate not only the company but the food as well."

"It was a nice gesture." *Dat* folded up his newspaper and set it on the end table beside him.

Mamm studied Glen. "Remember what I said about not

getting attached to her? You need to face the fact that she's not going to stay here."

"I'm enjoying getting to know her better. That's all." Glen stood. "I'm going to take a shower."

"Your *mamm* is right," *Dat* chimed in. "Laurel will most likely go back to Pennsylvania after a couple of years, so you shouldn't set your heart on her. There are plenty of other *maed* in our community."

But none of them are like Laurel. Glen kept his thoughts to himself. It was no use disagreeing with his parents. *"Gut nacht."*

His parents told him good night, and then he loped up the stairs.

"It's been a *gut* week," Rena said as she and Laurel stood by the fence around the schoolyard Friday afternoon.

Laurel scanned where the children played during recess. The younger children enjoyed the swing set and slides while the older children played softball. "I agree! I couldn't be happier with how it's played out."

At the sound of a crying child, Laurel stood up straighter. Her eyes roamed around the yard. Then she spun and spotted Lea on the ground beneath the swing set. The little one was gripping her knee, and Levi stood over her, his face twisted in worry and concern. "Teacher Laurel!" he called out. *"Dummle!"*

"*Ach* no!" Laurel rushed over to them. "What happened?"

Teardrops streamed down Lea's pink cheeks. "I fell off the swing. My knee is bleeding."

"Let me see." Laurel moved Lea's hands and found her knee was skinned. "Let's get you inside, and I'll clean you up." She scooped the little girl up in her arms and headed toward the schoolhouse while Levi jogged beside her to keep up.

"Do you need help?" Rena asked.

"No, *danki*. Please watch the other *kinner*." Laurel smiled down at Lea. "We're going to fix you right up."

Once inside the schoolhouse, Laurel set Lea down in a chair and then retrieved the first aid kit and a wet rag. When she returned to the twins, she found Levi standing beside Lea, holding her hand.

Laurel pulled over a chair and sat down beside Lea. "When I clean the wound, it's going to sting a little. Can you be brave for me?"

Lea sniffed and nodded.

Levi's expression was somber. "I'll be brave for you."

"*Danki*." Lea looked up at him.

Laurel marveled at the siblings' relationship and then turned her attention to the wound.

Lea cried out when Laurel cleaned it, and Laurel's heart twisted.

"It's okay," Levi consoled his twin.

Then Laurel put salve on the wound and covered it with a bandage. "You're *gut* as new now."

Levi wiped his eyes and sniffed. *"Danki* for helping *mei schweschder."*

"Gern gschehne," Laurel told him.

Lea wrapped her arms around Laurel's neck. *"Ich liebe dich,* Teacher Laurel."

Closing her eyes, Laurel hugged her. "I love you too." Then she stood and pointed toward the door. "You two run along and have fun now. Be careful on those swings."

"We will!" Levi promised as he took his sister's hand and led her out the door.

Laurel smiled after them. Taking care of these sweet littles ones was the joy of being a teacher.

CHAPTER 5

THE FOLLOWING SATURDAY AFTERNOON, Glen walked out onto his back porch just as Laurel climbed out of the driver's van with an armful of groceries.

"Let me help you." He ran down the steps and rushed over to her, gathering up her groceries in his arms.

"*Danki.*" She paid the driver, climbed the steps, and unlocked the front door before holding it open.

He carried the bags into the kitchen and set them on the counter. "Need help putting everything away?"

"I'd appreciate that." She opened a bag and began putting away produce while he set a box of cereal in a nearby cabinet. "I thought you were working in the shop today."

He turned toward her. "No, we're caught up. I actually came over to see if you wanted to go fishing."

"Fishing?" She turned to face him, her brow furrowed. "You want to go fishing this afternoon?"

"Why not? It's a *schee* day, and all of my work is done."

She blinked, looking surprised. "Oh. I was going to work on lesson plans and write a letter to my family."

"If I know you, your lesson plans for next week are done, and you're working on plans for October. And I know you write to your family nearly every day."

With a gleam in her eye, she wagged a finger at him. "You caught me."

"So, will you go?" He folded his hands, pleading with her. "I just have to hook the boat trailer up to my buggy, and I'll be ready."

"Okay. I'll pack some snacks. Are the *zwillingbopplin* going to join us?"

"Bethlyn and Roy took them to see Roy's family today, but they'll be back around suppertime."

She pulled a cheesecake out of a bag. "I bought this for your family. Would it be okay if I brought it over tonight to thank them for being so kind to me?"

A rush of gratitude overcame him. "That would be very nice."

"*Gut.*" She smiled. "I'll be ready to go soon."

Glen's heartbeat galloped as he hurried out to the barn and loaded up his fishing gear before readying his horse and buggy. He had just finished hooking up his jon boat trailer to the buggy when Laurel appeared with a small cooler.

She had changed into a blue dress, and her pretty smile was nearly as bright as the sun. "Are you ready?" she chirped.

They climbed into the buggy, and Glen pointed out landmarks along the roads as they headed toward his favorite pond. Conversation flowed easily between them, and he kept stealing glances over at her while he admired her long neck, pretty pink lips, and warm voice.

When they arrived at the pond, he unloaded the boat and gear. Soon they were out on the water, baiting their hooks and casting their lines.

The sun was high in the sky, and the sound of frogs croaking nearby mixed with the birds singing in the trees. He peered down at the murky water and spotted fish swimming by, shimmering in the light of the sun.

"It's the perfect day," Laurel said as if she could read his thoughts.

"It is."

"Did you fish with your *dat* and *daadi* when you were younger?"

He nodded. "I did."

"Tell me about your *daadi*."

"He loved to hunt and fish, and he enjoyed taking me. His influence is one of the reasons why I love being outdoors so much. I enjoy being a carpenter, but spending time out in nature is what makes me the happiest. *Daadi* was an intelligent man, too, and he loved the Lord."

"What are your favorite memories of him?"

Glen shifted on the seat and began describing the more

memorable hunting and fishing trips he'd taken with his *daadi*, and the time flew by as they laughed, shared stories, ate snacks, caught fish, and packed them up for future meals. He didn't want the afternoon to end.

"I suppose we'd better head home," he said.

"*Ya*, I think so. I still need to do some cleaning before I make supper."

While Laurel loaded up their fishing gear, Glen put the boat back on the trailer. During their ride home, Laurel told Glen about the lessons she had prepared for the week. Glen listened, a smile spread across his face, only stopping her to ask more questions about her plans for her students.

When they reached the house, sadness settled in Glen's chest. How had the day passed so quickly?

"I'll bring that cheesecake over later," she said.

He halted the horse at the barn and then turned toward her. "That would be perfect."

"*Gut.* Then I'll see you after supper. *Danki* for a fun afternoon."

"Let's do it again sometime?"

"*Ya*, I'd love to." She gathered up her cooler and then climbed out of the buggy.

As Laurel walked toward the house, he released a deep sigh. In spite of his mother's warning to not get attached, he couldn't stop his heart from craving more than friendship from Laurel. Would someone like her ever consider staying in Colorado for him?

Laurel squared her shoulders and then knocked on Glen's back door later that evening. She'd spent the rest of the afternoon cleaning her house, writing a letter to her family, and grading papers before making her grandmother's favorite chicken potpie recipe for supper.

After she ate, she cleaned up the kitchen, gathered up the cheesecake, and headed over to the Troyers' house, hoping they hadn't already had dessert.

Though she'd just seen him hours before, she couldn't wait to see Glen again. Oh, how she enjoyed getting to know him! He was such a kind man, and he had become a special friend. She felt her heart craving more than friendship from him, but she couldn't imagine how they could make a relationship work. Still, he was the kindest, most generous young man she'd ever known. He had become her confidant, the one person who went out of his way to help her feel at home in Colorado.

Footsteps sounded and then the door opened, and Glen greeted her with a warm smile that made her heartbeat tick up. "I was hoping you'd still come by to visit."

Voices sounded behind him, and she heard the twins and their parents talking in the kitchen as the aroma of pork chops whipped over her.

"I wanted to give you and your family time to eat."

"Please come in." He held the door open wide. "That cheesecake looks *appeditlich*."

She followed him into the kitchen, and the family looked over at her, smiles overtaking their faces. Their plates were clean, as well as the platters and bowls in the center of the table. She had managed to arrive just at the end of their supper.

"Teacher Laurel!" Lea clapped. "Our teacher is here, Levi!"

"Don't yell in the house, Lea," Bethlyn corrected her.

Magdalena divided a look between Glen and Laurel. "How nice of you to come by. Glen mentioned that you picked up a dessert for us."

Laurel held up the cake. "I saw this cheesecake while I was out shopping today, and I wanted to bring it over to thank you all for being so nice to me. I've appreciated your hospitality as I've learned my way around here."

"Oh, how thoughtful of you," Dorothea said.

Glen hurried over to the counter and prepared the percolator. "Please stay, Laurel. I'll put *kaffi* on."

"And I'll take care of the dirty dishes." Bethlyn stood.

Laurel set the cake on the counter. "May I help you with them?" She gathered up the empty platters and bowls, while Bethlyn took care of the dishes and utensils, and Magdalena picked up their drinking glasses.

Once the dirty dishes were in the sink, Magdalena ran hot water and added soap. Bethlyn pulled a stack of cake plates from the cupboard, and Laurel retrieved forks and brought them to the table. Glen smiled at Laurel as he handed out mugs.

After the coffee was ready, Laurel joined the family at the table, sitting beside Glen. When his leg brushed hers, a shiver raced through her.

Glen began cutting up the cheesecake and handing out pieces.

"I hope everyone likes cheesecake," Laurel began. Then she smiled over at the twins. "I just adore my scholars, and the community has been so kind to me. I can't thank you all enough."

Glen handed Dorothea a piece of cake.

Dorothea nodded over at Laurel. "This is lovely. *Danki*."

"We appreciate the treat," Roy said as he added creamer and sugar to his mug of coffee.

"I love cheesecake," Levi announced. "And *schweschder* does too."

"*Bruder* is right," Lea agreed.

Laurel laughed. "That makes me so *froh*."

Glen held out a slice for Laurel, and when her fingers brushed his, her skin hummed with excitement. She cleared her throat. Then she turned to Bethlyn. "How was your family visit today?"

"It was *gut*. We saw Roy's parents."

"We had so much fun," Lea said. "They have kittens in their barn. Me and *bruder* played with them all day."

Levi gestured widely. "They have a thousand kittens!"

"They don't have *quite* that many," Roy said, and everyone laughed.

"How are your parents?" Laurel asked.

Roy nodded as he enjoyed a bite of the dessert. "Very well. *Danki*."

Moses turned toward her. "I heard you and Glen went fishing today, Laurel."

Levi stuck his lip out. "*Onkel* Glen, you went fishing without me?"

"I'm sorry, buddy," Glen told him. "I promise we'll take you next time, right, Laurel?"

"Absolutely," Laurel agreed as she forked a piece of cheesecake. She savored the thought of more outings with Glen and his family.

Lea stuck her hand up as if she were in the schoolroom. "If Teacher Laurel goes, then I want to go too."

"It's a date," Glen said.

Laurel smiled at him, and when he blessed her with a warm expression, she felt a strange stirring in her chest.

"How did you like fishing?" Roy asked.

"It was fun. We caught quite a few trout," Laurel began before sharing the details. As she spoke, she glanced around the table and found the twins watching her with curiosity in their eyes. Meanwhile, Bethlyn and Magdalena looked at her with unreadable expressions.

"I love how you tell stories," Dorothea said.

Laurel smiled at her. "*Danki*."

"Have you spoken to your family?" Moses asked.

"*Ya*, I called them last night. I try to check in every couple of days, and I also write them letters every night. Everyone is well." She felt a familiar tug at her heart. Oh, how she missed them! "*Mei boppli schweschder* is having fun at school. She was struggling with reading, but she seems to have had a breakthrough. I just love when a child suddenly understands something. There's nothing like seeing that light in their eyes when it all clicks."

Laurel spent the rest of her time with the Troyer family discussing her classroom in Colorado as well as sharing stories about her students in Pennsylvania.

Once the cake was gone, Laurel helped the women clean up again. After she said good night to the family, Glen walked her home.

"Everyone enjoyed the special dessert," he said as they sat beside each other on the rocking chairs on her porch.

"I'm so glad." She took in his handsome profile as the sun began to set, sending glorious hues of red and orange across the vast sky. The Colorado sunsets were different from Lancaster County's but just as beautiful. Leaning back into the rocker, she accepted that she was seeing Glen in a new light too. He had become important to her, and she could feel their friendship turning into something much deeper.

But Laurel hadn't come to Colorado seeking a boyfriend or love. No, she had come seeking adventure before settling down back in Pennsylvania. She couldn't fathom falling in love with Glen and staying somewhere so far away from her family. The thought of not seeing them except for possibly once every year made her insides turn and drop.

He glanced over at her and lifted an eyebrow. "You okay?"

She forced her lips into a smile. "*Ya*, I was just noting how the sunsets here are glorious." She pointed to the sky. "And listen to those *froh* cicadas. It's as if they're singing their favorite hymn to God."

"I like how you see the world. You help me see the beauty here that I've taken for granted for too long."

"*Danki.*" A yawn overtook her, and she shielded her mouth with her hand. "I think the sun wore me out today."

"*Ya*, me too. I should get to bed." He stood. "Will you ride to church with me tomorrow?"

"Of course."

"Great." He held his hand out to her.

She took it, and once again, she felt that jolt of heat that warmed her from the inside out. "*Gut nacht*," she said, her voice breathy.

"See you in the morning."

As he walked toward his house, she felt a tingle of worry in the pit of her belly. She couldn't allow her heart to fall for Glen. She had to remind herself to keep him at a safe distance.

But somehow, she knew to the depth of her bones that it was too late.

CHAPTER 6

LAUREL RESTED HER ELBOW on the desk and her chin on her hand as she yawned on Friday night one month later. She shivered as the cold September air crept into the school-house, and she pulled her sweater closer against her body.

She sat up and rubbed her eyes before turning her attention back to the math papers she had to grade. She was determined to finish them tonight so that she could clean, grocery shop, and work on lesson plans tomorrow. She glanced out the window and found darkness creeping in. She had lost track of how long she'd been working, but she had to finish this tonight.

The past month had moved at lightning speed as she settled into a comfortable routine at home and at work, focusing on her students and staying busy in order to keep her homesickness at bay. She loved her job as a teacher, and she did her best to connect with her students every day she was in the classroom.

She'd also concentrated on being Glen's friend and ignoring her growing admiration for him. While she enjoyed spending time with him at Sunday youth group events, she'd avoided seeing him alone, only agreeing to go fishing and hiking when they included the twins or Faith and Jerome, who had started dating a few weeks ago.

Sitting up straighter on her chair, Laurel moved the Coleman lantern closer to her paper and tried her best to concentrate on the math assignment in front of her.

She had finished grading one paper and turned to another when she heard the doorknob turn and the door creak. Her heart thudded in her chest and her throat dried as she looked toward the back of the schoolroom.

"Hello?" Her voice scratched out as fear twined through her.

"Laurel? Are you in here?" Glen's voice sounded, and her shoulders relaxed.

She stood and met him as he walked up the aisle between the desks. "Glen! You scared me."

He gave her a hesitant smile. "I'm sorry. I was worried about you when you didn't come home. You haven't ever stayed out this late." He grimaced. "I know that makes me sound creepy, but I was afraid something had happened to you."

Her heart trilled in her chest. "*Danki* for worrying about me. I was just trying to finish grading papers."

"Can't you go on home? You can finish up tomorrow."

"No, I'm almost done."

He studied her, and concern flashed over his face. "I'm sure you're hungry. Why don't you come home with me, and you can eat with my family?"

"I don't want to—"

"You're not going to impose," he said, as if reading her thoughts. "Please just *kumm*." He started toward the door, and when she remained in the same spot, he turned toward her. "What are you waiting for?"

"Really, I'm almost done." She shivered again and noticed he was wearing a coat. He was prepared for this cold weather, but she was not.

He must have noticed too, because he shucked his coat and held it out to her. "Here, take this, Laurel."

"Oh, I couldn't."

He tilted his head. "Are your other siblings this stubborn? Or are you the only headstrong one in the Weaver family?"

She laughed. "Fine, you've convinced me." She pulled on his warm coat and breathed in his scent—wood, soap, stain, and a manly musk. "*Danki.*"

"*Gern gschehne.* Now, let's go. Pack up what you need, and let's get you home. The meal was almost ready when I left, which means we have to hurry. *Mei mamm* gets cranky when I'm late."

Laurel gathered up the papers she needed and loaded them into her tote bag. Then Glen lifted her bag onto his shoulder and walked her outside. He held up his flashlight as she locked the schoolroom door. Then they started down the road together toward the house. She could see her breath in the cold evening air. It was much colder in Colorado at night in September than it was in Pennsylvania.

"I haven't had a chance to really talk to you this week," he said as the beam from his flashlight bounced along the pavement. "How is school going? Seems like you're working too hard."

"Perhaps I am, but the *kinner* are working hard too. I just have one who is struggling with reading, and Rena has also been spending extra time with him. There's another *bu* who is having trouble with long division, and I'm trying to think of new ways to work with him. I have a few ideas I want to try next week."

"You're so *schmaert*, Laurel." The intensity in his eyes made it hard for her to speak.

"I, uh—well, *danki*. I just try to think of new methods to help them. Not every scholar is the same. The *kinner* that need extra help just need a different way to understand." Her thoughts turned to his niece and nephew. "Levi and Lea are very bright. They're doing so well with their reading and math. I saw Lea helping another scholar the other day. She's very kindhearted."

"They are *gut kinner*."

"I agree." She peeked over at him. "Do you want a family someday?"

"*Ya*, of course I do. Do you?"

"I do."

They walked up the driveway together, and when they reached his back porch, she held her hand out for her bag. "*Danki* for walking me home. I'll take my bag."

He sighed. "Are we really going to have this argument again?"

"I guess so."

"Please come eat with my family and me." He reached out and touched her hand, and she gasped and took a step back, surprised by the contact. "I'm—I'm sorry," he said. "I didn't mean to be that forward."

"Glen! Laurel!" Dorothea called from the porch. "Get inside now. The chili is getting cold."

He grinned. "You heard *mei mammi*. Let's go."

Laurel felt a blush creep up her cheeks. "Looks like you win again."

"That was the plan." His smile was smug, and she couldn't help but laugh. "You'll love *mei mamm*'s chili."

And Laurel was sure she would.

Glen held the back door open for her and then set her tote bag on a bench in the mudroom. After she handed him his coat, he hung it on a peg above the bench and then tossed his straw hat beside it.

He could smell the delicious aroma of chili and corn-bread as the sound of his family's discussions filtered out into the mudroom.

He gestured for her to walk into the kitchen first, and she hesitated. "Go on," he said. "They're expecting you."

She gave him a shy smile and then stepped into the kitchen. "Good evening, everyone. I hear the chili is fantastic."

Glen walked into the kitchen, and his mother shot him a concerned look. Ignoring her, he walked over to the sink. "*Danki, Mammi,* for inviting Laurel to join us," he called over his shoulder.

"I already set a place for her," *Mammi* said with a wink.

Lea waved to her. "Hi, Teacher Laurel!"

Levi also waved.

"Hi." Laurel moved over to the sink, and he breathed in the flowery scent of her shampoo mixed with her soap and something that was uniquely her.

After they each washed and dried their hands, Glen and Laurel sat beside each other at the table. She gave him a sweet smile, and his heart flopped around like a fish on land.

"You made it just in time," *Dat* said. "We were about to pray when your *mammi* said she saw you two walking up the driveway."

Laurel glanced around the table. "*Danki* for inviting me to join you."

"You're always welcome. Let's pray." *Dat* closed his eyes and folded his hands.

Glen closed his eyes and opened his heart to God. *Thank you, Lord, for this meal, for my family, and for my special friendship with Laurel. If it's your will, please guide me to an even more special relationship with her. I feel in my heart that she and I belong together, but I will listen to hear if you see fit for her to be with me.*

When *Dat* shifted in his seat, Glen looked up and found his father reaching for the pot of chili while *Mamm* took a piece of cornbread and then passed the platter to Bethlyn beside her.

"Why were you working late tonight?" *Mammi* asked Laurel as she scooped chili into her bowl.

Laurel took a piece of cornbread and then passed the platter to Glen. "I was grading papers. Glen scared me when he walked into the school. I wasn't sure who was walking in."

"You need to be careful." Roy clucked his tongue. "You should lock the door when you're there late. We don't have much crime around here, but you never know."

Glen retrieved a piece of bread, then cut it open and smothered it in butter. "That's true."

"Why would you stay late to grade papers on a Friday night?" Bethlyn asked.

"I wanted to get a head start on next week. It makes it easier if I stay organized." Laurel talked on about her schoolwork as she filled a bowl with chili and added shredded cheese. Then she handed the serving bowl to Glen.

While Glen fixed the chili to his liking, his mind wandered, and he imagined what it would feel like to have Laurel at all of his family's suppers and how it would feel to date her and call her his girlfriend. Excitement tore through his veins at the idea.

"The scholars are really doing well. I'm so grateful to

be their teacher," Laurel continued. "And Lea and Levi are such *gut* students. They are so bright, and they even help the other *kinner* in their grade." She smiled over at the twins, who beamed in response.

In that moment, Glen imagined Laurel as his niece and nephew's aunt. His heart turned over in his chest at the idea of marrying her.

But he was getting ahead of himself. First, he had to find out if she would even consider dating him. No sense in thinking about lifelong commitments just yet.

Those thoughts lingered in the back of his mind throughout supper and while Laurel fielded questions from his family about how she liked Colorado.

When supper was over, *Mamm* served a lemon cake for dessert, and Laurel participated while the family discussed the fall and the colder weather that had descended upon Rio Grande County.

Later when Glen walked Laurel home, he stood on the porch with her.

Then she smiled up at him. "I had a really nice evening. *Danki* for coming to the school and convincing me to come home."

"I'm glad you listened to me." Before he could catch himself, he stepped forward and cupped his hand to her cheek. The urge to kiss her overwhelmed him, but when her eyes widened, he shook himself from the moment and took a step back. "I'm sorry. I . . . Would you ever consider staying in Colorado?"

The skin between her eyes wrinkled, and she held her hand to her cheek. "I . . . I don't know. Why?"

"Just curious." He cleared his throat. "Well then, *gut nacht.*"

Glen jogged down the porch steps, shivering as he made his way back into the house, where his mother and sister sat in the kitchen together looking through cookbooks.

Mamm looked up at him, and her eyes narrowed. "What are your intentions with Laurel?"

"My intentions?" He gave a bark of laughter. "What do you mean by that?"

Bethlyn rolled her eyes. "It seems like the two of you like each other. Are you planning to date her?"

"That depends." He walked over to the sink, filled a glass with water, and took a long drink.

"Depends on what, Glen?" He could hear the impatience in his mother's voice.

"It depends upon if she likes me, if she wants to date me, and if she plans to stay here. I can't date her if she doesn't want to date me, you know." He set the glass in the sink. "Why are you concerned about it?"

Mamm's brow puckered. "I've already shared my concerns with you. You're setting yourself up to get hurt. It's obvious how much she misses her family. She talks about them all the time. She calls them a few times every week, plus writes them nearly daily. I see her putting the letters in the mailbox on her way to the schoolhouse. She's homesick and not planning on staying here."

"*Mamm* is right." Bethlyn nodded. "Her heart is in Pennsylvania, not here."

Then fear overtook *Mamm*'s face. "Would you consider moving to Pennsylvania with her?"

"Did I ever give you such an idea?" Frustration burned through Glen. "Besides, it's my decision who I want to date, not yours."

"Watch your tone," *Dat* warned from the doorway, his expression stern. "Your *mamm* is right, Glen. You need to slow down. Laurel hasn't been here two months yet. How could she possibly know if she wants to settle here for *gut*? And you have her *dat* to consider. Would he give her permission to date when her parents aren't here to chaperone?"

Glen looked toward the doorway for his grandmother. She would support him. He could see in her eyes how much she liked Laurel.

"This is a temporary stop for Laurel," *Mamm* said. "She just wanted to see the world before going home and settling down with a man in Pennsylvania. Tell me you wouldn't consider going to Pennsylvania with her." He could hear a tremble in her voice.

"I'm going to shower." Glen's voice sounded rough around the edges. He headed upstairs, his irritation clinging to him like a second skin.

His family was worried for no reason. Laurel could decide she wanted to date Glen and stay in Colorado. And the only way he'd find out was to ask her.

He just had to pray for the right words to convince her that he was worth the chance.

"Laurel!" *Mamm*'s voice sang through the phone. "I was hoping you'd call tonight. I received your letter today. Did you get mine too?"

After Glen had returned home, Laurel had found the key Moses had given her to the shop, along with a flashlight, and hurried back out through the cold to call her family. She sat on the desk chair in the office and wound the phone cord around her finger as she listened to her mother's voice sound through the phone.

"I did get your letter. *Danki*. How's everyone?" Her voice sounded thin and reedy.

"We're *wunderbaar*! Ervin has news," *Mamm* announced.

"Oh?"

"He and Rachel Ann got engaged!" *Mamm* exclaimed. "They announced it yesterday. They're getting married in December. We're so excited."

Laurel gasped as happiness filtered through her. "Oh wow. That's fantastic."

"I know, but I wish you were here to help plan. It won't be the same without you."

Laurel's chest squeezed. "I want to hear about everything."

"*Ya*, we have so much to do before the wedding."

"What else have I missed?" Laurel asked.

As her mother talked on about her siblings, Laurel's thoughts wandered to when she had stood on the porch with Glen. Her heart had nearly beat out of her chest when he had caressed her cheek, and she was almost certain he was going to kiss her. And she wanted him to!

"Laurel?" *Mamm* asked. "Are you still there?"

"*Ya*, I am. I'm so sorry."

"I should let you go. It's getting late here."

"*Ya*, it was so *gut* to hear your voice, *Mamm*. Please give everyone my love."

"I will. *Ich liebe dich.*"

"I love you too. *Gut nacht.*" As Laurel hung up the phone and headed back out into the cold, she once again considered her feelings for Glen. The idea of staying in Colorado and exploring a relationship with him filled her with pleasure and anticipation—but the accompanying notion of leaving her family behind had her feeling gutted.

Laurel climbed her porch steps and looked up at the stars sparkling in the sky above her. "Lead me, Lord," she whispered. "Show me where I belong."

Then she walked into the house and got ready for bed.

CHAPTER 7

ON SUNDAY NIGHT TWO weeks later, Laurel sat beside Glen in his buggy, a handmade quilt wrapped around her shoulders. He gave her a sideways glance, and the lantern at his feet cast a golden glow on her beautiful face. "Did you have fun today?" he asked.

"I always have fun at the youth gatherings," she said. Then she pulled the quilt tighter around her and shivered.

"I think there's another quilt in the back of the buggy if you want to grab it."

"I'm okay. I can't believe how cold it is for the second week in October. It was nice during the day, and then once the sun set, the temperature dropped like a rock. It's not this cold at night back home."

Back home. Oh, how he longed for her to consider Colorado her home, but he had to give her time.

"*Ya*, it gets colder sooner here. Just wait until it snows. It's not unusual to have our first snow in mid- to late October."

Laurel's smile was bright. "I love snow. That will be so fun!"

"You might get tired of it by April though. We have a long winter here."

"We'll see about that."

He grinned. "You seemed to have bonded with Faith. I saw you two talking during supper."

"*Ya*, she was telling me about how well it's been going with Jerome. She's been really *froh* since they started dating."

Glen nodded. For the past two weeks, he'd debated telling Laurel how he felt about her, and today he'd felt something inside of him break apart. He was ready to be honest with her and tell her that he cared for her. He just hoped she'd be receptive to the idea of dating him. If not, then he would certainly be left with a broken heart. And he hated the idea of an awkward friendship if she didn't care about him the way he cared for her.

"You looked like you had fun today too," she said. "I saw you and Jerome teasing each other during volleyball."

They continued to talk about their friends during the remainder of the ride home. When they reached the barn, Laurel walked in with him and stood by while he took care of his horse and the buggy.

"Would you like to sit on the porch for a few minutes?" she offered as he walked her toward her house.

His heart lifted. "I would. *Danki*."

"I'll grab a couple of quilts for us." She walked into the house and a few minutes later returned wearing a heavier coat and carrying two quilts. "Here you go."

"*Danki*." He sat down on a rocker and placed the quilt on his lap.

She wrapped the other quilt around herself and then sat down beside him. "It's beautiful out here."

He breathed in the scent of a wood-burning fireplace in the distance as the sound of traffic on a nearby road filled the air. "Wait until you see how *schee* it is when the snow falls."

"I'm excited to see."

"Have you spoken to your family this week?"

She angled her body toward him. "*Ya*, I have. *Mei bruder*'s wedding plans are already in the works. Rachel Ann is going to have her *schweschder* as her attendant, and they are going to wear rose-colored dresses. Ervin is going to have his best *freind*, Tim, as his attendant. Rachel Ann and her *mamm* are talking about the menu and table decorations."

"Sounds like everything is falling into place." Glen studied her expression, waiting to see if she would show her disappointment over not being involved in the planning, but she continued to smile.

"Rachel Ann is so sweet. I know that she and *mei bruder* will be so *froh*."

At that moment, Glen couldn't stop himself from telling her how he felt. He reached over and took her hand in his.

"Laurel, I need to tell you something I've wanted to tell you for some time."

She nodded, her eyes widening.

"I care for you deeply, and I want to get to know you better. You've only been here two months, but I feel as if I've known you for longer—much longer. You've become important to me, and I'd like to date you—if you would consider me." He held his breath and studied her eyes as she swallowed.

"I care for you too," she said, her voice soft.

He released the breath he'd been holding. "You do?"

"I do, but we have to ask *mei dat*."

Happiness soared through him. "I can do that, Laurel."

She bit her lip. "But I have to be honest with you. I'm not sure about staying in Colorado. The idea of not seeing my family is devastating, so I need to take it slow."

"I understand and respect that."

She relaxed her shoulders, and a smile crept back over her face. "Let's call *mei dat* tomorrow after I get home from school."

His pulse took on wings as he gave her hand a gentle squeeze. "I can't wait."

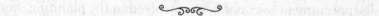

Rena sidled up to Laurel during recess the next afternoon. "You seem like your head is in the clouds today. What's going on?"

Laurel leaned back against the fence and glanced around

to where the children played. The blue October sky above her was dotted with white, puffy clouds while a horse and buggy moved past the school on the road.

Her heartbeat ticked up as she turned toward Rena's curious expression and debated how much to tell her. While she trusted Rena, she wasn't certain how her friend would react to the news.

"Last night Glen told me he cares for me." Laurel was careful to keep her voice low so that the children wouldn't hear her personal business.

Rena clapped her hands. "Oh, that's *wunderbaar*!"

"Shh," Laurel warned her. "Glen wants to date me, and we're going to call *mei dat* later when I get home from school. I'm not sure what he'll say. After all, I'm not supposed to stay here permanently, and my parents aren't here to chaperone us."

"But Glen's parents can chaperone you, can't they?"

"That's true."

Hope had warmed Laurel's chest since the moment of Glen's confession. She looked over to where Lea and Levi played on the slide, and she imagined what it would feel like to be their aunt. She felt anxiety mix with her excitement.

While her feelings for Glen grew each day, she couldn't deny how much she adored her family and would miss them if she were to stay in Colorado forever.

"Are you sure you want to stay here?" Rena said, as if sensing Laurel's anguish.

Laurel sighed. "That's the problem. I care for Glen, but

my heart is still in Pennsylvania with my family. I don't know if I can give up my family for him."

"You won't have to give them up. You might not see them as often, but they'll still be a part of your life. You can call them and maybe see them once a year."

"Not seeing my baby *schweschder* grow up would be terribly painful." The thought twisted her insides.

Rena touched her arm. "Have you prayed about it?"

"I've been praying."

"Keep praying. God will lead you."

Laurel nodded, hoping the Lord would show her the answer soon.

Later that afternoon, Glen walked into the workshop and found his father and Roy standing in Roy's work area while discussing the china cabinet that Roy had been sanding earlier. Glen had spent all morning thinking about what he would say to Laurel's father, and he was ready to share his news with his family.

He took a deep breath and then walked over to his father and brother-in-law. "I have something to tell you both."

Dat turned and gave him a curious look. "What is it?"

Roy sank down onto a nearby stool.

"I'm going to call Laurel's *dat* this afternoon and talk to him," Glen said, his body thrumming with nerves. "I'm going to ask his permission to date her."

Roy looked surprised. "You are?"

Dat's expression was solemn. "Aren't you setting yourself up to get hurt?"

Glen's excitement morphed into irritation. "I care about her, *Dat*."

"But I warned you that you were moving too fast."

"Moving too fast? I've known her for two months now. We're close *freinden*, and we care about each other. Why wouldn't I want to date her?"

"You should find someone in our community." *Dat* pointed to the floor. "This business, this place, is your future."

Glen felt his face contort with an angry scowl. "Laurel could fall in love with me and decide to stay. Then I'd have her in my future along with this business." He looked over at Roy, hoping for some support. "What do you think?"

Roy held his hands up. "I'm neutral."

"Surely you have an opinion. Just tell me the truth."

Roy sighed, and Glen felt his hope dwindle.

"I think you should be careful. She's not a member of our community, and she does talk about her family a lot. Your *dat* could be right."

Glen shook his head. "I thought I could count on the two of you to support me. I care about Laurel, and that's what matters. But if neither of you can see that, just forget I said anything."

A flare of disappointment and frustration surged through Glen as he stalked over to his stall and picked up his sanding block. He refused to allow his family to squash his hope for a relationship with Laurel. In his heart, he believed God had led him and Laurel together, and he would not give up on her.

"Lord, give me strength and guide my heart," he whispered, lowering his head and resuming the day's work.

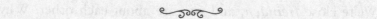

Laurel walked toward her house and found Glen standing on her porch early that evening. When he smiled, her knees wobbled.

"Hey, Laurel. I've been excited to see you all day."

"I know what you mean." She pointed toward her front door. "Just let me put down my things, and we can call *mei dat*. Is the office empty at the shop?"

"*Ya, mei dat* and Roy left about thirty minutes ago."

"*Gut.*" She stepped into her house and set her lunch bag on the kitchen counter while he put her tote bag on the floor by the sofa.

Then she walked over to the door. "I'm ready."

He held his hand out to her, and she threaded her fingers with his. Her skin burned, and her pulse tripled as she looked up at him.

"Let's go call your *dat*."

They walked into the shop together, and she allowed him to steer her into the office. She sat down on the office chair, and he pulled a stool over beside her. Then she dialed the number to her phone shanty and held her breath as the phone rang.

"Hello?" *Dat*'s voice sounded through the phone.

"*Dat. Wie geht's?*"

"Laurel! I'm so *froh* to hear your voice."

She smiled over at Glen. "*Dat*, there's someone here who would like to speak with you. I'm going to put Glen on the phone." She handed the receiver to Glen.

Glen took a deep breath and then held the phone between them so she could hear too. "Hi, Gideon. This is Glen."

"How are you?" *Dat*'s tone was friendly.

"Fine. *Danki*." Glen cleared his throat. "I wanted to talk to you about Laurel. She and I have been getting to know each other, and we care about each other. I would like your permission to date her." He looked over at her. "She's become important to me, and I promise you I will be respectful. Also, I live with my parents, and they can be our chaperones. But I need your permission before we can officially date."

"Oh." *Dat* sounded surprised. "How does Laurel feel about this?"

"I would like to date him, *Dat*," she said. "I'm listening in too." Her heart began to beat wildly as she waited for his response.

Dat hesitated for a moment. "Well, I'm not sure what to say. I'm a little surprised by this. Dating makes your stay in Colorado a bit permanent, and that's not what your *mamm* and I envisioned when we gave you permission to apply for the job."

Laurel's heart sank. "I understand. I wasn't expecting this either, but I truly care for Glen."

"Does that mean you see a future with him?" *Dat* asked.

She glanced over at Glen, and her heart gave a resounding *Yes!* Then her body began to vibrate with fear as she wondered if she could truly leave her family behind. The muscles in her shoulders tightened.

Glen's expression fell as he studied her.

Oh no! She was hurting him too!

"I'm—I'm not sure what the future holds yet, but I'd like to explore the idea," she said, hoping not to worry her parents.

Glen's eyes twinkled, and she felt her shoulders relax.

"Well, Glen," *Dat* began, "Laurel's mother and I had expected her to come home before she started dating, but she's old enough." He was quiet for a beat. "If you promise to be respectful, then I will permit it."

Glen released a breath. "*Danki*, Gideon. I won't let you down."

"*Danki, Dat*," Laurel said, relief flowing through her.

"All right then," *Dat* said. "I need to get back to the cows. You call again later in the week to talk to your *mamm*, Laurel."

"I will, *Dat*," she said. "Give my love to everyone." She hung up and then clapped her hands. "I'm so excited!"

"Me too." Glen pulled her against him for a hug, and she rested her cheek on his shoulder. "I'm so honored to be able to date you."

When he brushed his lips over her cheek, she closed her eyes, savoring the feeling.

"Let's go celebrate," Glen said.

He held out his hand, and she took it before they headed out of the shop and toward his parents' house.

"Are you sure it's okay if I come for supper?" Laurel asked as they climbed the porch steps.

"*Ya*, I told *mei mamm* I was going to invite you."

She followed Glen into the kitchen and greeted his parents before helping his mother serve the meal of hamburger casserole. Then she took a seat at the table across from Glen and bowed her head in silent prayer.

After everyone's prayers, Glen cleared his throat. "I have an announcement to make," he said, scooping a mountain of casserole onto his plate. "Laurel and I are dating."

Laurel smiled as she looked over at Glen. She turned, and when Magdalena's mouth twisted downward, Laurel's heart sank.

Moses looked surprised. "You are?"

"*Ya*, we are. We called Laurel's father, and he gave us permission." Glen's smile widened. "And I'm honored to call Laurel my girlfriend."

Laurel blinked as she took in his parents' scowls. Her hands began to tremble, and she stared down at her plate.

"That's-that's fantastic," Moses said. "I'm *froh* for you."

Magdalena looked down at her plate. "*Ya*."

"Laurel?" Glen asked.

"*Ya?*" Laurel pushed the ties to her prayer covering over her shoulders.

Glen gave her a concerned expression. "You're not eating. Are you okay?"

"I'm fine." She forced her lips into a smile, but it felt more like a grimace.

Glen seemed to study her, but she cast her eyes down and nibbled her casserole while he and his father discussed work.

After they were finished eating, she helped Magdalena clear the table and then wash the dishes. Laurel tried to pull Magdalena into a conversation about cooking, but Magdalena gave her short responses to any of her questions.

Laurel was relieved when the kitchen was clean and she and Glen stepped out into the brisk night air. He held out his arm for her, and she wrapped her hand through it as they walked together to her little house.

"You hardly said a word at supper," he said, the cold ground crunching beneath their feet. "Are you *naerfich?* Worried?"

"Your parents don't like me," she mumbled. The words nearly broke her heart.

"That's not true."

She spun to face him. "It was obvious your *mamm* was not *froh* with the news we're dating, and your *dat* seemed more stunned than pleased. How can this possibly work if your family doesn't approve of me?"

"Laurel, I care for you more than I've ever cared for anyone. If you care for me, then this can work."

Her lip trembled. "So, I'm right. They don't like me."

"They *do* like you. Just give them time to get used to the idea that we're dating, okay?" He moved his finger over her cheek with a featherlike touch, and she inclined her face toward him.

Cupping his hand to her cheek, he leaned down and gently kissed her. An unfamiliar quiver of wanting danced up her spine, and she closed her eyes and enjoyed the feel of his lips against hers. Laurel was certain she was dreaming, but the heat rushing through her veins was as real as the feel of his lips.

No, she wasn't dreaming. This moment was as real as any other. And as Glen's lips left hers and his eyes shimmered at her in the darkness, she was certain that everything would somehow be okay.

CHAPTER 8

LAUREL WALKED UP THE Troyers' back porch steps Saturday afternoon. She had spent the morning cleaning, writing to her family, and preparing for the next week of school. Now, she needed a break—and to spend some well-earned time with her boyfriend.

Her heart lifted at the thought. It had been five days since Glen had asked permission to date her, and she hadn't stopped smiling since. Her lips burned at the memory of their first kiss! She had joined Glen and his family for supper every night before they sat and talked on her porch. She was so happy. In fact, she couldn't recall a time when she'd been so happy.

She felt as if the Lord had led her to Colorado to meet Glen and fall in love. And that notion sent bliss curling through her.

But she still couldn't shake the feeling that his family wasn't pleased with their new relationship. If only she could figure out why they didn't approve. Her gut told her they preferred he date a member of their community, but what did that matter if she was a baptized member of the Amish church?

When she climbed the back steps, she glanced up at the gray clouds in the sky and breathed in the scent of rain. She shivered and pulled her heavy coat closer to her body as a cool breeze moved over her.

Squaring her shoulders, Laurel knocked on the back door. She heard footsteps and then the door opened, revealing Bethlyn.

Laurel smiled. "*Gut* to see you, Bethlyn."

"Come in." Bethlyn beckoned her to enter the house.

Laurel followed her into the kitchen and greeted Magdalena, who looked over from the counter, where a large bowl, a cookbook, and ingredients sat.

Laurel looked back and forth between Magdalena and Bethlyn as they watched her with uneasy expressions, sending more anxiety coursing through her. "I was looking for Glen. I knocked on the shop door, but no one answered. I thought maybe he was here."

"They went for supplies," Bethlyn offered.

Laurel forced a smile. "Oh. Will you tell him I stopped by?"

"Of course," Magdalena said. "We'll see you later." Then she turned back to the counter and looked down at her cookbook.

Bethlyn nodded and then sidled up to her mother.

Laurel opened her mouth, ready to ask if she could join them, but then she stilled. If they had wanted her to cook with them, they would have invited her. A coldness swept through her as the truth smacked her in the face: She wasn't welcome in their kitchen.

She heard little voices in the family room, and she peeked in to where the twins were coloring. They sat on the floor and leaned against a coffee table, their backs to the doorway. She lingered for a moment and considered saying hello, but the overwhelming urge to leave the Troyers' home propelled her toward the doorway.

When she reached the mudroom, she looked down and found her shoe untied. She rested her foot on the bench and began to tie her laces.

"I'm not *froh* about any of this," Magdalena grumbled in the kitchen. "I have this terrible feeling she is going to convince Glen to move to Pennsylvania with her, and I'll lose *mei sohn* forever."

Laurel froze, her breath caught in her throat.

"I understand," Bethlyn said. "I keep praying he'll break up with her and find someone in our community. I don't want to lose *mei bruder* either."

"She's made it clear that she's homesick," Magdalena continued. "She never should have come here if she knew in her heart that she didn't want to leave her family. Why does she have to break up mine?"

A black feeling settled in the pit of Laurel's stomach. She

gasped and choked on a sob as she finished tying her shoe-lace. Then she hurried out the back door, closing it gingerly behind her before she stepped out into the cold, misty rain.

She looked up at the sky as the truth rained down on her with the raindrops—the Troyers didn't approve of her. They only saw her as a threat to their family. She didn't belong here. She needed to go back home.

Laurel started toward her house and then stopped and looked over at the shop. She needed her family. No, she needed her mother.

She rushed over to the shop and was relieved when she found the door unlocked. She stepped in and hurried to the office. Then she dialed her family's number and prayed her parents would hear the phone ringing.

Please, God. Please let them be home. Please let my family help me heal my broken heart.

"Hello?" Her middle sister's voice sounded through the line after several rings.

"Maranda?" Laurel sniffed and wiped her face with a tissue from her pocket.

"Laurel? Are you okay?"

She couldn't catch her breath with her grief packed around her heart. "No, not really. Is *Mamm* around?"

"What happened?" Maranda sounded frantic. "Are you hurt?"

"I just need to talk to *Mamm*." She needed her mother so badly it felt like a hunger pang.

"Hang on."

Laurel held her tears at bay and wiped her eyes and nose while she waited for her mother to come to the phone. After a few moments, her mother's soothing voice rang through the line.

"Laurel," *Mamm* said. *"Was iss letz?"*

"I don't belong here." Her hand fisted and she held onto the truth as she shared her concerns about Glen's family. Then she repeated what she'd heard them say. "I never should have come here at all. I want to come home."

"Ach, mei liewe. I'm so sorry. I thought you were so *froh* there."

"I was, but I've realized I made a terrible mistake."

"Have you spoken to Glen about this?"

"Not yet."

"Talk to Glen and then pray about it. Then if you're still certain you want to come home, tell the school board."

"You and *Dat* won't be disappointed in me if I come home?"

"No, *mei liewe.* Your *dat* and I just want you to be *froh.*"

"Danki."

"Go make yourself some tea and calm down. Call me later."

"Okay. *Ich liebe dich, Mamm."*

"I love you too," her mother said.

Feeling heavy and yet hollowed out, Laurel hung up the phone and then headed back out into the rain. As she walked toward her house, her heart broke a little more with every step.

Glen walked into the kitchen later that afternoon and breathed in the delicious scent of carrot cake.

"Oh, it smells heavenly in here," he told his mother and sister as they sat at the table together looking through a catalog.

Mamm looked up at him. "Laurel stopped by earlier. She was looking for you."

"What did she want?" He moved to the refrigerator and poured himself a glass of water.

"She didn't say," Bethlyn responded as she turned a page in the catalog. "She asked us to let you know she was here."

He drank the water and then set the glass in the sink. "I'll go see her."

The cold rain soaked through his coat and dripped from his straw hat while Glen walked toward the *daadihaus*. He climbed the back steps and knocked on the door.

After a few moments, the door opened, and Laurel stood before him, her eyes bloodshot and her cheeks bright pink as if she'd been crying.

Panic scratched his throat. "Laurel! *Was iss letz?*"

"It's time for me to go home." She turned and walked toward the kitchen.

He followed her and reached for her arm. "What do you mean?"

"I don't belong here." She stepped away from his touch and yanked a tissue out of the box on the counter. "I stopped

99

by your parents' *haus* earlier and asked where you were. Your *mamm* and *schweschder* were cold to me, and when they thought I had left, I heard them talking about me." Through tears, she shared what his mother and sister had said.

Glen's mouth fell open as confusion and ire warred inside of him. "Are you sure they said that?"

She gave a derisive snort. "Why would I make that up?"

"I-I don't know what to say." He felt a stab of shame.

She wiped her eyes and nose with the tissue and then stared down at the counter. "Coming here was a mistake. I'm going to tell the school board that I quit and then book a ride home." Her face crumpled.

"No, don't say that." He walked over to her, and she backed away from him. "Please, Laurel. Don't leave. We can work this out."

"No, we can't. It's obvious your family doesn't want me here, and if they feel that way, then certainly other members of your community do too." Her voice was gravelly as her eyes shimmered with unshed tears.

He shook his head as his throat dried. "No, that cannot be true. Faith and Jerome like you. And Rena does too. Everyone in the youth group likes you as well." He pointed in the direction of his sister's house. "And look at how much *mei bruderskinner* love you, and all the good you're doing for the students."

Then he pointed to his chest. "And I love you, Laurel. I've known if for a while now, but I was afraid to tell you because I thought you might feel it was too soon for me to say it. *Ich liebe dich.* And if you left, it would break my heart."

"And that's the problem. I'm a threat to your family. They don't want me to steal you away. You need to give up on me and find someone in your community, just like Bethlyn said." Her lower lip and chin quivered as she spoke.

Oh, how he longed to take away her agony! He reached over to brush away her tears, but she moved away from him.

"Please leave, Glen." She looked pained.

"You don't mean that."

"*Ya*, I do." She lifted her chin. "We can't date or be together. I want to be left alone."

Her words were like a knife to his stomach. "I'm so sorry. I—I don't know how to fix this."

"Go now." She brushed past him and disappeared into the bathroom, her sobs sounding through the little house.

He started toward the bathroom and then stopped. His heart shattered as he listened to her cry. He looked up toward the ceiling and opened his heart to God.

Lord, help me! What am I supposed to do for the woman I love?

Suddenly, his anguish transformed as white-hot anger boiled under his skin. His family needed to know how badly they had hurt Laurel.

Glen wrenched open the door and stalked back toward his house, his body vibrating with his rage. He found his mother, sister, and grandmother sitting in the kitchen.

Mamm looked up at him, and her expression flickered with worry. "Are you okay?"

"No, as a matter of fact, I'm not." He pointed toward the *daadihaus*. "I just spoke to Laurel, and she's planning to quit and go home. Do you want to know why?"

Mamm's mouth opened and then closed, reminding him of a fish.

He sat down across from them. "I'll tell you why. She stopped by earlier looking for me, and when she went to leave, she heard you and Bethlyn talking about her." Then he shared what she overheard.

Mamm glanced over at Bethlyn, and his sister's cheeks reddened as she looked down at the tabletop.

Mammi gasped. "Did you say that about her?"

Mamm gave a solemn nod.

"She's a sweet *maedel*, and she and Glen obviously care for each other. Why would you want to break them up when Laurel makes your *sohn froh*?" *Mammi* demanded. "Don't you want your *kinner* to have a happy life?"

Mamm also studied the tabletop.

"*Mammi* is right," Glen said as admiration for his grandmother swelled within him. "Laurel is a sweet, *schmaert*, and kind *maedel*, and I love her. Do you realize how much you hurt her and me? Now she wants to leave!" His voice rose as his body shook with renewed fury. "She'll be leaving the schoolchildren behind, and you've ruined everything between her and me to boot!" His voice was flinty and sharp.

"What's going on in here?" *Dat*'s voice boomed.

Glen turned and found *Dat* and Roy standing behind him.

After Glen filled him in, *Dat* peered over at *Mamm* and Bethlyn. "Is this true?"

Mamm and Bethlyn both gave him sullen nods.

Dat drew his brows together. "I understand you're afraid of losing Glen, but the Lord is the one who will lead him on the right path. You should have kept your thoughts to yourselves."

"More than that, you both should be *ashamed* of yourselves," *Mammi* snapped. "Laurel is *gut* for this family. She's vibrant and funny. And she's sweet and hardworking. Of course Glen has fallen in love with her! Don't you remember how Lea told us that she fell at school and Laurel took such *gut* care of her? Why wouldn't you want Glen to marry a *maedel* like her, whether she lived here or in Pennsylvania?"

Glen shook his head as his heart sank. "*Mammi* is the only one here who understands how I feel. The rest of you are too blind to see what I see. You were worried about Laurel breaking my heart, but you're the ones who broke it." His words sent a shaft of ice through his chest as he stood. "I'll be in my room."

He made his way upstairs and then sank down on the edge of his bed. "God, help me repair my broken relationship with Laurel. Give me the right words to convince her to stay. Losing her will break me apart."

CHAPTER 9

GLEN KNOCKED ON THE front door of the *daadihaus* the following morning. He had barely spoken to his family since their confrontation last evening, and he'd been up half of the night praying and trying to figure out a way to make things right with Laurel.

When the door opened, Laurel studied him with sad eyes.

He plastered a smile on his face. "*Gude mariye.* Would you like to come to youth group with me today?"

"No, *danki.*"

"Jerome and Faith will be there."

"I'm going to rest today, but you have fun." She started to close the door, and he shot his foot out and stopped it.

"Please give me a moment. I'm sorry my family is too narrow-minded to see we belong together, but I meant it when I told you I love you. I was up nearly all night praying and trying to figure out a way to fix this, but all I can think to do is tell you how much I care for you and how much it would destroy me if you left. Please give me another chance."

She shook her head. "I'm sorry, Glen, but it can't work between us. It's better if we're just *freinden*."

Her words were like shards of glass to his heart, but he tried to mask his pain. "I understand, but I will miss you."

"Have a *gut* day. Tell Faith I said hello."

He stepped back, making room for her to close the door.

As Glen walked toward the barn for his horse and buggy, a new determination seized him. He would find a way to convince Laurel to stay.

"Where's Laurel?" Faith asked as she sat on a folding chair between Glen and Jerome in Randy Smoker's barn later that afternoon.

Members of their youth group laughed and talked while playing Ping-Pong and eating snacks. The smell of hay, animals, and moist earth surrounded Glen.

"She didn't want to come." Glen kept his eyes focused on his lap.

Jerome nudged Glen with his elbow. "You've been glum all day. Did you two have an argument?"

"Sort of."

"About what?" Faith asked.

As Glen summarized what had happened with his family, Faith gasped and Jerome cringed as the story moved from bad to worse.

"That's terrible," Faith said. "You and Laurel are great together. It's obvious how much you care for each other."

"Apparently only *mei mammi* can see that."

"You can't give up on Laurel," Jerome added.

"I'm not giving up, but I don't know what to do from here." Glen kicked a rock with the toe of his shoe as indignation ripped through him. "I'm so disappointed in my family, but how can I make things right when *mei mamm* and *schweschder* hurt her so deeply?"

"With God all things are possible," Faith said.

Glen nodded as hope took root in his chest. *Lord, show me how to fix this before it's too late.*

"I made your favorite this morning," *Mamm* said, her voice sugary sweet as Glen sat at the kitchen table the next morning. "French toast and sausage."

"*Danki,*" Glen muttered as he stared down at his pile of French toast, which he doused with butter and syrup.

The muscles in his shoulders were coiled as he worked to suppress a yawn after another sleepless night. He had prayed, tossed, and turned nearly all night long while he worked to find an answer to his conundrum with Laurel. Despite his best efforts, Glen had come up short. And then the reality that he would lose her truly hit, landing like a punch to his gut.

"Would you like more sausage?"

Glen looked up and found his father studying him while *Mamm* held out the platter of food. "No, *danki*." He looked down and focused his eyes on his half-eaten breakfast.

"We need to get started on that dining room table order today," *Dat* began. "It's going to be a big project. It will seat twelve, and they want it done quickly."

Glen nodded and tuned his father out while his thoughts continued to swirl with sorrow over Laurel.

"Did you hear what I said, Glen?"

His head popped up when he heard his mother say his name. "What, *Mamm*?"

"I said I'm sorry." Her voice shook as tears stung her eyes. "I'm sorry for hurting you."

Glen sat back in his chair as he studied his mother with suspicion. "If you were truly sorry, then you'd see Laurel and I belong together. And you'd apologize to her yourself."

Mamm nodded and sniffed.

"Don't disrespect your *mamm*," his father warned.

"You know what, *Dat*, I think I have a right to my anger," Glen seethed. "I love Laurel, and I want to plan a future with her. But I can't since my family ruined it. How would you have felt if *Mammi* and *Daadi* had ruined your chances with *Mamm*? Don't you think you'd be upset too?"

Dat stared at Glen over his coffee mug.

"I'm done. *Danki* for breakfast." Glen pushed back his

chair and carried his plate to the counter. "I'm going to the shop." He started toward the door.

"Glen," *Mamm* said.

He spun and faced her.

"I am truly sorry." *Mamm* wiped her cheeks as tears began to trail down them.

He studied his mother. "If you truly are sorry, *Mamm*, then you need to make things right."

Before she could respond, he stalked out to the workshop and hoped he could lose himself in a project and somehow forget his fractured heart.

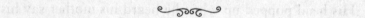

"*Was iss letz,* Laurel?"

Laurel looked up from her desk and found Rena watching her with a concerned expression later that morning at the schoolhouse.

Laurel sighed. "Coming here was a mistake. I'm going to give the school board my resignation later this week, and hopefully I can go home before Thanksgiving."

Rena hurried over to the desk. "Why?"

Laurel glanced at the clock. "The scholars will be here soon, and it's a long story. I'll have to tell you later."

"Tell me now."

Laurel shared an abbreviated version of how Magdalena and Bethlyn had hurt her feelings and then explained that she and Glen broke up. She felt a fresh crush of sadness when she thought of leaving Glen. "I care for him, but I can't stay here knowing his family doesn't approve of our relationship."

"Magdalena and Bethlyn are wrong about you and Glen. Plus, you're a *wunderbaar* teacher. The *kinner* love you, and I'm honored to call you *mei freind*." Rena touched Laurel's shoulder. "Please don't go."

Laurel felt the grief that had followed her around like a shadow for the past few days well up inside of her. She tamped it down, pushed back her chair, and stood. "*Danki*, but I've made my decision. I'm going to go greet the *kinner* at the door, and then I'll pass out our work papers. We have a busy day ahead of us."

As Laurel turned her attention to her school day and her beloved students, she sent up a silent prayer to God, asking him to help her get through the day.

Later that afternoon, Laurel stood in front of the class. "Okay, everyone. It's almost time to go. *Danki* for your hard work today."

"Teacher Laurel," Rena said as she walked to the front of the schoolroom. "I'm sorry to interrupt, but the scholars have something special for you."

"What do you mean?"

"Earlier today, when the *kinner* had some free time at their desks, I asked them to create something for you." Rena smiled at Lea. "Lea asked if she could present it to you."

Lea stood and walked over to the desk carrying a stack of colorful pages. She set them on the desk and then pointed to the mural of the Pennsylvania dairy farm that Laurel had created. "Since you made a picture to show us why you love Pennsylvania, we made you pictures to show you why we love Colorado."

Laurel looked down at the colorful stack of papers, finding drawings of snowmen, horses, mountains, and log homes. "These are lovely. *Danki*." She looked over at Rena, who gave her a warm expression.

Then Lea handed her a picture showing nine stick people. "This is my family." She pointed to a person standing on the end. "This one is you. *Ich liebe dich*, Teacher Laurel."

Speechless, Laurel cupped her hand to her mouth as tears filled her eyes.

"It's time to go, scholars," Rena announced. "We'll see you tomorrow."

Laurel continued to study the drawings as the children left for the day.

"They love you," Rena said as she walked over to the desk. "Can you imagine leaving them now? And the school board had such a terrible time finding a teacher for our community."

"You could be their teacher." Laurel's voice sounded hoarse.

Rena shook her head. "I don't have enough experience. I'm learning so much from you, but I'm not ready to take on the classroom by myself. Don't you see how much your leaving will upset the community? We need you. I know you're hurt, but please give everyone a chance to show you how much you mean to us."

Laurel sniffed as a heavy feeling knotted up her stomach. Coming here had been such an easy decision. Leaving would prove to be harder.

Laurel climbed her porch steps at the end of the day and found a note tacked to the door. She pulled the note down, and her eyes widened as she read it.

Laurel,

Would you please come over and bring your grand-mother's barbecued meatloaf recipe?

Thank you,

Magdalena

Suspicion taunted Laurel as she walked into her house and wondered what Magdalena wanted. She considered not complying, but it was the Amish way to forgive. Plus, Rena's words about how much the community needed her continued to echo in the back of her mind as guilt had begun to mix with her hurt. Laurel would be leaving the community in a lurch if she quit the teaching job. She had made a commitment, and the school board needed her.

Laurel huffed out a deep breath. Perhaps Magdalena

wanted to apologize, and Laurel hoped that if she did, she was sincere.

After freshening up, Laurel retrieved her grandmother's cookbook and walked over to the Troyers' house. She knocked on the door and then hugged the cookbook to her chest.

"Hello!" Magdalena's expression seemed too bright and also a little nervous as she opened the door wide. "I'm so *froh* you came over. Did you bring the recipe?"

Laurel held up the book. "*Ya.*"

"Please come in. Bethlyn and I have been expecting you." Magdalena pointed toward the kitchen.

Laurel walked through the mudroom and stepped in the kitchen, where Bethlyn stood at the counter. "Hello."

"Hi." Bethlyn gave her an awkward wave.

"Here's the book." Laurel set the cookbook on the counter. "I marked the page. Enjoy." Then she pivoted and started toward the door.

"Wait," Magdalena called after her.

Laurel spun to face them, hugging her arms to her chest to shield her fragile heart.

Magdalena's expression was hopeful. "Will you cook with us?"

Laurel hesitated. While it was their way to forgive, she couldn't stop their hurtful words from echoing in her mind. If they didn't approve of her, then the invitation felt artificial. "I have a lot of papers to grade, and I—"

"Please?" Bethlyn asked, interrupting her.

Magdalena walked over to Laurel and touched her hand. "We're sorry, Laurel." Her voice quavered. "What we said about you was wrong. We want to show you that we truly would like to start over."

Laurel studied her and couldn't find any sign of a lie.

Bethlyn walked over to them. "*Mei zwillingbopplin* love you. Lea can't stop talking about you, and I understand what she sees in you. You're a kindhearted, sweet, loving, gifted teacher, and our community is blessed to have you. And Glen is also blessed to have you in his life."

"You've blessed *mei sohn* abundantly," Magdalena added. "You've made him so *froh*, and since you broke up, I've never seen him so distraught. Please don't leave." Her voice caught and then recovered. "It's breaking my heart to see him so very *bedauerlich*. Please give us another chance."

Bethlyn nodded with vigor. "*Ya*, please. We want you here."

Laurel sniffed as tears filled her eyes. "I want to stay, but I'm not sure."

"I was overwhelmed by the idea of Glen wanting to move away from us," Magdalena said. "To the point where I lost sight of what a sweet *maedel* you are. Will you give us another chance?"

Laurel smiled as forgiveness flooded her. The Lord had sent her here for a reason, and she needed to give Magdalena and Bethlyn some grace. Plus, she owed it to the school board to honor her commitment. "Of course I will."

"*Danki!*" Magdalena pulled her in for a hug.

"I'm so grateful." Bethlyn joined them, wrapping her arms around them both.

Laurel wiped her eyes as she pulled away.

"Now, will you help us cook your *mammi*'s recipe?" Bethlyn asked.

"I will." Laurel's heart turned over in her chest as she moved to the counter. "I hope you have barbecue sauce."

Shock rained down on Glen as he stood in the kitchen doorway later that evening and found *Mamm*, Bethlyn, *Mammi*, and Laurel sitting at the kitchen table laughing together. He blinked and rubbed his eyes, certain he had imagined it, but he hadn't. The delicious smell of meatloaf drifted over him as he stepped into the kitchen.

"What's going on here?" he asked.

"Hi, Glen." Laurel waved at him. "We made *mei mammi*'s barbecued meatloaf."

Mammi grinned at him. "I can't wait to have a piece."

"It should be ready soon." *Mamm* stood and crossed to the counter, checking the timer.

Bethlyn pushed back her chair and stood. "I'll start setting the table."

"Laurel," Glen began, "may I speak with you alone?"

"Of course." She wiped her hands on a dish towel, then followed him out to the porch.

"What happened?" he asked once they were alone.

"Your *mamm* left me a note asking me to bring *mei mammi*'s meatloaf recipe. When I got here, your *mamm* and Bethlyn apologized and asked me to stay and give them another chance."

"What did you say?"

"I said of course I will."

His heart came alive. "Are you saying you'll stay in Colorado?"

She nodded. "*Ya*, I am."

"Does that mean you'll give me another chance too?"

"*Ya*. I just couldn't stay knowing your family didn't approve of me. But if they won't give up on me, I won't give up on them or your community. And to be honest, we had a really nice time this afternoon while we cooked. I think I can have a *gut* relationship with your *mamm* and Bethlyn if they're being sincere with me."

She rubbed her thumb across his cheek, and he leaned into her touch. "The truth is, *Ich liebe dich*, Glen. I want to be with you, and I'm certain in my heart that God will bless our relationship."

"I'm so grateful to hear you say that. I love you too." He leaned down and pressed his lips against hers, and the contact sent a new warmth and happiness flooding his every cell. When he broke the kiss, he threaded his fingers with hers. "Let's go inside for supper. We can talk later on the porch."

As he walked back into the house with Laurel at his side, he silently thanked God for bringing her back to him.

EPILOGUE

"I'M SO FULL. THAT was the most *appeditlich* Thanksgiving meal I've ever had." Laurel placed her hand on her abdomen as she sat beside Glen in the porch swing on his parents' back porch. "But don't tell *mei mamm* I said that."

Glen chuckled as he looped his arm around her shoulder. "I promise I won't tell your *mamm*." He smiled over at her, and her stomach swirled.

The past month had flown by since Laurel had decided to stay in Monte Vista. His mother and sister had both gone out of their way to include Laurel in family dinners, even inviting her to their quilting circles with their friends.

Laurel had also continued to enjoy her time in the classroom as she bonded with her students and learned new ways to help the struggling children learn. She was happy, really happy, and even though she missed her family, she loved

Monte Vista and felt comfortable there. She no longer felt like an outsider but instead like a member of the community.

"I wanted to talk to you about something."

Laurel turned toward Glen, and his expression seemed sheepish, or possibly nervous. "What is it?"

"I talked to your *dat* the other day."

"You did?" She searched his eyes. "Why?"

"I wanted to ask him a question, and he gave me his answer."

"What question?" She angled her body toward him.

Glen cleared his throat and shifted in his seat, which caused the swing to move. "These past few months with you have been the happiest of my life. I'm so grateful God led you here and that he found a way for you to stay." He paused, looked down at the porch, and then looked up. "So, I wanted to ask you something."

Laurel held her breath as anticipation gripped her.

"Laurel, would you marry me?"

Laurel could barely speak, but she squeaked out a yes. She wrapped her arms around his neck. "I would be honored," she said, pulling back and meeting his warm gaze.

"*Gut.*" He leaned over and kissed her, sending happiness buzzing through her like a honeybee. "We can make a home wherever you'd like. We can live here or we can go back to Pennsylvania. As long as I'm with you, I'll feel like I'm home. You gave up everything when you came here, and I'm willing to make that same sacrifice for you, Laurel. I love you, and my future is with you."

She leaned her head on his shoulder and smiled. "I love you too. At first I was afraid to leave my family, but I feel the same way you do—I believe in my heart that I belong here with you. I feel like I'm home when I'm with you, no matter where we live. And I know that I will still have my family in my life through letters, phone calls, and yearly visits."

"I'm so *froh* to hear you say that, but if the Lord leads us down a new path, I'm willing to go wherever he leads us."

"*Danki.*" When she saw something white and fluffy twirl through the air, she sat up. "Look! It's snowing!" She stood and walked to the edge of the porch as snow began to fall like pretty glitter.

"Look at that." Glen rubbed her back. "Your first Colorado snow."

She looked up. "I can't wait to experience more Colorado snow."

Glen pulled her into his arms for a hug, and she rested her head on his shoulder. Closing her eyes, she silently thanked God for leading her to Colorado. She couldn't wait to see what God had in store for their love and the rest of their lives.

ACKNOWLEDGMENTS

AS ALWAYS, I'M THANKFUL for my loving family, including my mother, Lola Goebelbecker; my husband, Joe; and my sons, Zac and Matt.

Thank you to my mother and my dear friend Maggie Halpin who graciously read the draft of this book to check for typos. I'm also thankful for my special Amish friend who patiently answers my endless stream of questions. I'm grateful for the story she shared that inspired this story.

Thank you to my wonderful church family at Morning Star Lutheran in Matthews, North Carolina, for your encouragement, prayers, love, and friendship. You all mean so much to my family and me.

Thank you to Zac Weikal and the fabulous members of my Bakery Bunch! I'm so grateful for your friendship and your excitement about my books. You all are awesome!

To my agent, Natasha Kern—I can't thank you enough for your guidance, advice, and friendship. You are a tremendous blessing in my life.

Thank you to my amazing editor, Jocelyn Bailey, for

your friendship and guidance. I'm grateful to each and every person at HarperCollins Christian Publishing who helped make this book a reality.

Thank you to editor Becky Philpott for polishing the story and connecting the dots. I'm so grateful that we are working together again!

Thank you most of all to God—for giving me the inspiration and the words to glorify you. I'm grateful and humbled you've chosen this path for me.

DISCUSSION QUESTIONS

1. Laurel traveled from Bird-in-Hand, Pennsylvania, to Monte Vista, Colorado, for a teaching job. What do you think of her decision to move across the country to serve as a teacher?
2. Glen is devastated when he finds out his mother and sister hurt Laurel's feelings. What do you think about his mother and sister and what they said about his relationship with Laurel?
3. Rena had the students in the schoolhouse draw pictures to represent what they love about Colorado as a way to try to convince Laurel to stay. How do you think the pictures made Laurel feel about her decision to leave?
4. Glen is furious with his mother despite her effort to apologize to him for hurting Laurel. Did you think he was right when he told her to fix what she'd done to ruin his relationship with Laurel?
5. Which character can you identify with the most?

Which character seemed to carry the most emotional stake in the story? Was it Laurel, Glen, or someone else?

6. At the end of the story, Laurel decides to give Glen's family and the community another chance. What do you think made her change her mind about leaving?

A LESSON ON LOVE

KATHLEEN FULLER

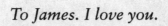

To James. I love you.

CHAPTER 1

I NEVER THOUGHT I'D be back here again.

Priscilla Helmuth stared at the Wagler's Buggy Shop sign in front of her, lost in her thoughts. When she returned to the Amish last year, she'd expected to spend the rest of her days in Shipshewana, her hometown. But here she was, in tiny Marigold, Ohio, ready to buy a buggy. Marigold was home to fifty people, all Amish. Quite a difference from Shipshe, and a world apart from her former life. But she knew better than anyone that the best laid plans didn't work out. God had a way of seeing to that.

Glancing to the right, she saw two buggies parked on the side of the large workshop. The doors were wide open, but she didn't see anyone inside. Hopefully one or both of the buggies were for sale. If they weren't, she would have to ask the guy who owned the shop where she could buy a used one. She couldn't afford to buy a brand-new buggy.

She tugged on one of the strings of her white prayer *kapp*. There was a time she never thought she would wear a *kapp* again, or a calf-length dress like the lavender one she had on now. Although it had been six months since she left Nashville and returned to her Amish roots, she still thought about her English clothes from time to time. She had loved jeans, high heels, crop tops, red lipstick, and highlighting her light-brown hair with streaks of blonde. Now the only two pairs of shoes she had were black tennis shoes and black winter boots, and she hadn't worn lipstick since she went back to Shipshe.

"Hi." A man's voice, low and pleasant sounding, brought her out of her thoughts. He was approaching her from around the back of the shop. He wiped his hands on a rag, then stuffed the corner of the cloth into the back waistband of his broadfall pants. "Can I help you?"

Priscilla stilled, then nodded. Wow, he was a handsome guy. Blond hair and blue eyes had always been her weakness, whether she was Amish or English. But that wasn't the only thing that drew her attention. He was big, at least half a foot taller than her, and had a body the size of a football player, thick and well muscled. He also looked like he ate well, which added to his attractiveness. She appreciated a man with a big appetite.

She brought her thoughts up short. What was she doing, admiring this man? She was thirty-five years old, and he looked to be several years younger. Not only was she old but she had also newly returned to her faith. Her old maid status was a given. Besides, someone as good-looking as him had to be taken already. He was clean-shaven, but that didn't mean he didn't have a girlfriend, or even a fiancé.

He tilted his head and caught her gaze. "Did you need something?"

Her face warmed, and not only because of the afternoon summer heat. She had to look like a fool standing here staring at him like this. "I'd like to purchase a buggy. A *used* buggy, that is."

"All right. I happen to have one available." He pointed to one of the two near the shop. "Would you like to take a look at it?"

She nodded and followed him to the vehicle. Now that she saw it up close, she realized it was in rough shape. The wheels were warped, the body needed to be replaced, and the doors were dented in.

"I rehab old buggies," he said, giving it an affectionate pat. "Don't worry about what it looks like now. It won't take long to fix her up *gut* as new."

"*Mei* horse is due to arrive in two weeks." She had purchased the retired racehorse at an auction in Holmes County when she first arrived in Marigold, and she made a deal with the owner to board him until she built a barn and bought a buggy. She hadn't made any progress finding someone to build the barn, but hopefully she could make a deal with this man concerning the buggy.

"That's *nee* problem. I can get this finished in a week, tops."

Priscilla liked his confidence. "How much will it cost?"

"How does four thousand sound?"

It sounded like a lot, but she knew she was getting a good deal. A new buggy would cost twice that or more, so she couldn't be choosy. "I'll take it."

"Great." He gestured to the plain white house behind him. "We can *geh* to *mei* office and discuss the details."

Her good feelings about him shifted. "That looks like a residence."

"It is. I keep *mei* office in there, too, right up front near the door. That way I can use up every bit of shop space."

She hesitated, her self-preservation kicking in. Then she reminded herself that she wasn't in a cutthroat city anymore, and this man was Amish, and what he was saying made sense. The likelihood of him taking advantage of her was basically zero. She relaxed, sensing she could trust him.

A warm summer breeze kicked up, but it offered little relief from the August heat. She thought she had acclimated to hot and humid weather during her time in Tennessee, but she'd forgotten that there were days in Ohio that rivaled the muggiest southern summer weather.

"Come on inside and you can tell me what you want done to the buggy." He started walking toward the house. "*Mei* name is Micah, by the way."

She quickly followed, pushing her musings as far away as she could. "I'm Priscilla," she said, then added, "Helmuth."

"Wagler's *mei* last name." He grinned and opened the screen door. "I guess you already knew that. Name's on the sign." He held open the door for her. "Office is to the left."

She walked inside, surprised to catch the scent of a home-cooked meal in what appeared to be a bachelor's home. The front room was obviously a living area, and to the left was a nondescript desk and a chair.

He inched past her and picked up a spiral-bound steno pad from the desk, then took the pencil from behind his ear. The pencil and pad looked small in his brawny hands. "That buggy is a two-seater. I could make it a four-seater for the same price if you need me to."

"Two only."

"Two it is."

The rest of the ordering process was straightforward since Priscilla had found out when she arrived here that all the buggies in Ohio were the same no matter what district a person lived in. Micah wrote down the list of everything he would do to refurbish and upgrade the buggy, including a warm, plush blanket for extra cold days. "I can upholster the seat in the same color as the blanket," he said. "Some folks like things to match."

"No upholstery," she said. That would be extra, and right now she couldn't afford anything other than the basic model. She almost laughed, remembering some of the fancy cars she had ridden in, and now she was purchasing a simple, used buggy. For some that might be considered a step back. *More like a step in the right direction.*

"Got it. Anything else?"

"Are you sure it will be ready in a week? I don't know much about buggy repair or restoration, but it looks in bad shape to me."

"You're right about that. The old girl is in a sad state right now. But I'll have it done. Things are slow at the moment. That's kind of how things *geh* around here. Business, like life, ebbs and flows."

"That it does," she said, noticing he sounded more like an old sage than a young man.

"Do you live nearby?" He scribbled one last thing on the paper before tearing it off the pad.

"I just moved to Marigold last week."

Micah handed her the slip. "I didn't think I recognized you. Welcome to Marigold. We're small, but we're . . . well, small." He grinned again.

She couldn't help but chuckle as she looked down at the four-thousand-dollar amount he'd written down, along with all the buggy specifications they'd discussed. "*Danki*," she said, looking up at him again. Attraction hit her harder than it had when she first laid eyes on him. She'd been around a lot of good-looking English men during the fifteen years she lived in Nashville. She'd even gone out with a few, but those dates had never gone anywhere. That was partly due to her focus on her dream. Dating only got in the way of that. But none of the men she'd met had ever brought out the butter-flies in her stomach the way Micah was. *Focus on the buggy, not on him.* She wasn't in Marigold to find a man, no matter how kind and handsome he was.

Priscilla tapped on the receipt, shifting her thoughts to the matter at hand instead of . . . *never mind.* "Your price is very reasonable."

"That's how I stay in business." He smiled again.

The fluttering intensified, and she knew she had to get out of here before she said something stupid, like ask him if he was single. She was supposed to be getting her ducks in a row, not hitting on the buggy maker. "See you in a week then."

"Oh, I forgot." He picked up the pad again. "How do I get in touch with you and let you know the buggy is done? Sometimes I finish them early."

Priscilla told him her address. She had used what was left of her savings to buy a tiny house that was once owned by an English family, and last week she removed most of the electrical herself, thanks to getting a book from the local library two towns over that showed her how to be an amateur electrician. She was pretty proud of herself for accomplishing that. Then she had to check herself. Humility was the goal, not pride. A total reversal of her life in the English world.

"You don't live too far from here," he said. "Glad you didn't have a long walk." Then he paused. "It's almost quitting time. I can give you a ride home if you need one."

She almost dropped the paper in her hand. She couldn't believe he was offering to take her home. The distance was hardly worth the trouble of hitching up a buggy. *What a good guy.* "I don't mind walking. The weather is nice."

"It sure is. Pretty hot, though." He walked over to the screen door and opened it. "Don't worry. I'll get that buggy done as soon as I can."

"I appreciate it." She walked through the door and into the small gravel parking lot. She resisted looking behind her to see where he was, annoyed that it mattered to her. It wasn't like she didn't have a lot of things to keep her occupied, like a new house and a new job. Hopefully soon she'd have a new barn for her new horse and buggy. She needed to focus on her new life, not the buggy maker. *Priorities, Priscilla. Priorities.*

Micah stood in front of his house and watched Priscilla walk away. Strange, since he normally didn't do that when customers left his parking lot. Then again, he didn't have too much to do today. Business had been down to a crawl lately. Not surprising, considering he had just come off a busy time over the past three months, enough that he had to hire temporary help. Fortunately, there were a few young teenage kids in the district who were eager to learn something new while picking up a little extra cash. That alleviated any guilt he had for laying them off when things slowed down. His latest helper, Christopher, had just finished eighth grade. Micah wished he could have kept him on, but the business just wasn't there. He was pleased to find out Christopher got another job quickly after Micah let him go.

Although he'd lived in Marigold a little over three years, some of Micah's family and friends still questioned the wisdom of his decision to leave Lancaster and live in this tiny community no one knew about in Knox County. He told them what he believed—he wouldn't be here if God didn't want him here. Owning his own buggy shop had been his dream since he was sixteen and worked as an apprentice in his great-uncle's business. But he'd always known he couldn't open a shop in Lancaster due to the competition. Instead he trusted that God would lead him to the right district, so much so he had closed his eyes and pushed a pin in a map of Ohio, vowing to go wherever the pin stuck. Three years later, he still had no regrets.

Not that owning his own business was always easy, but he was careful with his money during the busy times so he would have margin during the slow ones. Now that he wasn't swamped with work, he was free to help the community build the new schoolhouse. That's where he would be this Saturday, when all the available able-bodied men would help build the school.

I wonder what Priscilla's doing on Saturday . . .

He gave his head a hard shake. Where had that come from? Sure, she was a nice-looking woman, but so were a lot of the women he knew. He appreciated her directness, and that she knew exactly what she wanted when she ordered the buggy. She carried herself gracefully. He also thought her eyes were pretty. They were an unusual shade of light green, a color he hadn't seen before. He could tell she was older, probably in her thirties if he had to guess.

He shrugged and went back to the shop. The only thing he needed to think about concerning Priscilla was rehabbing her buggy to the best of his ability, as he did for all his customers.

Half an hour later, Micah went inside his house and headed straight for the kitchen. The pot of chili he'd made right before Priscilla showed up was simmering nicely on the stove, and he quickly whipped up a batch of cornbread and put the pan in the oven. Then he sat down at the table, stretched out his legs, and—unbelievably—thought of her again.

But this time he knew why she came to mind. Although he was twenty-five and had lived on his own for three years, he'd never had a problem feeling lonely until recently. He couldn't pinpoint why he felt that way, but he chalked some of it up to not being as busy as he normally was when business was bustling. Usually after work he had only enough energy to make himself supper, read the newspaper while he ate, and then hit the hay. But for the last two months or so, even though he had been busy, being in this empty house was getting to him. He had even thought about getting a dog for company, which was a huge deal because he was allergic to pet dander. That could be fixed with a little antihistamine. There wasn't such an easy solution to his loneliness.

He got up and walked to the counter, then poured himself a glass of iced tea from the pitcher he'd made that morning, and drained half of it. The timer went off on the oven, and he grabbed a potholder to pull out the golden cornbread. One thing he knew for sure was that since he'd been living alone, he had learned how to cook. Next week he planned to make cherry turnovers. He'd never made those before, but he was feeling adventurous.

Does Priscilla like turnovers?

Good grief, he had to stop thinking about her. Maybe he really did need to get a dog.

CHAPTER 2

ON FRIDAY EVENING, PRISCILLA was still thinking about Micah Wagler, much to her annoyance. She couldn't afford to be distracted, especially for two whole days. She sat at the small table in her kitchen, the last bit of evening sunlight streaming through the window, a fan hooked up to a gas generator cooling off the inside. Due to the heat, she couldn't bring herself to cook anything, not that she cooked that much anyway. Instead she slapped together a quick cheese and butter sandwich and munched on a few corn chips. Not the healthiest supper, but then again, she didn't have to worry about her figure anymore.

She had just finished the last corn chip on her plate when she heard a knock on her front door. When she answered it, she saw Leah Yoder, the former schoolteacher of Marigold school, standing there. She was holding a basket, and by the yummy smell emanating from it, Priscilla could tell she had brought food. "Hello," she said, smiling at the younger woman as she opened the door and gestured for her to come inside.

"Hi, Priscilla." Leah walked into the living room. She turned around and held out the basket. "I brought a few goodies to welcome you to Marigold. And to thank you for taking on *mei* old job."

"That's so thoughtful of you," Priscilla said in English as she closed the door. Then she switched to *Deitsch*. "The food smells *appeditlich*."

"I just whipped up a few things," she said. "It's *nix* special."

But Priscilla could tell by Leah's small smile that she was pleased by the compliment. "I'll put this in the kitchen," she said. Then she glanced at her tiny living room, filled with exactly one chair and a small love seat. Eventually she would fully furnish her small house, but right now the sparse furniture would have to do. "Make yourself at home. Would you like some *kaffee*? I can make a fresh pot. Or would you rather have iced tea?"

"A glass of water would be nice, if it's not too much trouble."

"*Nee* trouble at all. I'll be right back."

When Priscilla entered the kitchen, she set the basket on the counter and peered underneath the white tea towel covering the food. There was a tin foil–wrapped loaf, still warm, and from the smell of it she presumed it was meatloaf. There was also a container of whipped potatoes, a broccoli salad, and what looked like a peach cobbler for dessert. Her stomach growled. Clearly the cheese sandwich and corn chips hadn't satisfied her. This also wasn't "just a few goodies." This was a bona fide feast.

As she put the food away and then prepared the glass of water for Leah, she marveled at how easily she had fallen back into her hospitable Amish ways. She filled up two glasses with water and started to go back to the living room, then paused. Water wouldn't be enough, and she scrambled for something else to bring her guest. When she saw the bag of corn chips on the table, she grabbed it, poured a few into a plastic bowl, and tucked the bowl in the crook of her arm. Then she picked up the glasses and left the kitchen.

But when she got there, she realized there wasn't a place to put the snack. She handed Leah her water, then held out the bowl. "Corn chip?" she said.

"*Nee.* I'm still full from supper."

Priscilla looked around, finally deciding to balance the bowl on top of the fireplace mantel. Martha Stewart would be appalled, but Leah didn't seem to mind.

"I heard you took all the electric out of here yourself." Leah took a sip of the water as she glanced around the room with wide-eyed interest. "I'm impressed. I could never do something like that."

"Oh, I'm sure you could. It wasn't that hard." Priscilla sat down on the chair across from her, pleased with how she had smoothly deflected Leah's compliment.

"I don't have a handy bone in *mei* body." She smiled, her light-blue eyes sparkling with mirth. "*Gut* thing I know how to cook, and Ben knows how to fix everything."

"I'm not much of a cook." Priscilla looked down at the water in her glass.

"You didn't cook with *yer mamm* growing up?"

"Oh, sure. And she's a great cook. But her teaching didn't stick with me much. There were other things I wanted to do besides cook."

"Like teach."

Priscilla smiled. "*Ya*. Like teach." She hadn't revealed much of her past to anyone in Marigold, although she hadn't met all the residents yet. That would change when she attended church next week. She met Leah before at the board member meeting when she had interviewed for the teaching job. "I'm eager to meet *mei* students."

"You'll get a chance for that." Leah placed her hand over her stomach, and Priscilla wondered if she was expecting. Leah had resigned from her position at the end of the last school year, and Priscilla knew from her own school district in Shipshe that when a teacher resigned, it usually meant she was pregnant, or she was hoping she would be soon. But Priscilla wasn't going to pry.

"If you need any help, just let me know," Leah said. "I've got notes on every student, and I can give them to you before the school year starts."

"That would be wonderful." Priscilla smiled. She had liked Leah from the first time they met, and her opinion of this woman was growing higher by the minute. They chatted for a little while about the students and the schedules Leah had used with the younger and older grades. Priscilla was surprised when she checked the small clock she hung on the wall two days ago and saw that almost an hour had passed.

"I should be heading home," Leah said, getting up from the couch. "I told Ben I wouldn't be gone too long. Will you be at the school tomorrow?"

"*Ya.* I've never seen a school built from the ground up before." The school she attended had been in their district for twenty years already. Then she stilled. She had completely forgotten that she needed to take something to share for the meal that would be served in the middle of the day. Her pantry had only the essentials, and not Amish pantry essentials either. In the English world, if she ever went to a potluck, she stopped by the local grocery store and picked up something premade. It wasn't that simple in Marigold. The nearest store from her house was nearly a three-mile walk, and that meant shopping was an all-day event. She would be worn out by the time she got to the building site. What was she going to do? She glanced at the bowl of corn chips. *I can't bring those.* Besides, there was only a quarter of the bag left.

"Our town is growing, so we needed the new building," Leah added. "The old school won't be going to waste, though. A cabinetmaker moved into Marigold recently, and he's going to open up his shop there."

"Sounds like a *gut* solution for everyone."

"*Ya*, it is. And don't worry about bringing anything tomorrow," Leah said, as if she had read Priscilla's earlier thoughts. Then again, she might have, considering how mortified Priscilla felt about the situation. Surely her distress was written on her face. "We'll have plenty of food. All the women have been cooking up a storm. It has to be difficult moving to a new house and trying to get settled alone—oh, I'm sorry."

"Don't be." She smiled at Leah, who was obviously guileless. If there was one thing she'd learned from her time in Nashville, it was that she could judge a person's character. And similar to how she had felt with Micah, she knew Leah was a good person. "I don't mind being alone."

Leah's heart-shaped face turned pink. "I'm glad I didn't offend you."

"Not at all. And I promise I'll bring something next time."

After Leah left, Priscilla picked up the bowl of corn chips, went back into the kitchen, and then turned on her gas oven, intending to warm up the meatloaf. As she waited for the oven to heat up, she got out a plate. When she touched the meatloaf, which was wrapped in several layers of thick aluminum foil, she realized it was still plenty warm. So were the potatoes, and she decided to turn off the oven. Then she filled her plate with meatloaf, potatoes, and a slice of fresh bread. She walked to the table and sat down, bowing her head for silent prayer. Slipping back into the habit of prayer after being away from it for so long hadn't been difficult, and she'd turned back to praying a few months before returning to Shipshe. Now, not a day went by that she didn't talk to the Lord, even outside of her prayers before meals. Then again, wasn't that the main reason she had come back to her faith? To reconnect with God permanently? *Yes, but there are other reasons too.*

After her prayer, she looked at the meatloaf and potatoes.

Fat and carbs. Two no-no's in her life for the last fifteen years. She grinned and dug in.

Micah arrived at the school building site early in the morning, ready to go to work. He didn't have any customers yesterday, which had given him plenty of time to get a good start on Priscilla's buggy. He had been particularly fastidious as he worked, making extra sure the frame was as perfect as it could be. Since he had the spare time, he could afford to be. At least that's what he told himself. But for some reason deep inside, he wanted Priscilla to be pleased. And maybe a little impressed. He frowned. *Watch that pride.* Nothing good came from being prideful.

He pulled into the makeshift driveway and parking lot next to the future school. After parking his buggy, he got out and tethered his horse to the hitching rail. Two Amish men in their district who were masons had already built a cinder block foundation a week ago, and a week later several other men had dug the two latrines. Today's goal was to complete the schoolhouse, which could be done with plenty of the community's help and cooperation. The fact that school was starting next week added to the urgency.

Five other men were mingling around the site, even though it was barely sunrise. Soon more folks would show up, including the women, who would be bringing food for the midday meal. He smiled, already anticipating the delicious lunch.

Would Priscilla be here?

His smile faded. Why couldn't he get her out of his mind?

Ben Yoder, the husband of the former schoolteacher, strolled up to him. "Ready to build the outhouses?"

Micah rolled his eyes. "Of course, you would give me that job."

"At least they're empty." Ben laughed, hitching his thumb into his black suspenders. "With you doing the job we'll get it done in *nee* time."

Unlike Micah, Ben was whip thin and on the short side. Micah had never minded his large size, and in fact, he liked that he was called on to help out with hard and heavy tasks. Constructing the outhouse buildings was neither, but he was ready to get started. "Did they hire someone to replace Leah yet?"

Ben nodded. "*Ya*, and Leah visited her last night. I can't recall her name, though. You know how I am. It took me a year to remember Leah's."

Micah knew he was kidding—somewhat. Ben was notorious for being unable to put names to faces. "Guess I'll find out soon enough."

A short while later, as he expected, more than enough help had shown up, including a few teenagers. After working hard for the next several hours, around noon, everyone broke for lunch. Along the side of the parking lot, which was now almost covered in gravel, the women had set up several tables laden with a variety of foods. Nearby were a few other tables and chairs for the workers to sit at and eat, in addition to three large standing coolers of water on another table and four bottles of hand soap so everyone could wash up for lunch. Once his hands were clean, Micah sidled up to the first serving table and grabbed a sturdy paper plate and plastic silverware, his stomach grumbling. "I'm starving," he said to Ben, who was standing right behind him.

As he made his way down the line, the women served up the food. By the time Micah got to the desserts, his plate was piled high with macaroni ham casserole, crunchy potato balls, a few mini corn dogs, two soft pretzels, a large helping of broccoli and cauliflower salad, and a few lime pickles. He inspected the desserts, wondering which one to choose. That was a challenge since he could have picked them all. When he looked up, he saw that only two women were manning the table—Leah and . . . Priscilla.

Micah looked at his overflowing plate. Everyone knew he liked healthy portions and they hadn't been shy about giving them to him. Suddenly he was a little embarrassed. Maybe he should skip dessert. But he was already holding a smaller plate and he didn't want to put it back. He didn't want to keep Ben waiting for his dessert either.

Leah held out a huge piece of chocolate-and-white cream cake. "Here you *geh*, Micah. I cut this extra-large piece of Ho Ho Cake just for you."

Oh, the Lord knew how he loved a good piece of Ho Ho Cake. But he didn't want to look greedy in front of Priscilla. Ultimately, he had no choice because Leah plopped the piece on the right side of his dessert plate. "Uh, *danki*," he mumbled, quickly bypassing the other desserts, which consisted of several platters of cookies and candy. Then he stopped when he saw a cake he didn't recognize, wondering what it was. When he glanced up again, Priscilla was right in front of him.

"Hi, Micah," she said, gesturing to the cake. "Would you like a piece?"

Fortunately, the cake, which was chocolate flavored with white frosting and cherry pie filling on top, had already been cut into smaller pieces. His appetite got the best of him and he nodded. "Sure. I've never had this before. What is it?"

"I don't know," Priscilla said, looking over the pieces. She selected the largest one and picked it up. "Leah, what's this dessert called?"

Leah was cutting another slice of Ho Ho Cake for Ben. "My True Love Cake."

For some strange reason, his cheeks heated. Then again, it was hot today and he had been working hard. But this was a different type of heat, one he hadn't experienced before, and despite his excuses, he knew he was blushing because of Priscilla. She still held the piece of cake on the serving utensil, her expression impassive. Of course it was. She probably hadn't given him a second thought since she left his shop. He was the one with the issue and he need to get a grip. "Set it right here," he said, holding out his plate.

Priscilla placed the piece on his plate. "I've been staring at this cake all morning. It looks *appeditlich*. I might have a piece myself later."

Micah couldn't help but smile. There was nothing more

attractive than a woman with an appreciation for quality desserts. He nodded his thanks, then left and sat down at an empty table. He had just picked up a mini corn dog when Ben plopped down in the chair across from him.

"I'm surprised you're not eating the True Love Cake first." Ben picked up a slice of buttered bread and took a bite.

Micah shot him a look. "Dessert is for after the meal."

"Not when it's a *special* dessert."

Micah was confused. He peered at the cake, wondering if he was missing something. "It's different, but I don't see what's special about it."

"Perhaps it's not the cake so much as the person who served it to you." Ben grinned and took another bite of bread.

Great. Now Micah could feel his ears turning red. Was he being that obvious about his attraction to Priscilla that Ben had noticed? Worse yet, what if *she* noticed?

"Hey," Ben said, his expression turning serious. "I'm just teasing you, big guy. By the way, that's the new schoolteacher. Wish I could remember her name."

"Priscilla," he said, staring at his food.

"That's right. You two seemed to know each other."

Micah explained about Priscilla purchasing the buggy from him. When Ben returned to eating, Micah started to dig in too. But his mind was still on Priscilla and whether she had noticed his interest in her. As he bit into the corn dog, he hoped she hadn't.

CHAPTER 3

PRISCILLA FINISHED OFF THE last bite of her piece of True Love Cake and sat back, satisfied. After Micah left, she asked Leah who had made the cake. "*Mei mamm* was trying out a new recipe, and she decided to use all of us as guinea pigs," she said. "I had a small bite earlier and I think it's *sehr gut.*"

Priscilla thought the cake, along with all the other food, was very good too. She had to be careful because she might not be able to fit into her clothes if she kept eating like this. But after so many years of being weight conscious, she was glad to have some freedom. Wearing such a modest dress helped to hide some flaws, and while she had resented her Amish clothing when she was younger, she now appreciated the simplicity of her wardrobe.

Once everyone was finished eating and the men went

back to work, she helped the other ladies clear the tables, clean up the dishes, and put up the chairs. By the time all the work was done, two hours had passed. A few of the women pitched in with helping to spread the gravel on the parking lot, while the mothers of the younger children were sitting around and visiting as their offspring played.

During the day, Leah had pointed out Priscilla's students. She thought she might introduce herself to them today but decided to wait until school started. She still needed to get her seating chart, lesson plans, and grade book in order, but she was looking forward to teaching. There was a time when she thought about being a teacher before she decided to leave the Amish. Now she was getting ready to do a job she had wanted to do in the past, but never thought she would. *God works in strange ways.* No, not so strange. More and more she was realizing she'd made the right decision to return to her faith.

She picked up a spare shovel and joined the other women as they worked on the gravel parking lot, not only because she wanted to help but that way she could focus on something else besides Micah. When he smiled at her after she told him she thought the cake looked delicious, her heart had fluttered. There was no doubt she was attracted to him, and she couldn't help but watch him as he ate his lunch with Ben, although she made sure she wasn't being weird about it. He ate every crumb off his plate. Considering how much work he and the other men were doing, she wasn't surprised.

She also wasn't surprised when she saw him talking to the young woman who had stopped by his table while he was still eating. Emphasis on young. She was also pretty. Leah, who had not only pointed out Priscilla's future students but had also told her everyone's name, introduced the young woman as Suetta. The girl had lingered at the table longer than she needed to, considering she was bringing around a jug of water for anyone who needed a drink. A green thread of envy had wound around Priscilla, and she didn't like that one bit. Throwing herself into spreading gravel had been a good distraction.

By suppertime, the school building and the parking lot were finished. There was still more work to do on the inside of the building, but it wouldn't take an entire day and the whole community to finish the job. Everyone was tired but satisfied. They packed up the tools and empty dishes they'd brought, gathered their families, and left for the day.

Priscilla was about to leave when she saw a small empty patch of dirt at the back edge of the parking lot. She didn't bring a shovel with her, so instead she used her hands as she crouched down and evenly spread out the gravel. When she was finished, she brushed off her hands on her light-green dress, which was already dusty from the day's work, and turned around. "Oh!" she said, as she almost bumped into Micah. She looked up at him. "I thought everyone had already left."

"I wanted to finish up the back part of the boy's restroom," he said. He pushed back his hat, revealing his damp bangs.

His shirt also had dark spots of perspiration on it, and his face was red from exertion.

But she didn't mind any of that. She liked that she was back with people who did a good, honest day's work. That hadn't always been the case with the crowd she ran around with in Nashville. "I was just covering that last patch of dirt," she said.

"I know. I saw you. Looks *gut*." He put his hands on his waist, his tool belt slung low on his hips. "I heard you're the new schoolteacher."

"You heard right." She stared at the brand-new building in front of her. "This is a wonderful building. Once everything is finished, my students and I are really going to enjoy it."

"That's *gut* to know. Makes all the work worthwhile." He paused. "I, uh, wondered if you needed a ride home."

Stunned, she wasn't sure what to say. Although the day had been hot, clouds now cloaked the sky, cooling off the summer heat. She could walk the two miles back home but didn't relish the idea. She was worn out, and now she just wanted to get home and put her feet up.

But what about the little flutter that had appeared in her chest again? *And what about Suetta?*

Now she was being absurd. She already knew Micah was a nice guy, and he'd offered her a ride home before. She'd be nuts not to accept. "I'd like that," she said. *"Danki."*

He grinned, and instead of simply fluttering, her heart skipped a beat. He had a great smile, straight, white teeth, and full cheeks that made her think of a big, cuddly teddy bear. Her gaze drifted to his arms and his impressive biceps. *Oh boy.* Maybe she should have refused the ride after all.

She followed him to his buggy, and as he untied his horse from the hitching rail she climbed inside. The interior was clean, and the seat was upholstered in a royal blue fabric. When she sat down, she noticed how comfortable the cushion was. She shifted her feet, and her heel struck something. When she looked down, she saw a shiny object next to her foot. As she picked it up, she realized it was a harmonica.

Micah stepped into the buggy and looked her way. His gaze shifted to the harmonica in her hand.

"I found it on the floor." Priscilla handed it to him. "Do you play?"

He sat down and took the instrument from her. "Sometimes. It's been a while. I guess I forgot I left it in here." He examined the harmonica like he'd never seen one before.

The *Ordnung* back home had a rule against any instruments, including harmonicas. The way Micah reacted, she assumed Marigold didn't have the same restrictions. It had been so long since she'd heard music, other than being in a big-box store with canned sounds over the store's speakers. Priscilla couldn't help herself. "Would you mind playing it now?"

"I can try." He lifted the harmonica to his lips. "Like I said, it's been a while." He started to play, tentatively at first, as if he were getting used to the instrument again. Then he hit his stride.

She leaned back in the seat and closed her eyes, listening

to the haunting tune he played. The music reminded her of bluegrass, one of her favorite music genres, especially when played in a minor key.

He finished the song, waving his hand over the harmonica as the note faded into oblivion. When he looked at her, his expression was apprehensive. "I guess I put you to sleep."

She shook her head, then she turned to him. "Not at all. That was beautiful. What's the name of the song?"

Micah shrugged. "I don't know. I must have heard it somewhere when I was young because it didn't take me long to learn the tune." He rolled the harmonica in his hand. "I've missed playing this thing."

"How long have you been playing? Who taught you how?" She sat up and angled her body toward him so she could face him.

"*Mei daed* showed me," he said. "When I was about five or so. The district we lived in didn't allow instruments, but he bought me a harmonica anyway and gave me lessons. The rule was that we could only play in the barn. I thought that was fair, and as I grew older, we would play duets. Mostly hymns, some old songs he knew when he was a kid."

"Did you have sheet music?" she asked.

He frowned. "What's that?"

"Music printed on a page. Like in our hymnals."

"Ah," he said, nodding. "*Nee*, we just played. Sometimes I would *geh* out to the barn by myself and just make up some songs."

"Can you play one now?" She thought for a quick second

that she might be keeping him from plans he had at home. But the sweet music that came through his harmonica had touched her deeply, as all music did. That was the hardest thing to give up when she came back to her faith—the music she loved so much.

"Sure."

Priscilla smiled, and Micah began to play. When he was a few bars in, she began to hum a few notes of melody, the pitch of her singing a little higher than the harmonica's dulcet tones. It wasn't long before she fully joined in with her improvised singing and his vibrant playing.

They finished at the same time, and he turned to her, amazement in his eyes. "How did you do that?" he asked.

"Do what?" She couldn't help but smile.

"Whatever you were humming went perfectly with the song. It sounded beautiful too."

She glanced down at her lap, warmed by his compliment. But it wasn't just the words he'd said, but the way he looked at her, the music they'd made, and the coziness of being close to each other in the buggy. She shouldn't be feeling such intense emotions so soon after they had just met, but she refused to question that right now. All that mattered was this beautiful feeling in her heart and soul, the spark when they first met already growing stronger. "*Danki*," she said, looking at him. Then she realized she didn't answer his question. "I've had a lot of practice."

"Singing in church?"

"*Ya*. And by myself. I've always liked music. We couldn't

have instruments either, but I loved to sing." She glanced at the harmonica again. "Are you going to get in trouble for playing?"

He shook his head. "The bishop doesn't mind, as long as it's just a harmonica. No fancy guitars or anything like that. Now that I think about it, I haven't played for anyone else in a long time. Usually it's just me and the horse in the barn."

Pricilla laughed. "Why are you playing in the barn if you don't have to hide?"

He shrugged. "Old habits are hard to break. But playing here in the buggy with you beats the barn any day."

When she met his gaze, she couldn't pull away. "I think so too."

❧

Micah had taken a risk when he asked Priscilla if he could take her home, and that risk was paying off more than he'd hoped. He'd been a little nervous to play his harmonica for her, mostly because he was rusty, and even though some of the rust disappeared after two songs, he knew he could play better. But all that was forgotten because of two things— her breathtaking voice and the way she was looking at him now. He'd never believed in love at first sight. But right now, alone in his buggy with Priscilla, he was starting to change his mind. *Rein it in. I don't want to scare her off.*

"I should be getting home." She turned and faced forward, her expression blank again.

He tucked the harmonica into his tool belt and tried to hide his frown. A second ago, she seemed so open and warm. Now she was back to acting like they were strangers. Which they were. He was the one that was reading more into it. "*Nee* problem," he said, keeping his voice steady as he tapped the reins on the back of his horse, Billy. "We'll be there real soon."

She was silent on the way home, and he didn't try to make conversation with her. But the echoes of their duet still played in his mind. If her humming was so mesmerizing, he couldn't imagine what her singing voice sounded like. All he knew was that he wanted to find out. He just didn't know how, other than to ask her straight out, and he wasn't sure how receptive she would be.

A short while later he pulled into the driveway of a small, blue vinyl-sided house. He'd never met the previous owners, since the house had been for sale before he moved to Marigold three years ago. But it was obviously English, and not just because of the color of the siding. There was an attached garage door painted pale yellow, white shutters on the windows, and a cement driveway.

When Billy halted in the middle of the driveway, Priscilla turned to him. Instead of a blank expression, she looked a little sheepish. "I still have a lot of work to do on the house. I'm going to get the siding replaced, paint the garage door, and redo the landscaping."

He frowned a little. "That's going to be a lot of work."

"I'm not going to do it all at once. I have to focus on teaching first, of course. But I'll get things done a little at a time."

Micah nodded. She was obviously independent, and he liked that about her. He wasn't a fan of clingy women, like Suetta Keim. She'd annoyed him a little today when she kept talking to him while he tried to finish his lunch. She was a nice enough girl, but there was no attraction there on his part. Not like there was with Priscilla.

Problem was, he was liking Priscilla a little too much. What he didn't like was the amount of work facing her to get this place in shape, especially since she would have to complete what she could in her spare time. That didn't set right with him.

"I guess I'll see you at church tomorrow," she said.

Church. He'd forgotten all about it, and now he realized she'd have to walk a little over two miles to get to the Keims' place, where the service was being held. "Can I give you a ride there tomorrow?" he blurted. "It's a fairly far walk from here."

"I was going to leave early so I would be there on time."

"I can pick you up," he said, then quickly added, "That way you won't have to get up so early."

"I don't mind."

Disappointment filled him, but he wasn't surprised she'd turned him down. *Independent, that's for sure.*

"I better get inside," she said, moving to get out of the buggy. "*Danki* for the ride, Micah. I appreciate it."

"You're welcome." Although he wished she would have agreed to let him take her to church, he accepted her decision. "I'll see you tomorrow."

"See you then." She stepped out of the buggy and walked toward the house.

Frowning, he gripped Billy's reins, trying to stem his disappointment. Then again, it was probably for the best. He didn't need to get more attached to Priscilla than he already was, especially when she didn't return his feelings. He would make sure to finish her buggy this week, though. She didn't need to be hiking all over Marigold any more than she had to. He didn't begrudge long walks, but having a horse and buggy saved time.

He reversed his buggy out of the driveway and turned toward home. Back to his empty, lonely house, which was the last place he wanted to go. Maybe he would stop by the bishop's house for a little while. He and his wife, who had grown and married children and lived alone in a small house nearby, were always up for visitors. Then he nixed that idea. Bishop Miller would be preparing for tomorrow's service and Micah didn't want to intrude. He had no choice but to go home.

"Wait!"

Micah pulled Billy to a stop, the buggy wheels at the edge of the driveway. Priscilla was running toward him, waving her arms.

Priscilla wasn't sure what compelled her to change her mind and flag Micah down. Common sense mostly, she assumed as she hurried toward his buggy. He was right—if he did give her a ride to the service tomorrow, she would have at least an extra hour of sleep tomorrow morning.

But that wasn't the only reason. There had been a finality in his eyes when she refused his offer, and she realized she did want to see him again. Impulsivity had been a problem for her when she was young, but as she grew older and more jaded, she also took more time to think about her decisions. On the ride home she had talked herself out of any feelings she had for Micah. Getting involved with someone at this point in her life would be a mistake. She still believed that, but the knowledge didn't stop her from changing her mind.

"Is everything okay?" Micah said, leaning his head out of the buggy.

She nodded. She had almost reached her front door, and although the driveway wasn't that long, she wasn't exactly in prime physical shape. Catching her breath, she said, "If it's all right, I wouldn't mind a ride to church after all."

A grin broke out on his face. "I'd be happy to give you one."

Priscilla couldn't help but smile back, and the flutter returned full force. He was such a genuinely nice man. Having been around a lot of men who weren't, she could usually peg someone who had ulterior motives. But there was no guile in Micah, she was sure of that. *"Danki,"* she said, glad she had made a sensible decision, despite her feelings being the exact opposite of sensible.

He told her what time he would pick her up, still smiling. "I'll see you then," he added, then drove away.

She turned and walked to the house, wondering what she would wear tomorrow. Then she chuckled. The question was so automatic and moot now that she was Amish again. She would wear her navy blue dress, white *kapp*, and black stockings. Regular church clothes. Nothing fancy or impressive. *What a relief.*

She opened the door and went inside, then turned on the small gas lamp in the living room. After fixing a plate of leftover meatloaf and mashed potatoes, she sat down at the kitchen table and said a silent prayer of grace. When she opened her eyes, she ate with gusto, a little surprised that she could be so hungry after eating a huge meal at lunch. Then again, she had done a lot of physical labor today.

One of her teacher manuals was lying on the table, and she read a few pages while she was eating. But she ended up closing the book, unable to concentrate on anything other than Micah, the lovely music they had made together, and the fact that she would be seeing him tomorrow.

CHAPTER 4

ON THE WAY TO church the next morning, Priscilla enjoyed the comfortable conversation between her and Micah. He told her a little more about Marigold and about how he had moved from Lancaster to start his own buggy business. "I had to get used to making a different type of buggy," he explained as sunshine filtered through the front opening of his buggy. "The ones back home are more square-shaped. Some are gray, some are yellow. Here in Ohio they're all black."

"I noticed that. They're different in Shipshewana too."

"It didn't matter to me, though. I like learning new things." He glanced at her with a half smile, and she couldn't look away. No man could compare to Micah Wagler in his Amish church clothes. "Sometimes we have to *geh* where we can find the work too."

She nodded. "I couldn't find a teaching job in *mei* nearby

community. That's how I ended up in Marigold." She wasn't ready to reveal her complete past to Micah, but she could tell him about how she ended up in Ohio. "*Mamm* has a friend in Birch Creek."

"That's about half an hour from here," Micah said.

"*Ya. Mamm* mentioned to her that I was looking for a teaching position. Her friend suggested looking for a job in this area, and that's how I found out that the Marigold teaching job was available."

"How big of a *familye* do you have?" he asked.

"Not that big. I've got an older *schwester*. She's been married a long time and has three kids. They're all married now too." Priscilla paused, feeling a touch of homesickness. Even when she had announced that she was leaving to go to Nashville, her parents and sister were supportive. Since she hadn't joined the church yet, she wouldn't be shunned, and they could maintain their relationship. But she hadn't been back in Shipshe for a year when she took the job in Marigold, again with her parents' blessing. As soon as she was able, she was going back for a visit. Eventually her house would be ready for guests so they could visit her too.

"I've got four sisters. I'm the oldest." Micah turned into what Priscilla assumed was the Keims' driveway.

"Was your *familye* okay with you moving?"

He nodded. "They understand the competition in Lancaster. *Daed* is an accountant, and I've got *nee* interest in numbers, other than the bookkeeping I do for *mei* business. I've always worked with *mei* hands, and the idea of sitting at a desk all day never appealed." He pulled the buggy to a stop. "We're here."

She looked around and saw many of the people she had met yesterday milling around outside the Keims' barn.

"Hi, Micah!"

Priscilla turned to see Suetta standing near the driver's side of Micah's buggy. Up close, the young woman was even prettier and younger than Priscilla thought. With her dark hair and Micah's blond locks, she had to admit they would make a striking couple. Then a horrible thought occurred to her. Maybe Suetta was already Micah's girlfriend. Her stomach twisted into a tight knot.

"I made some double-loaded chocolate brownies last night for lunch today," Suetta said, smiling at Micah as if he had hung not only the moon but the stars and planets too. "But I forgot them this morning. I was wondering if you could take me home to get them after the church service."

Priscilla couldn't help but inwardly cringe. This lovely young girl's feelings for Micah were painfully obvious. *She has good taste. That's for sure.* Suetta reminded her of a time back when she was sixteen and had been smitten with Paul Raber, who was nineteen at the time. Fortunately, he hadn't returned any of her awkward attempts at getting his attention, and he ended up marrying his wife six months later. That had been embarrassing to say the least, but like most childhood crushes, she quickly got over it.

Micah glanced at Priscilla, then looked at Suetta again. "I'm sorry, Suetta, but I have plans right after the service.

I'm sure Samuel Yoder wouldn't mind giving you a lift, though."

Suetta scowled. "Never mind. I'll *geh* get them myself." She glared at Priscilla, then flounced away.

"Sorry about that," Micah said as he started to get out of the buggy.

"She likes you." Envy struck her again, even more so than yesterday when she had seen him and Suetta talking during lunch. She fought to keep her tone even.

"Nah. She's just a *kinn*."

"How old is she?"

He paused, his large body halfway out of the buggy. "Twenty? Twenty-one? I reckon I don't really know."

Priscilla smirked. "She's too close to *yer* age for you to be calling her a *kinn*. Now I can call her a *kinn* because—" She pressed her lips together. She couldn't believe she came so close to revealing how old she was. Maybe he wouldn't notice.

"Because why?"

Oh boy. Well, he would find out sooner or later. "Because I'm thirty-five."

He shrugged. "Well, we should head for the service or we'll be late."

She gaped at him. Didn't he care that she was so much older than he was? And then there was the envious knot in her stomach that wouldn't go away. Great. She was jealous of a girl who was fifteen years younger than her. *Pathetic.* She hurried to the other side of the buggy. "Did you hear what I said? I'm thirty-five."

"I heard you." He smiled. "Age is just a number." Then he walked toward the barn.

She watched him go. If he wasn't going to make an issue of it, she wouldn't. Or at least she'd try not to. Trying to focus on the service due to start in a few minutes, she walked inside the church and searched for Leah, the only person she knew well enough in the community to feel comfortable sitting with. She was relieved when she spotted her, but as she walked over, she saw Suetta sitting next to her. These two were friends? *Great, just great.*

"Hi, Priscilla," Leah said, motioning for her to sit down next to her. "You remember *mei* cousin, Suetta," she added as Priscilla sat down.

Cousin? She didn't recall Leah telling her yesterday that they were related. Leaning forward, she said, "Hi, Suetta."

Suetta crossed her arms, her face pinched into an unattractive glower as she stared straight ahead and refused to acknowledge Priscilla.

The singing started, and as Priscilla stood to sing, making sure to temper her voice so as not to gain anyone's attention, she thought about what Micah had said about Suetta being a child. She was starting to think he was right. But that didn't change the fact that the girl liked him or that she was more appropriate for his age . . . and that Priscilla definitely wasn't. That truth hit her like a buggy at breakneck speed.

Whatever feelings she had for Micah, she needed to get rid of them, and fast. If she didn't, she would be in for a world of pain.

After the service, Micah took Priscilla back home. He'd expected to get a little ribbing from Ben when he arrived with her at church, so he ignored his friend and sat on the back pew for the service. He wasn't in the mood for teasing.

On the way home from church, he glanced at Priscilla. This morning they had gotten to know each other better, and he'd hoped they would continue that conversation during the return ride. But she was angled away from him, watching the landscape pass by. He couldn't blame her for enjoying the weather. The temperature was slightly cooler than yesterday, the sparse clouds helping to temper the hot sunshine. Birds chirped and sang, the grasses and lawns were a deep, vibrant green, and the air was refreshing.

Or maybe Priscilla just made everything better.

Still, there was something different from the ride this morning to the one now, and he couldn't figure out what it was. The drawn-out silence made him ill at ease, so he said, "Nice weather today, *ya*?" Small talk seemed so superficial compared to their conversation this morning, but he didn't know what else to say.

"It's nice."

Oh boy. She had a bee in her bonnet for sure. His mother would get like this when she was irritated with *Daed*, although to her credit she often got over things quickly. Micah had inherited that trait from her. "Priscilla, did I do something wrong?"

She turned to him, a surprised expression on her face. "Of course not." She sighed and faced forward. "*Yer* the nicest man I've ever met."

He shifted in his seat. Women didn't make sense sometimes. "That's a problem?"

Shaking her head, she looked at him again, and this time there was a slight smile on her lips. "*Nee.* And you're right, it is a nice day. That's something I missed when I was in . . ." She glanced at her lap. "Never mind."

He wondered why she hadn't finished her statement, but he also wasn't the kind of man to pry into someone else's business. They were close to her house anyway, and a few minutes later he pulled into her driveway and brought Billy to a halt. When he saw her house, he remembered the long list of things she said she had to get done. She shouldn't have to do all the work herself, and he couldn't abide letting her. "I'll be finished with the buggy this week," he said, still holding onto the reins, but relaxing his grip. "After that, I can help you with some of those renovations you were talking about yesterday."

"Oh, I couldn't ask you to do that. I'll get them done in the future." She smiled, this time a full one. "I appreciate the offer, though."

Wow, she was so pretty. He even liked the tiny lines around her eyes when she smiled. He didn't care that she was ten years older than him. She was beautiful. And she was turning him down again. "I don't mind," he said quickly. "Like I said, business is slow right now. I need something to fill *mei* time. Besides, that would free you up to work on your planning and stuff for school."

"But it's a lot of work—"

"I like working." *Especially when you're near.* He bit the inside of his cheek, reminding himself that his interest was one-sided. "It's *mei* Christian duty to help you out," he said, hoping that putting his offer in that perspective would make her reconsider. That wasn't his primary reason, of course, but it was also true. "I could take a look and see what needs to be done at least."

Priscilla paused. "All right. You'll probably change your mind after that."

He knew he wouldn't, but he nodded anyway. He drove his horse closer to the house until he was in front of the garage door.

"I plan to have a small barn in the back," she said. "When I first moved in, I tried finding someone to build it, but knowing that the community was building the *schoolhaus*, I didn't want to ask anyone in Marigold. When I tried some other nearby businesses, they were busy. There is one other place I plan to call tomorrow, though."

Her explanation didn't make much sense to him. So what if the community was building the school? Micah knew they would pitch in to build the teacher a barn too. What kind of community did she come from in Shipshe that she didn't think she could depend on them?

He got out of the buggy and unhitched Billy. As he followed her to the backyard, he decided he would take care of building the barn for her. From what he guessed, she needed one big enough for the horse and maybe an awning next to it to shelter the buggy. That wouldn't take too long to build, and if Christopher was available, they could get it done in a few hours. He made a mental note to mention it to her later.

While Billy munched on the grass in the fenced-in backyard, Priscilla showed him where she planned to have the barn. Then she gave him the grand tour of the backyard, which included a shaded, concrete patio. She didn't have any patio furniture, but he saw a pile of hay bales stacked up against the house and well underneath the short roof overhang in case of rain. "I bought them at the same auction where I got *mei* horse," she said. "They were on sale, so I got a *gut* deal."

He was glad to see she had started a supply, but she would have to get more once winter set in. "I'll make sure the barn has plenty of storage space."

"Wait a minute," she said, holding up her hand. "I didn't agree to you building the barn or doing anything else around here."

No one could call Priscilla Helmuth a pushover, that was for sure. "You're a practical woman, *ya?*"

She lifted her chin. "I like to think so."

"Then think about this practically. You need a barn. I'm willing to build you one. Not only that, but I can do it at a *gut* price and get it done quickly. You saw me working on the *schoolhaus*. I take any job I do seriously, and I always do *mei* best. You may not find that in an English company."

Her gaze held his, defiance in her eyes. Then she nodded. "You're right. Okay, I give. You can build the barn."

He grinned. *"Danki."*

Priscilla laughed. "I should be thanking you . . . so, *danki.*" She tapped her chin. "I've never had a barn built before. *Mei daed* has, of course, but this is the first one I've owned. I guess the next step is to figure out the size."

"I can help with that too." He walked over to her and put his hands in the pockets of his black pants and explained his ideas.

"That sounds perfect. Are you sure it's not too much work?"

"I'm sure, Priscilla." He met her gaze with a direct one of his own. "I helped *mei daed* build our barn back in Lancaster. It was larger than yours, but it didn't take long to put up. *Mei daed* called me his workhorse."

Frowning, she said, "That doesn't sound nice."

"Oh, I didn't mind because he was right. I liked working on the barn and taking care of the animals. It was *mei* job to get them settled for the night."

"I wondered if they enjoyed listening to your harmonica music," she said, walking over to the stack of bales. Then she turned around. "I imagine it would have been soothing to them."

"Oh, I don't know about that. They never voiced an opinion one way or another."

She laughed. Then she looked up at him and met his gaze with a smile. "Maybe you could try it on *mei* horse sometime?"

His heart did a tiny flip. "Only if you sing with me."

CHAPTER 5

SO MUCH FOR GETTING rid of mei feelings . . .

Priscilla hadn't been this comfortable or happy with any-one in a long time, with the exception of her family. It felt good to laugh, to not have to judge Micah's motives and guess how he was going to use her to get ahead, or worry that she was saying or doing the wrong thing around him. She hadn't realized how much she had walked on eggshells while she was in Nashville, or how much she was willing to put up with to reach her dream. How many men would offer to build a barn for someone they barely knew? Then again, she felt like she'd known him forever. Maybe he felt that way too.

Now he was asking her to sing with him, and although the right thing to do would be to turn him down, she couldn't. She nodded, then gestured to one of the two hay bales that wasn't in the stack. She sat down, making sure to give him enough room. Then she asked, "Did you bring your harmonica with you?"

"*Ya.*" He looked a little sheepish as he pulled the harmonica out of his pocket. "I was hoping I'd get the chance to play again." He glanced at the empty seat beside her for a second, then sat down.

Due to his large size, his knee almost touched hers, but she didn't move over. Instead she glanced around. Her little house had more than an acre of property, even though it was almost all overgrown. The next nearest house was several blocks away. She and Micah would have privacy as they sang and played. "Do you take requests?" she asked.

"*Nee* one's ever asked before. I gotta admit, though, I don't have a large repertoire of songs."

When he grinned, she noticed the right side of his top lip curled a little higher than the rest of his mouth, but that was something she could only see when they were this close to each other. "That's okay. You just start playing and I'll come up with something."

Micah paused for a moment, then lifted his harmonica to his mouth. Soon he was playing another melancholy tune. Oddly enough, instead of filling her with sadness, her heart grew light listening to the beautiful song. Like she had last night, she started to hum, adding a light melody to the somber notes.

When they finished the song, he asked, "How do you do that?"

"Hum?"

"*Nee.*" His blond brows knitted together. "Come up with the perfect melody?"

She breathed out a sigh. She'd known when she moved here that people would want to get to know her better, but she hadn't expected to divulge anything so soon. Yet she couldn't hold back the truth from him. "I used to be a singer," she said.

"Like in the shower?" he joked.

Priscilla shook her head. Of course he wouldn't expect her to be a professional, or even sing solo in church, which was forbidden due to the attention-drawing aspect. "When I was eighteen, I wanted to be a famous country singer." She glanced at him, expecting to see shock on his face.

Instead he nodded, as if what she had revealed wasn't a surprise at all. "*Geh* on."

"I hadn't joined the church yet, but all *mei* friends had, and *mei* parents were expecting me to." She dug the heels of her hands into the prickly hay bale. "But there was something inside of me that wanted to be a star. I know it sounds silly and prideful, and it was. Still, I couldn't get the idea out of *mei* mind, enough that I couldn't sleep or eat. I had to make a choice." She turned to Micah. "I chose the world."

"Where did you *geh*?"

"Nashville. I lived there for fifteen years trying to make it. I cut some demos—those are recordings that *mei* agent used to help me get signed with a record company or to get some airplay on the local radio stations. That didn't work out, so I ended up doing a lot of gig work."

He took off his black hat and batted at a fly. "What's that?"

"Singing jobs that were usually for one night or maybe a week. I did a lot of backup singing. Rarely any solo work." She turned to him, her face heating. "I might have had a *gut* voice in Shipshe, but I was *nix* special in Nashville."

"Your voice isn't just *gut*," he said, angling his body toward her. He set his hat in his lap. "It's the most beautiful sound I've ever heard."

"You must not get out much," she mumbled, averting her gaze but unable to stop from looking at him again. From the sincerity in his eyes, she could see he wasn't flattering her, and she shouldn't expect him to. She knew he wasn't the type of man to engage in empty compliments.

Micah frowned. "I don't get to places like Nashville. That's true. But I know what sounds *gut* and what I like."

A pleasant shiver slipped down her spine. His simple words meant more than any praise she'd gotten from other musicians, some who had been supportive of her. Even her agent hadn't criticized her talent, only her circumstances. "It's a matter of timing and luck in this business," he'd said after representing her for five years . . . and before ending their contractual agreement. After that she had been on her own and wasn't any more successful.

"What made you come back to the Amish?" Micah asked.

She threaded her fingers together. "For the first few years, I was so focused on *mei* goal that I didn't realize how miserable I was. The last two years I was in Nashville, I cried every time I received a letter from home. I finally realized that God wanted me to go back to *mei* faith. I would never become famous because I wasn't meant to. I'm meant to be Amish and to do something else."

"Like teaching?"

"*Ya*. When I was considering joining the church before I left Shipshe, I wanted to be a teacher. I taught voice lessons on the side for years in Nashville—I enjoyed that much more than getting on stage and singing in front of a group of people. I still feel that way, which is proof that I'm where God wants me to be. Becoming a famous singer was what I wanted, or so I thought. The truth is that fame and fortune weren't what God wanted for me."

Micah rolled the harmonica in his hand, and Priscilla could tell it was a habit of his when he was thinking. "That's quite a story," he finally said.

She tensed. Had she read him wrong? Did he think she was weird? Or worse, that she was bad news? "When I left Nashville, I left *mei* worldly life behind," she said, wanting to reassure him that she wasn't about to take off again. She was older, wiser, and knew better. "There isn't anything there for me. I hope you believe that."

"Oh, I do." He smiled. "I was just thinking about how you've had an adventurous life, and I've just been building buggies."

"I'm starting over, though. You are miles ahead of me."

"I don't know about that. We all have our paths to travel in life. Some are straighter than others, some more exciting.

As long as God is with you during the journey, the rest doesn't matter."

She nodded. He was telling the truth, although she'd had to learn her lesson the hard way.

"How about another song?" he said, lifting up his harmonica again.

Grateful not only for the subject change but for the opportunity to do something she loved, she nodded. When he started to play "Amazing Grace," she joined in on the third note. The hymn was one of her favorites.

After they finished, she sat back against the stack of bales behind her. "That was lovely," she said, stretching her legs out in front of her. When she turned to him, he was gazing at her.

"*Ya*," he said, his voice low. "It definitely was."

Later that afternoon Micah drove back home after spending the next two hours with Priscilla. After they finished their "Amazing Grace" duet, she offered to fix him a sandwich for lunch. Never one to turn down food, he followed her into the kitchen and found out she had as much to do on the inside of her house as she did on the outside. Even he was daunted by the amount of work involved, but she didn't seem fazed. "I've lived in worse," she said as he noticed the uneven kitchen floor. He imagined if he set an apple on the floor and pushed it across the room it would roll downhill.

But when he mentioned it to her, she just shrugged and took another bite of her ham salad sandwich.

He smiled as he thought about that moment. What a remarkable woman. Hearing about her past as an aspiring country singer had surprised him, but only the part about her moving all the way to Tennessee by herself. He could easily see her being a success with her beautiful voice, not to mention her gorgeous looks. But he also believed in God's timing, and obviously being English and famous wasn't what God wanted for her. *Thank you, Lord.*

His smile faded. Just because they got along well and both loved music didn't mean there was anything between them. But as he continued home, he wondered if there could be. She wasn't going anywhere, and he was happy living in Marigold. They were both single, and he was very, *very* attracted to her. If she felt the same, wouldn't he know? Then again, how could he tell? It wasn't as if he had a lot of experience with women. *None, to be exact.*

But he'd always believed that when it was time for him to date someone, God would put that person in his life, and he would be sure she was the one for him. He just hadn't expected it to happen quite like this, or with a former country singer. Not that it mattered when or how. God's timing was always perfect. All Micah had to do was figure out if he was listening to his own desires or obeying God's.

The one thing he did know was that if he decided to pursue Priscilla, he had to be patient. She was starting a new job, and he had to finish her buggy for her, plus all the work he promised to do at her house. If his business started getting busy again, he'd have to set her projects to the side until he got another break. He didn't like that idea, but business was business. As he continued to think, he also didn't like the idea of having patience either. But he'd always been a practical man, and waiting seemed to be the practical thing to do.

The minute the time was right, he was going to ask Priscilla for a date. And if she accepted, he would make sure it was the best date of her life.

As he pulled into his driveway, he saw someone sitting on his front porch steps. As he neared, he frowned. What was Suetta doing here? Dread filled him as he remembered what Priscilla had said. *She likes you.* He found that hard to believe. But he couldn't think of any reason why Suetta would be waiting for him.

He parked his buggy and got out. Normally he would have settled Billy in the barn, but he trusted his horse not to take off, and whatever Suetta's business was with him, he would take care of it quickly. He patted Billy on his flank and walked over to the porch, where Suetta was already standing, a beaming smile on her face. *Uh-oh.*

"You've been gone for a long time," she said, walking toward him. "I've been waiting for you for over an hour."

"Why?" Micah made sure to keep his distance. "I told you I had plans this afternoon."

"I didn't think they would take you all day." She rolled her eyes. "Anyway, I brought you some of those brownies."

She turned and picked up a platter off the porch. "I made them just for you."

"I thought you said you made them for the church lunch."

Her eyes widened for a moment. Then she laughed. "Oh, I made some for that too. These are the extra." She held out the plate. "I know how much you love sweets."

Micah eyed the plate. Even the thought of eating those rich, fudgy brownies made his stomach turn. "Suetta, we need to talk."

"I agree." She moved closer to him. "You need to stop spending time with Priscilla."

"What?"

"I know she's the new teacher and all, and that you were just being nice giving her a ride to and from church. But it doesn't look *gut*, Micah. Some people might think you like her."

He crossed his arms over his chest. "What if I do like her?"

Suetta's mouth dropped. Then she choked out a strained giggle. "You can't expect me to believe that."

"Why not?" His irritation with her was growing. She was an okay-looking girl, but she thought too much of herself. That was something he had noticed. Otherwise he barely noticed her at all.

"Because she's *old*. She's at least forty, I'm sure."

"Thirty-five," he ground out.

"Whatever." She waved a dismissive hand. "I can understand her liking you," she said, batting her eyes at him. "But you liking her? That's a funny joke, Micah."

He was about to tell her he wasn't joking, but knowing Suetta, she would run her mouth and tell the entire community he had a crush on the new teacher, and he didn't want Priscilla dealing with a bunch of gossip. "Suetta, I appreciate the thought, but I can't take your brownies. And I don't want you dropping by *mei* place all by yourself. That's not appropriate and I don't want people to get the wrong idea."

"But you're fine with people seeing you with Priscilla," she snapped.

He held out his hands, palms up. "All I did is give her a ride," he said.

That seemed to mollify her a little. "Just a ride?"

"Just a ride." Guilt nagged at him for not telling Suetta the whole truth. On the other hand, it was none of her business. "But that doesn't mean there's anything between you and me."

"How do you know?" She stuck out her bottom lip in an immature pout. "We've never gone out."

Despite being irritated with her, he gentled his tone. "Because I'm not interested. You're a . . . nice *maedel*," he said, inwardly flinching at giving her a compliment he was fairly sure wasn't true. "There are several single guys that would give their hat to date you."

"But they don't own their own businesses," she huffed.

Ah, there it was. This had nothing to do with him and everything to do with money. His stomach turned again. Now he wouldn't wish Suetta on any of those young men.

"That shouldn't matter. If you love someone, you love *them*, not what they have."

"You don't understand anything." She brushed past him, then turned around. "I'm sorry I wasted *mei* brownies on you!"

Micah nodded. "I'm sorry you did too."

Suetta marched down his driveway. He would have chuckled at the childish display, but there was nothing funny about her attitude. Maybe he should mention it to her father, who owned a bricklaying business. In fact he'd been one of the men to lay the foundation for the *schoolhaus* and had donated all the materials. The man was kind and generous . . . and that might be the problem. Suetta was obviously entitled, which meant bad news for any man foolish enough to date her.

Thank God he wasn't that man.

He put Billy up and tried to shove Suetta out of his mind. He'd been as plain as he could be without hurting her feelings directly, even though she wasn't happy with him. But she'd get over it. What really chapped him was how she insulted Priscilla. Who cared about her age? He didn't, and he didn't care if anyone thought she was too old for him.

What if Priscilla does?

He hoped that wasn't the case. And if it was, he would make sure to set her straight.

CHAPTER 6

DURING THE WEEK FOLLOWING Priscilla and Micah's Sunday afternoon together, Micah started on the barn. He worked all day on her buggy at his shop. Then he came over to her house and put in two or three hours in the afternoon. Christopher, the young man who Micah had hired to help him, didn't say much but was a hard worker. Between the two of them they made good progress on the barn.

But Priscilla still couldn't shake the idea that she was taking up so much of his time. She brought it up to him on Tuesday. "I don't want you to get too tired working in both places," she said as she handed him and Christopher glasses of lemonade. She had finally made it to the store yesterday and had stocked her pantry until it was overflowing.

"Things are still slow." He tilted his head at her and smiled. "I've got the time, Priscilla. Don't worry about that.

Just focus on getting ready for the first day of school on Monday."

"All right." Relieved, she had gone into her house and worked on her lesson plans. For the rest of the week she was busy with school tasks, including ordering books for her students and meeting each one of them when they came to visit at her house. Soon she would be able to visit the students at their homes, thanks to Micah not only building her buggy but the barn too. That was another thing she had missed when she was in Tennessee—the eagerness of the community to help each other out, including her own community in Shipshe. Micah was just doing his duty in helping out others, just like all Amish people do.

But as she stood on her patio on Friday afternoon and watched him pick up a large board and place it on the sawhorse, she couldn't stop looking at him. No, he wasn't like anyone else. Not even close. He was a special man, and she was falling harder for him every day.

Sighing, she went back inside. She was finished with her school plans, and she felt confident that the first day of school would run smoothly, while still being aware that she was working with children, and children were rarely predictable. But she was prepared to handle any problem that came her way. Needing a break from teaching tasks, she decided to make a detailed list of all her indoor projects and created a budget to get them done, along with an estimated start date for each job. Unfortunately, she kept adding to the list, and by the time she finished, she figured it would take her almost three years to accomplish everything. But she was determined to get her house in order, even if it took longer than that.

A knock sounded on the door, and she jumped. She glanced at the clock on the wall above the sink. Seven thirty already? When she opened the door, she was surprised to see Micah standing there. "I thought you would have gone home by now. I should have brought you and Christopher another drink."

"*Nee* problem. I brought something from home." He was holding his hat, and his blond bangs were plastered on his head. Even though it was evening, the late summer air was warm and muggy. She opened the door wider.

"Let me get you some ice water," she said, motioning for him to come inside. "Where's Christopher?"

"He went home an hour ago." Micah set his hat on the table next to a book of teaching tips.

You should have left too. But she knew by now not to argue with him when it came to managing his time. He was a grown man, and if he said he wasn't overworking himself, she would have to believe him.

She walked over to the cooler that was on the counter. There was still some ice inside, but she reminded herself to get another bag tomorrow. She took a clean glass from the cabinet, filled it with ice cubes, then shut the lid of the cooler and turned on the tap. Fresh water flowed into the glass, and when it was almost full, she turned off the faucet and handed the drink to him.

"*Danki.*" He drained it in almost one gulp.

"Sit down and cool off. I'll get you another one." She gestured to the only other chair she had at the small table she had picked up at a thrift store shortly after she arrived. A couple minutes later she handed him the glass and sat next to him.

"Guess I got a little overheated," he said. Then he looked at the list on the table. "More school stuff?"

She grabbed the slip of paper. "I'm working on *mei* budget. I needed to take a little break from teacher prep."

"Then you're ready for Monday?"

"*Ya*, I am." But without warning, her nerves jumped. In less than three days she would be teaching a group of children for the first time. That was totally different from giving voice lessons to one student per session.

He peered at her. "Something's wrong."

She was about to deny his words, almost falling into her prior habit of pretending she was ready to go on stage when she was really a nervous wreck. Instead she told him the truth. "I'm a little worried about the first day of school."

He finished off the water and set the glass on the table. "I would be, too, if I were in your shoes."

"Really? Are you uncertain when you're around a lot of *kinner* too?"

He shook his head. "*Nee.* I love *kinner.* At *mei* old church I sometimes volunteered to babysit some of the *yung* ones while their *mutters* helped with lunch."

Priscilla's shoulders slumped. "You sound like you would

be a natural. Maybe you should teach on Monday instead of me."

Micah laughed, a deep booming sound that seemed to come straight from his heart. "Sorry, but *nee*. Business is slow, but it isn't that slow." He smiled. "You'll be fine. Everyone has first day jitters when they start something new."

"How did you become so wise at your young age?"

He paused, his brow flattening. "I'm not that young. And I've been told I have an old soul, whatever that means." He picked up the teaching book. Opening it to the middle, he read aloud, "Whatever you do, don't let them see you sweat."

She frowned and moved closer to him. "I don't remember that tip being in the book," she said, searching the open page.

"It's not." He snapped the book shut. "That's the Wagler family's rule number one."

"You were sweating buckets a little while ago," she pointed out, trying not to chuckle.

"Oh. Well, except on a hot summer evening. Then everyone is allowed to perspire a little."

She gazed into his blue eyes, mesmerized by their color and the wisdom she saw in them. He smelled like sweat and sawdust and hard work, a wonderful change from the meticulous, cloying grooming of most men she'd been around for so long. Then she brushed the tip of her index finger on the skin below his left eye. "You had some sawdust there," she said, her breath catching in her throat.

"*Danki.*" His voice was low and husky, sending a warm shiver down her spine. "Wouldn't want to *geh* home with sawdust on *mei* face."

She was close enough to him that she could easily slip into his arms. A dozen excuses ran through her mind about why thinking such thoughts was a bad idea, but she ignored all of them. All she wanted was to feel Micah's huge embrace.

"Priscilla . . ." He slowly reached out and touched the white string of her *kapp*, the pupils of his eyes growing wide, making their blue hue darken. "I—"

"It's past time for me to turn in," she said, jumping up from the chair. *Whew, that was close.* Too close, and if she had stayed in her seat a second longer, she would have kissed him.

"It's not even eight o'clock."

"Well, you know how us old people are." She grabbed the glass off the table and went to the sink, keeping her back to him. "We like to *geh* to bed early."

"Stop it."

She turned around, surprised at the irritation in his tone. "Stop what?"

"Talking about the difference in our ages."

She arched her brow at him. "I didn't realize I was."

"Aren't you?" He walked toward her. "That crack about me being so young, and now you're saying you're old. Which is *dumm* because you're only thirty-five."

"Thirty-five," she mumbled, looking at her feet. "Ten years older than you."

"So what?"

She snapped her gaze to him, ready to tell him that ten years was a huge gap. Then she realized that ten years meant nothing between friends. And that's what they were, friends. He clearly saw them that way. Wow, he must think she'd lost her mind. "You're right," she said, mustering a smile. "I won't mention it again."

"*Gut.*" He took another step toward her.

She had to get him out of here before she said anything else stupid. "I am tired, though. It's been a busy week getting ready for classes."

Was that disappointment she saw on his face? "Oh. Right. I imagine that is tiring." He moved away until he was closer to the door. "I'll be here tomorrow to finish up the barn."

Pricilla was relieved. And disappointed. There would be no reason to see him again after tomorrow, other than to pick up her buggy or at church. But that was for the best, and eventually she would lose these feelings for him. And eventually he would date and marry a young woman closer to his age, as it should be. Maybe that woman would be Suetta, although after meeting the girl, she hoped not. But she wouldn't begrudge him that happiness.

As for her, she would be satisfied with teaching. When she was in Nashville, she hadn't dated much, and getting married wasn't even a thought in her mind all those years. Now she was in her midthirties and Amish. Had the probability of marriage and a family passed her by? She hadn't even seriously thought of those things when she joined the church, but since she met Micah, the idea had been brewing in the back of her mind.

"Guess I'll see you tomorrow," he said, breaking into her thoughts.

"*Ya*," she said, his handsome face coming into focus. "Tomorrow."

He picked up his hat from the table and left.

She sat down and rubbed her forehead, her mind confused and her heart unsettled. Why did she have to be so drawn to this man? She'd never been this infatuated before, not even with her teenage crush. But like her singing career, Micah was out of reach. And just as she had accepted that being a famous singer wasn't meant to be, she had to accept that there wasn't a future for the two of them.

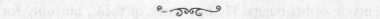

Micah slammed his hat on his head as he trudged to his buggy. He couldn't tell if he was annoyed with her or with himself. First Suetta made a big deal about his and Priscilla's age difference, and now Priscilla was. At least she had agreed not to bring it up again. But he couldn't shake the feeling that she'd wanted to get rid of him.

After he hitched Billy back up to his buggy, he climbed in and picked up the reins. Then he blew out a deep breath. He'd never been this indecisive before. When he wanted to do something, he wasn't wishy-washy about it. He just did it, like moving to Marigold and starting his own business.

When it came to romance and a future spouse, he had always trusted God. And now God had brought Priscilla into his life, and he didn't have the courage to be honest with her about how he felt. Did he trust God, or not?

He didn't have to guide Billy home. The horse knew his way around Marigold, which gave him time to think until he was tired of thinking. He had to take a chance on telling Priscilla how he felt about her. Now that he knew their age gap bothered her, he would have to convince her that age didn't matter. Feelings did, and he was overwhelmed with how much he cared about her. And after the way she had looked at him when they were sitting next to each other at her table, he thought she might care for him too.

Billy's hooves clip-clopped against the asphalt as dusk descended. He turned on the battery-operated lights on the outside of his buggy. He had three of them, but only for safety purposes and not to be fancy like some young adults would do. *Guess I really am an old soul.* Right now, he needed an old man's patience. Even though he was going to tell Priscilla how he felt, he wanted to do it right. He just had to figure out how.

CHAPTER 7

PRISCILLA STOOD IN FRONT of the brand-new school-house and tried to settle her nerves. School wasn't starting until tomorrow, but she couldn't resist coming by one more time by herself. The interior of the building had been finished two days ago, and she'd gone inside yesterday and decorated her classroom. Since there was no service this morning, she took a long walk and ended up here.

She hadn't been this jittery when she auditioned for her first record label. Then again, the stakes were much higher and more important now. The idea that the education of twelve young students was in her hands was far more valuable than getting a record deal. *I pray I can teach them well.*

She heard a horse and buggy pull into the parking lot, and for a moment she panicked, thinking she wasn't supposed to be here. Then she realized she was being foolish. She was the schoolteacher. Of course she could be here, even on a Sunday, as long as she didn't work. All she was doing was admiring the brand-new schoolhouse. Who wouldn't appreciate such a fine building?

Priscilla was surprised when Suetta jumped out of the buggy and marched toward her. She was stunned a second time when she saw Leah stepping out of the buggy too.

"Leave Micah alone!" Suetta yelled as she approached.

Taken aback, Priscilla said, "What?"

"Suetta!" Leah hurried toward her cousin. "What are you doing?"

Her face red with anger, Suetta glared at Priscilla, ignoring Leah. "You'll never have Micah," she said, her hands fisted at her side. "He's mine."

"I'm sorry, Priscilla." Leah reached for Suetta's arm. "We visited the Birch Creek church this morning, and we were on our way home when she screamed for me to stop or she would jump out of the buggy." She latched onto Suetta. "I'm taking you home."

"*Nee.*" Suetta shook off Leah's hand. "Not until I say so."

Priscilla's patience was disappearing. "Look, Suetta, I have *nee* idea what you're blabbering about, and you're being rude to your cousin."

"You're not *mei mamm*," Suetta scoffed.

"If I was, you'd get a *gut* talking to."

"I'm not scared of an *old* woman," she said, lifting her dainty chin. "It's hilarious that you're trying to take Micah from me. He doesn't want some dried-up prune."

Leah gasped. "Suetta!"

"I'm just telling the truth." Suetta scowled at Leah and turned back to Priscilla, her expression suddenly as sweet as peach pie. "I'll make Micah a *gut* wife. I don't have any wrinkles or gray hair."

Priscilla almost touched her *kapp*. Did she have gray hair already? She hadn't paid attention lately.

"And we'll have lots and lots of children," she continued. "Thirty-five is past childbearing age so you won't ever have any."

Priscilla's head nearly exploded. This . . . this *brat* had no idea what she was talking about. While she didn't have as many years to bear children as Suetta did, she could still have a child or two before she was too old.

"I'm so sorry, Priscilla," Leah said, trying to corral Suetta again. But when she went to grab her, Suetta jumped out of the way.

"I'm not finished yet!" Suetta shrieked.

"Oh yes you are." Priscilla stormed to her until she was practically stepping on the girl's shoes. "Are you and Micah dating each other?"

"*Ya*," she said, averting her gaze.

Priscilla caught the doubt in her eyes. "Are you telling the truth?"

"We will be going out soon. As long as you stay out of the way."

The girl wasn't looking at her, and now Priscilla was positive she and Micah weren't together. "You will leave with

Leah right now, and you won't give her a bit of trouble. Do you understand me?"

Suetta crossed her arms over her chest, a smirk on her face. "Who's going to make me?"

"I am." Leah yanked Suetta by the elbow. This time when she tried to pull away, Leah held on fast. She mouthed the words "I'm sorry" to Priscilla again. Then she dragged her cousin back to the buggy. Priscilla couldn't hear what Leah was saying, but from the way Suetta stopped resisting, she could see she had finally gotten through to her.

Priscilla refused to leave until Leah's buggy was out of sight. Then she started shaking. She'd never been insulted like that before, and even though it was clear that Suetta was troubled, that didn't make her words any easier to swallow.

"Priscilla?"

She froze at the sound of Micah's voice. Did he hear everything Suetta said? When she looked at him, she could tell he had.

It had taken every bit of Micah's willpower not to intervene in Suetta's tirade against Priscilla. He had walked from the back of the school building in time to hear what she'd said. He was ready to intervene when he decided Suetta might only get angrier if she knew he was there. So he stayed out of view, and only when he was sure Suetta and Leah were gone did he approach Priscilla.

"I guess you heard all that," she said, her head down.

"You're shaking." He moved closer to her, but she stepped away.

"I'm fine." She tilted up her chin, but she was still staring at the schoolhouse, not him. "I can take a little meltdown. I'm sure a few of *mei* students will have them in the future."

"That wasn't a meltdown. That was an attack." Micah went to her, and when she tried to move away, he blocked her path. "Please, Priscilla. Let me explain about me and Suetta."

Her gaze snapped to his. "So you two are together?"

"Absolutely not." He explained to her about Suetta's visit last Sunday. "I thought I'd set her straight. I guess I should have been even more direct. But I meant it when I told her that there would never be anything between us."

"Because she's troubled," Priscilla said, looking at the *schoolhaus* again.

"Because I've fallen for someone else."

After a long pause, she turned to him, her eyes shiny. Then she smiled, her bottom lip trembling. "Whoever she is, I hope she realizes what a wonderful man she has."

Micah moved closer and tenderly held her shoulders, looking down into her eyes. "Priscilla, don't you know that woman is you? From the moment I saw you at *mei* shop, I fell hard."

She shrugged off his hands. "You don't have to say that to make me feel better. I'm a grown woman—"

He drew her into his arms and kissed her with all the emotion he had in his heart. When he reluctantly pulled away, he said, "And I'm a grown man. I know what I'm feeling, and I know who I want. And that's you." His spirit plummeted when she didn't respond and only gaped at him. He'd made an impulsive move, and he might have ruined everything, but he didn't regret kissing her. "If that's okay with you, I mean."

Priscilla brought her fingers to her lips, her eyes wide with shock. "Micah," she said. "Didn't you hear what Suetta said? I'm old."

"I already told you I don't care about that."

"But you should." Tears shone in her eyes. "I don't have many childbearing years left."

"I know, Priscilla. I can count."

"And that doesn't matter to you? You said you love *kinner*."

"I do. And I want to have them." He gazed into her eyes. "God determines that, not us. I could marry someone younger and not have any *kinner* at all. If I loved her, that wouldn't matter." He wiped the tears that had fallen down her cheek. "I could tell when I kissed you that you felt something for me too. Would you at least give me a chance?"

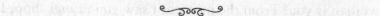

Priscilla didn't know what to say. She was still reeling from his amazing kiss, from Suetta's verbal assault, and from the overwhelming feelings she had for this man. But she couldn't agree right away. "You should think about this some more,"

she said, trying to gather her emotions. "In case you're confused."

For the first time she saw him turn angry. "I'm younger than you, but I'm not a *kinn*. I've thought about this. I've thought about *you* every day since I met you." He shook his head and moved away from her. "Maybe you're the one who's confused. Or maybe you're just scared." He turned on his heel and walked away.

Pain slashed at her. She had hurt him, and he didn't deserve it. He had asked her for a chance, and she'd treated him like a child.

As she watched him walk away, her heart squeezed. *This is for the best. He's hurt, but he'll get over it. This is less complicated. He'll move on . . .*

"Micah!" She ran after him as fast as she could. He slowed down and turned around, and she sped faster. By the time she reached him, she was out of breath.

"Hey," he said, gripping her shoulders. "You didn't hurt yourself, did you?"

"*Nee.*" She shook her head, gasping for air. "I'm . . . sorry . . . I . . . hurt . . . you."

"You didn't have to race after me to tell me that."

"That's . . . not . . . all."

He waited patiently while she steadied her breathing. "Are you all right now?"

"*Ya.*" She straightened and looked at him. "You're right, Micah. I'm scared." She wrung her hands together. "I'm terrified. I've never been in a relationship before."

"That makes two of us."

"So I don't know what to do. But here's what I do know. People are going to talk. I'm sure Suetta won't be the only one to think it's strange for us to be together."

He frowned. "Let them talk. If they're gossiping, they'll get their comeuppance one day."

"I wish I could be so confident."

"Priscilla, I'm not talking about eloping or anything. I just want us to get to know each other. Spend time together. Maybe even play and sing a time or two."

Her heart warmed. "That sounds lovely. But there's still the age issue."

He looked up at the sky, as if he were saying a prayer for patience. Then he met her gaze again. "I told you, your age doesn't make a difference to me."

"It might when I'm fifty and you're only forty. Or when I'm seventy and you're sixty."

A smile spread over his face, and then he started his deep rumbly laugh that normally would have her chiming in if she weren't so annoyed.

"I don't see what's so funny." She crossed her arms over her chest.

"You." He leaned forward. "A minute ago, you wouldn't give me a chance, and now you're talking about us sitting in rocking chairs on the front porch while our *grosskinner* play in the yard."

"Oh. Well, I wasn't imagining that much detail."

"I was." He grew serious. "Trust me. You could be twenty years older and I wouldn't care." Then he paused. "I went about this the wrong way. I shouldn't have kissed you first and then explained how I felt. And *nee*, I don't regret the kiss, if that's what you're thinking."

"You don't?"

"No, I don't. But I hope I didn't offend you. The kiss wasn't planned. It's just that I've been thinking about kissing you . . ." His cheeks turned bright red. "See? I don't know what I'm doing either." Then he frowned. "You've really never had a boyfriend before?"

"*Nee*. I was too focused on *mei* career to think about romance."

"And now?"

He looked so apprehensive—and so cute, she had to admit—that she couldn't keep him waiting any longer. "We take things slow. I need to focus on *mei* job, and I don't want anything to get in the way of that."

"I understand. Speaking of teaching." He reached into his pocket and pulled out a shiny red, wooden apple and handed it to her. "For your first day of school."

She took it, marveling at how perfect it looked. "Where did you get this?"

"In Birch Creek. There's a couple that lives there, the Detweilers. They're woodworkers, although the husband is also a farmer. I had seen these little apples at the shop she has in her house, and I bought one the other day."

Touching the smooth surface, which was so shiny she could almost see her reflection, she smiled. "*Danki*, Micah. It's perfect."

"I'm glad you like it. One other thing, I got two orders for new buggies on Saturday, so it's a *gut* thing I finished the barn."

"*Ya*, it is." She rolled the small apple in her hand, then looked at him. "I suppose we'll both be very busy the next month or so."

"*Ya*. But if you're not too busy, maybe we can *geh* out sometime."

Priscilla grinned. She couldn't resist him if she tried. "I think I can pencil you in."

CHAPTER 8

"HAND IT OVER, ARTIE." Priscilla crossed her arms and stared at the third grader standing in front of her. The rest of the children were spending their recess playing baseball, with a few of the younger ones chasing each other around the swing set several yards away. Except for Artie. She had seen him trying to put a frog down Katie Anne's dress. Fortunately, she called him over before he could do the nasty deed.

"Hand what over?" he asked, all wide-eyed innocence.

In addition to being a troublemaker, Artie was also one of her brightest students, and he knew how to weasel out of things. She had only been teaching for a month and a half, but she'd learned a lot in that amount of time, and one important lesson was that she had to make sure to keep an eye on Artie Miller. "The frog."

"You mean this?" He thrust his hand at her, a slimy brown creature in his grasp. "It's not a frog. It's a toad."

She forced herself not to flinch. Micah might not have known it, but his rule about not letting anyone see you sweat was actually good advice when it came to dealing with discipline. "Excuse me. The toad."

"Here." He held it out in front of her. "You said you wanted me to hand it over."

Now she was regretting not telling him to let the thing go free. Unwilling to bend, she took it from him, trying not to think about how the frog—uh, toad—had gotten so slimy. And didn't they have warts? "Sit down on the bench," she said, gesturing to the wooden bench a few feet away next to the schoolhouse. "That is where you'll spend the rest of your recess."

His bottom lip poked out and he dragged himself over to the bench and plopped down. Priscilla bent down and set the toad in the grass, making a mental note to scrub her hands as soon as recess was over. Now she had to deal with Artie. She turned and sat down next to him. "What do you think your consequences should be for trying to put that toad down Katie Anne's dress?"

He turned to her, his eyes growing wide. "You're asking me?"

"*Ya.*"

Artie stared out at the boys and girls playing baseball. "How about *nee* homework for a week?"

She almost laughed but caught herself. "Try again."

He sighed. "Extra homework for a week."

"That's better. And I think it's appropriate, considering you didn't actually put the frog—"

"Toad," he corrected.

"*Toad*," she said, trying not to think about her dirty hands. "But if you had been successful, your consequences would have been much more severe. Do you understand?"

"*Ya*," he said, sounding serious. "I understand." He looked at her. "I'm sorry."

"You're forgiven. But you still have to stay on the bench for the rest of recess."

He nodded, and she got up from the bench and walked around the playground, keeping an eye on the children.

By the end of the day—and after she had given Artie his extra homework assignment—she was tired but satisfied. Being a teacher was the most exhausting and rewarding thing she had ever done. She spent the next hour and a half grading papers, preparing the next day's lessons, and sweeping out the schoolroom. Her last task was making sure the outdoor bathrooms were in order for tomorrow. After she shut the boys' bathroom door, she headed for the front of the schoolhouse to wait for Micah to take her home. She had her own buggy now, and her own horse, Calypso. But she'd rather ride with Micah.

As always, he was right on time. She smiled as she saw him pull into the gravel parking lot. As much as she enjoyed teaching and the students, this was the best time of the day, when she could spend some alone time with Micah. He pulled Billy to a stop, and she climbed in.

"How was your day?" he asked, turning the buggy around and heading to her house.

"*Gut.*" She told him about Artie and he laughed, then complimented her on letting him choose his own consequences. Then he told her about the progress he and Christopher had made on the buggy they were building for a family in a nearby district.

"We got three more orders in today," he said. "Any more and we'll have to put people on a waiting list."

Priscilla smiled and sat back in the buggy seat, enjoying the cool fall air filled with the scent of wood-burning fireplaces and stoves. "Oh," she said. "I almost forgot. Leah stopped by today to let me know how Suetta is doing." Leah had explained that Suetta and her father left Marigold to go to New York and stay with family. "There's a treatment center near my great-aunt's district," Leah had said when she visited Priscilla the week after Suetta verbally attacked her. "We've known for a while that Suetta needed help we couldn't give her. Sunday was the last straw. She was such a sweet *maedel* growing up, but after her *mamm* died, she changed. Understandable, but *mei onkel* indulged her too much. I think seeing someone will help her."

"How is she?" he asked, genuinely interested.

"She's doing better. She likes living in New York, and counseling seems to have a positive effect on her."

"I'm glad to hear that. I hope she continues to get better."

"Me too." Priscilla leaned back against the seat and closed her eyes.

"Sing for me," Micah said.

She obliged, expecting his request since he often asked her to sing for him when they were together. First she sang "How Great Thou Art" and then broke into a country song she had frequently performed when she was pursuing her music career. By the time he pulled into her driveway, she was finishing up another hymn. When he halted the buggy, she got out and retrieved her mail. Then she climbed back in and he drove up to her house.

She scanned through the letters in her hand. "Do you want to stay for supper?" she asked.

"*Nee.*"

She glanced at him. "Is anything wrong?"

He shook his head, but his gaze darted back and forth.

Billy snorted as Priscilla grew alarmed. She was used to Micah's easygoing, calm manner and had come to appreciate that quality in him, along with everything else. The fact that he was so tense alarmed her. "It looks like there is."

He drew in a deep breath. "Priscilla, I've been thinking about this for a while. Will you—"

Billy lurched, jerking the buggy forward, and the letters flew out of Priscilla's hands. Micah grabbed the reins and settled him down while she picked up her mail. When the horse was still again, Micah glanced down at the letter near his feet. "You missed one," he said, picking up the envelope and handing it to her.

"*Danki*—" She froze, her eyes focused on the return address. *Preston Fulbright.* Her agent.

"Priscilla, I wanted to talk to you about something—"

"Can it wait a second?" She ripped open the envelope and read the contents.

Dear Priscilla,

I hope this letter finds you well. It's been a long time since we last talked, but I have a surprise for you. Somehow the demo you cut eight years ago landed on the desk of the head of RC Records, and he's been trying to get in touch with you. His secretary contacted me two weeks ago and I've been trying to hunt you down ever since. One of your former music students said you returned back to Indiana, and after some detective work I found you moved to Ohio.

This is an excellent opportunity for you, Priscilla. He's eager to sign you as soon as possible. Get ready to dust off your stage name. Heather Love is about to break into the big time.

Contact me as soon as you get this, and we will hash out the details.

Best,
Preston

The letter fell into Priscilla's lap. She couldn't believe it. After all these years, after she had been so sure she wasn't meant to be a star and that God wanted her to be a simple Amish schoolteacher. Now her dream was only a signature away from coming true.

"Priscilla? Is everything okay?"

She turned to Micah, still numb. She couldn't speak, so she handed him the letter.

He scanned the page, then asked, "Who's Heather Love?"

"Me," she managed to say. "That is *mei* stage name." Suddenly what Preston had said sank in. She turned to Micah and clasped her hands together. "Can you believe it? A record label wants to sign me!"

"What does that mean?"

"It means recording an album, going on tour, doing interviews . . ." She sat back in her seat, still dumbfounded. "*Mei* dream isn't dead after all."

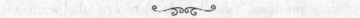

Micah's heart shattered.

When he picked up Priscilla, he had planned to propose. He'd been thinking about it for the last few weeks but didn't want to put any pressure on her while she was still adjusting to teaching school. It wasn't a secret that they were courting, and as it turned out, the community didn't question their relationship, at least not openly. He was falling more deeply in love with her every passing day. Still, it had been difficult to bring up the subject, and he'd been so close to asking her when Billy decided to rile up. Now his dream of marrying Priscilla was in pieces.

He looked at her, saw the happiness in her eyes, the way she looked at the letter when he handed it back to her.

And he couldn't blame her. She had worked fifteen years to have this opportunity. Of course she would be excited. He thought about how she had said she was never going back to Nashville or the English life. But there had never been anything to draw her back there before. Now there was.

She turned to him, her excitement palpable. "You were going to ask me something?"

Marry me. But he couldn't speak those words. Not now. And he loved her too much to stand in the way of her getting something she'd wanted more than anything else. *I just wish she wanted me more.*

He dug deep and gathered his emotions. "Nah, it can wait." He swallowed. "So, that's *gut* news, *ya?*"

"Very *gut* news." She sighed. "A record label wants me. I didn't think I'd ever hear those words. Oh, I better answer Preston. He's expecting to hear from me." She picked up her teacher's bag, filled with student homework, books, and other tools of her trade. "Can we have supper together another night?"

"Sure." The stone in his throat felt like a boulder now. "Anytime."

She touched his shoulder. "*Danki* for the ride." Then she got out of his buggy and hurried to the house.

He watched her disappear through the front door, and the ache in his heart grew. *I love her so much.* Enough to let her go.

CHAPTER 9

FOR THE REST OF the work week, Micah kept his distance from Priscilla. He had picked her up the next morning and took her to school but begged off giving her any more rides in the near future, using work as an excuse. She seemed a million miles away that morning, giving him one-word answers when he tried to make small talk. He could see that her mind was already in Nashville, and it wouldn't be long before she was physically there too. Soon she would become Heather Love, and she would leave him and her Amish life behind.

On Saturday afternoon, he put a pot of stew on the stove to simmer and went back to his workshop. He had plenty of work, but not enough for Christopher, who was now officially his apprentice, to have to work the weekend. Micah could close shop right now, but he never knew when a customer would show up. *Like Priscilla.* But no one could ever compare to her. The sooner he got over her, the better, but he knew that wouldn't happen for a long, long time.

By four o'clock he gave up and locked up the shop. He checked his stew and found it was ready, so he took down a bowl from the cabinet. But he only filled it halfway. Lately his appetite wasn't what it used to be. He set the bowl of steaming stew on the table, then sat in the chair and stared at it. *Another lonely meal.*

He had just closed his eyes to pray when he heard a knock on the door. Frowning, he got up. Every once in while someone would ignore the sign and try to do business with him since it wasn't five o'clock yet. He always humored the customer, but today he wasn't in the mood to deal with anyone. "I'm closed!" he yelled as he walked toward the door.

"Even to me?"

Priscilla. His heart leapt then sank to his knees. He stared at the door, knowing why she was here. She was going to tell him she was leaving. She wasn't the type of woman to skip town without letting him know . . . and without letting him down. He closed his eyes, steeling himself for the inevitable heartache, and opened the door.

"Hi," she said. She didn't come inside like she usually did when she visited.

"Hi." He didn't invite her in.

"Can we talk?"

He paused. If he sent her away, he wouldn't have to deal with hearing her reject him to his face. But that wouldn't be right. He needed to focus on her happiness, not his sorrow. Mustering a smile, he said, "Come on in."

She walked inside. He shut the door behind her, but she didn't walk farther into his house. Instead she put her hands on her hips and stared him down. "Why are you avoiding me?"

"Huh?"

"You're pushing me away." Fire sparked in her eyes. "And I want to know the reason."

Bewildered, he said, "I wanted to give you time to get everything in order."

"In order for what?"

Did she really not know what he was talking about? "For when you *geh* to Nashville. Resigning your job, getting your house ready for sale, selling Calypso and . . . your buggy."

"For goodness' sake, where did you get the idea that I was leaving?"

"Your letter? The record deal? Your dream finally coming true after all these years?" Was she being obtuse on purpose? That wasn't like Priscilla at all.

"Micah." She walked over to him and cradled his face in her hands. "You big goof. I'm not going anywhere."

"What?"

She dropped her hands and stepped away from him. "This is all *mei* fault. I can see how I left you with the impression I was going to tell Preston that I wanted the contract." She smiled, her gaze meeting his. "*Nix* could be further from the truth."

"Did you write him back?"

"I did, that night. I told him thanks, but I'm staying here."

"But what about your dream?"

"I have new dreams. Better ones that are coming true. At least most of them are." She put her arms around his neck. "I'm staying here in Marigold. I belong here with *mei* students . . . and hopefully with you."

He wrapped his arms around her waist and kissed her, relief flooding through him. When he pulled away, he said, "I'm sorry, Priscilla. You're right. I was pushing you away."

"To protect yourself."

Micah nodded. "*Ya.* But I want you to know, if you had decided to become Heather Love again, I wouldn't have stopped you. I want you to be happy."

She wrinkled her nose. "I definitely wouldn't be happy as Heather Love. What a dumb name."

"Why did you choose it?"

"I didn't. Preston gave it to me. He didn't think Priscilla Helmuth was a name for a star."

"I think it's perfect." He rested his chin on her head, his pain forgotten. "I love you, Priscilla."

"I love you too." She paused. "You were going to tell me something the last time we were together. What was it?"

He held her away from him enough that he could meet her eyes, but he continued to hold her tight. "Will you marry me?"

"*Ya.*" She beamed, her smile lighting up her face. "I can't wait to marry you."

Micah kissed her again. "That's what I was hoping you'd say."

After a few more kisses, which neither of them rushed, Priscilla said, "Something smells *gut.*"

"Stew," he said. The bowl on the kitchen table had grown cold by now.

"Do you have enough to share?"

He laughed and nodded. "Let's eat. I'm starving!"

EPILOGUE

PRISCILLA GIGGLED AS MICAH carried her over the threshold of his house, which was now their home. She still owned the small house where she had lived for the past several months until her and Micah's wedding. Both she and Micah worked on the house together, and it was almost ready to go on the market for sale. But their wedding had interrupted the final touches.

Micah carried her as if she weighed nothing—which for sure wasn't the truth—over to the couch and gently set her down. On the coffee table in front of them was a fruit, cheese, and cookie tray, courtesy of Leah and Ben. They had spent the last week after the wedding visiting family, including hers in Shipshe and his in Lancaster. Now they were home, and she couldn't be happier.

He looked at the food in front of them, then turned to her. "Are you hungry?"

She gazed into his eyes. *"Nee."*

"Me neither."

That surprised her, since his appetite was so huge. "You're not?"

"Maybe a little." He settled her in his lap and kissed her. "But this is the first time we've been alone. I can eat later."

She looked at him and smiled. "So can I." She started to kiss him when a knock sounded on the door.

Micah groaned. "Can we tell them to *geh* away?" he muttered.

"That would be rude." She climbed out of his lap and opened the door. A large brown delivery truck was backing out of the driveway. She was surprised she hadn't heard the driver pull in. Then again, she was preoccupied. She glanced at the porch and saw a box at her feet. Picking it up, she saw that it was addressed to her. She went inside and shut the door.

"Oh, *gut*, it came." Micah sat up and gestured to the package. "I thought it would arrive tomorrow."

"You know what this is?"

"Ya."

The excitement on his face was so cute she couldn't help but tease him a little. "Hmm. Maybe I should wait until later to open it."

He patted the empty space next to him. "It will only take a second." He pulled out a pocketknife and handed it to her when she sat down.

She slid the knife through the tape and opened the box, then picked up something covered in layers of bubble wrap. Inside the bubble wrap she found a piece of sheet music framed in a simple, pale wooden frame. "What is it?" she asked.

"Our song."

"I can see that." She pointed to the title at the top of the page. Then she looked at the notes. Two bars in and she put her hand over her heart. "It's *our* song," she whispered.

He laughed. "That's what I said."

"But how? When?"

"I talked to one of the local churches here, and they have an organist. I played the notes, and he wrote them down. Then I found a company to print out the sheet music." His eyes sparkled. "What do you think?"

She hugged the frame against her chest. "I think it's perfect, just like you." She set their song down on the table, then climbed into his lap again. *Dreams do come true.*

ACKNOWLEDGMENTS

THANK YOU TO THE editors who helped me with this story—Becky Monds, Karli Jackson, and Laura Wheeler. Another thank you to my agent, Natasha Kern, who always cheers me on. And as always, my appreciation to you, dear reader. I hope you enjoyed Micah and Priscilla's journey.

DISCUSSION QUESTIONS

1. Micah tells himself to "watch his pride." Why is it important to not be prideful?
2. Micah tells Priscilla that "age is just a number." What do you think this popular saying means?
3. Priscilla discovered that her goals weren't the same as God's plan for her. Discuss a time when this happened in your life.
4. As I was writing this story, I thought back to the times when I was a teacher and a student. What was your favorite school memory?

WENDY'S TWENTY REASONS

SHELLEY SHEPARD GRAY

Joyful is the person who finds wisdom,
the one who gains understanding.
PROVERBS 3:13

We make our decisions, and then our
decisions turn around and make us.
AMISH PROVERB

For that first group of students I taught back in Mesa, Arizona. Even after all this time, I still remember all the lessons y'all taught me about life.

CHAPTER 1

AT FIRST GLANCE, WENDY Schwartz figured it wasn't much to look at. Roughly five hundred square feet, the building had four walls and a wooden floor built from reclaimed white oak, walnut, and maple. In the corner stood a small enclosed bathroom. There were no lights.

Being an Amish schoolhouse, there was, of course, no electricity. The only heat source was a kerosene oil stove that she was more scared than appreciative of. At least it was March and not November. Before long, all she'd need to do was open a few of the windows that lined one of the walls. The fresh breeze would be familiar and welcome as the days turned warmer.

It wasn't the building itself that mattered, though. At least not all that much. Neither the heat nor the windows were why Wendy had jumped at this opportunity. Even the twenty desks, the coat racks, and the print and cursive alphabets that had been painstakingly painted at the top of one of the walls by Mrs. Wagoner, the former teacher, hadn't been what claimed her heart.

The children had done that.

From the first moment she'd been introduced to her twenty scholars, they'd meant so much to her. For most of her life she'd yearned to be a teacher, and at long last her dream had come true.

And what a group! They were a varied lot, ranging in age from six to fourteen. They all lived within walking distance of the old wooden schoolhouse and arrived soon after she did at eight every morning. Some were sweet and shy. Others were loud and argumentative. A couple seemed to be dreamers, and one or two of them were extremely smart. And for the last three months of the school year, they were hers. For better or worse.

It was just too bad that, so far, she'd had more "worse" days than good ones.

It was currently close to three o'clock, and the day was almost finished. As she continued to write math problems on the chalkboard at the front of the room, most of the students watched her with looks of consternation. A few even looked irritated.

Wendy had been their replacement teacher for almost two weeks. Knowing the children would find it difficult to adjust to a new teacher with just three months left of school, she'd been more lenient than she might normally have been. Common sense told her that implementing new rules wasn't a good idea, especially since she was so different from their beloved Mrs. Wagoner.

However, yesterday Wendy had decided enough was enough. She'd been hired as their teacher, not a fill-in babysitter. And she wanted to prove herself capable so that she'd receive a contract for the upcoming year. That was why she'd decided to give them a test of sorts—especially since Mrs. Wagoner had left her almost no notes about each student's progress.

Today, she planned to assess each child's math level. She'd started with basic addition, then moved on to subtraction, multiplication facts, then more complicated problems, and finally long-division problems with remainders. Nothing was too difficult. At least it shouldn't have been for her oldest scholars—her fourteen-year-old eighth graders. She'd figured she'd hear some complaining, but not the current reaction. Two of the eighth graders actually looked upset.

By the time she finished writing at last, most of the students were staring at her with apprehensive expressions.

Little seven-year-old Becca raised her hand. "I only know how to add, Teacher," she whispered.

Knowing all the children were listening, Wendy again tried to alleviate their worries. "I know, Becca. But remember what I said? Only do the problems you know how to do."

"What if I've forgotten how to do some of the work?" Paul, one of the fourteen-year-olds, asked.

"Then I will know what I need to help you with. Remember, scholars, this isn't for a grade. All I'm trying to do

225

is figure out what you know and don't know." She smiled encouragingly yet again.

Unfortunately, no one smiled back.

When it looked like a couple of her more squirrelly students were considering asking additional questions, Wendy leveled a hard—and hopefully tough—look around the room. "This isn't an option, students. You may get started now."

At last, everyone's pencils got busy.

Wendy felt like raising her hands in victory . . . and banging her head against one of the walls at the same time. Her foray into teaching had been far more challenging than she'd thought it would be. Back when she'd dreamed about finally getting her first job, she'd imagined having a few rocky days, but that was all. But so far? Well, it was as if her brief honeymoon had ended and she and her students were stumbling into their first weeks of married life.

Of course she didn't actually know what that was like, given that she was nineteen and unmarried, but she had a pretty good idea that her analogy was close.

When she'd been asked to finish out Mary Wagoner's class from March until the beginning of June, she'd been overjoyed. She might have felt secretly prideful as well. Ever since she'd graduated the eighth grade, she'd been volunteering in Amish schools, tutoring teenagers, and collecting and making items for bulletin boards.

She'd so badly wanted to be a teacher.

Unfortunately, her age had worked against her. No matter

how many people she reached out to or wrote to regarding an opening for a teacher, Wendy had heard the same thing: she was too young to be in charge of a whole Amish school.

It had been beyond frustrating. After all, it wasn't her fault she didn't have much actual teaching experience. Everyone had to start somewhere. She'd graduated after eighth grade the same as everyone else in her church district. Next, she'd spent two months in Mexico with other members of her New Order Amish church district, tutoring young children at an orphanage.

After that, she'd divided her time between volunteering, tutoring, and helping her mother at home in their community near Middlefield.

It was only when Mary Wagoner fell in love and decided to move to Shipshewana to get married that this school's board decided to give Wendy a try.

She realized she hadn't been their first choice. Not the second or third choice either. *Nee*, she'd been hired because no one else had wanted to take over a class at the very end of a school year.

She was all right with that, however. After all, her favorite verse was Galatians 6:9: *Let's not get tired of doing what is good. At just the right time we will reap a harvest of blessing if we don't give up.*

She had taken to saying that verse aloud to herself every morning as she walked to work. No matter what, she was not giving up.

"Teacher," Jonas called out.

"My name is Wendy Schwartz, Jonas. Remember? You may call me Miss Wendy or Miss Schwartz."

"But Teacher. Look." He pointed to the clock.

It was three o'clock. For a boy who couldn't remember her name, he could tell time real well.

All the students were now staring at her with hope in their eyes. She supposed she couldn't blame them.

She cleared her throat. "Scholars, it seems Jonas is right. It is time to end our day. Put your names on your papers, hand them to me, and then get ready to leave."

And just like that, a new breath of life filled the room. Children rushed to turn in their papers, gather their materials, and pull on their coats.

"Don't forget to stack your chairs and pick up around your desks!" she called out.

Less than five minutes later, the floor was clean, the chairs were stacked, and her students were all in line. As she stood next to the door, she gazed at them until they stood silently.

At last she smiled. "Goodbye, scholars. I'll see you tomorrow."

The door opened, and like a rush of wind, they escaped. All of them had made it through another day. Feeling marginally better, she walked to the doorway and watched the children leave. Some walked home together. Others rode their bikes. A couple of her students went right to their waiting mothers. Minutes later, after a few of them waved in her direction, they were gone.

Wendy breathed a sigh of relief.

She'd achieved her dream. It just wasn't exactly the wonderful experience she'd always imagined it would be.

With another deep breath, Wendy went back inside and got ready to do it all over again tomorrow. Hopefully things would go better. One of these days, she felt sure that it had to.

CHAPTER 2

THEIR NEW BOARDER WAS pretty as a picture—cheery, smart . . . and completely off limits. No way should he ever be thinking about her in a romantic way.

It was really too bad Lewis Weaver couldn't seem to *stop* thinking about her.

When his mother walked into the living room, she scanned the area and propped one hand on her hip. "Wendy still hasn't arrived?"

"Mamm, supper isn't for another ten minutes. She'll be here soon."

"I know I shouldn't act like she's late. I know she isn't." She lowered her voice. "It's just that Mervin and Fern are already in the dining room."

Their two other boarders had been with them for years. Mervin was in his late sixties and had moved in a few months after his wife passed away. Fern was a spinster in her mid-forties who liked to knit and crochet but not cook. Both were rather set in their ways. "That ain't Wendy's fault. They come in early to eat every day."

"And Wendy always walks in at five on the dot."

"Don't fault her for being punctual," he chided.

She sighed. "I'm not. It would just be easier if I didn't have to remind Fern and Mervin of that every evening," she muttered under her breath as she wandered back to the kitchen.

Lewis sat down. By all appearances, he was relaxing for a few minutes before going into the dining room to eat with his family and their three boarders. In actuality, he was looking for Wendy too. He'd gotten home around the same time she did today. They'd spoken for a few moments, but she'd been far quieter than her usual chatty self. He hoped nothing was wrong.

Two minutes later, his father wandered in, his hair still damp from his shower. "Lewis, everything *gut*?"

"I reckon so. Fern and Mervin are in the dining room, *Mamm* and Judith Rose are in the kitchen, we're here, and Wendy hasn't come inside yet."

"Which means your mother's in a tizzy."

Lewis grinned. "Those are your words, not mine . . . but *jah*."

His father chuckled. "So everything is how it always is."

"Pretty much."

"Has your *mamm* wandered out to complain yet?"

"*Jah.* About two minutes ago."

His father sat down and propped a foot on the ottoman. "The more things change, the more they stay the same. Ain't so?"

"You're right, *Daed.*"

About six years ago, his parents had decided to start taking in boarders. There were three sizable rooms attached to the barn that Lewis's great-uncle had once used as storage for furniture he'd been building. After they had lain vacant for more than a decade, Lewis's father decided they would be good places for some single members of their community to rent.

His parents had learned that there were some older members of their community who either didn't have younger families to live with or, for one reason or another, had elected not to live with them.

Before long, Lewis and his *daed* had remodeled the rooms to each include a small sitting area and a full bathroom. They'd been rented out almost immediately, and since then they'd all gotten used to having a few older folks around the farm.

However, when Esther got sick in January, she'd moved in with her niece, leaving an opening. When word got around that Wendy Schwartz was going to take the teaching job but needed a place to stay, it felt like a match made in heaven.

They were all going through a bit of a learning curve, though. Wendy was young, busy, and actually thought his mother wanted her to come to the supper table at five, not ten or fifteen minutes early because Mervin and Fern didn't want to wait one extra minute for the meal.

Daed glanced at the large brass wall clock that had been his and *Mamm*'s twenty-fifth wedding anniversary gift to each other. "Looks like she's got three minutes now."

"Wendy'll be here on time. She always is."

His father raised his eyebrows and crossed his legs. "That's true, but I fear she's cuttin' it a bit close this evening."

"Not so much. Five is five."

"*Jah*, but—"

They heard footsteps pattering down the hall.

"Here she is," *Daed* said with a smile.

Lewis stood up right as Wendy blew into the room. Today she wore a dark-pink dress, the color of a ripe raspberry. Over it, she had put on a light white sweater. Her wide-set brown eyes were bright, and her brown hair was neat and pinned securely under her white *kapp*. She wore rubber flip-flops on her feet.

"Hiya, Wendy."

"Hello, Lewis." She turned to his father. "Hi, Frank."

"You're just on time, Wendy," *Daed* said. "I'm glad about that."

She looked at him in confusion. "Why? Were you worried I was going to be late?"

"Oh, only a little bit. *Mei frau* runs a tight ship, you know."

"I do know that," she murmured as they made their way into the dining room. Now looking worried, she added,

"The sheet does say that supper begins at five. Is that not true?"

"It is," said Lewis.

"All right. Then I'm afraid I don't know what I've done wrong. Is Bonnie upset with me for some reason?"

Lewis gave his father a pointed look.

Luckily, he caught on. "Not at all, child," his *daed* said with a chuckle. "I was only making conversation, that's all."

Wendy raised her eyebrows at Lewis, causing him to laugh.

"Don't worry about it," he whispered to her as they sat down. "My parents are a handful."

"Oh. Mine are too." She smiled at him, then greeted Fern in the polite way she always did. "*Gut* evening. How was your Thursday?"

"It was productive. I mailed off a sweater to one of my customers, then finished a crossword puzzle before taking a long walk."

"It was a lovely day. I'm sure the walk was pleasant."

Fern nodded. "It was, indeed."

Wendy turned to Mervin. "And how was your day?"

"I was under the weather, I'm sorry to say."

"Oh?"

"No worries. It might be a touch of the flu."

Her eyes widened. "Really?"

"Oh, *jah*."

Mervin began describing his sniffles and stomach ailments in detail, and Wendy's expression eased when it became apparent that he was something of a hypochondriac. Soon, it became clear she was trying not to laugh.

Obviously not wanting to be rude, she jumped to her feet. "Let me go see if Bonnie and Judith Rose need any help."

As she disappeared into the kitchen, Mervin leaned back. "That girl certainly brightens up the place, doesn't she?"

Grinning, his father said the exact words Lewis had been thinking to himself. "Wendy does, indeed. I'm starting to wonder how we managed without her."

CHAPTER 3

WENDY COULDN'T DENY IT: it was nice not to have to walk to school by herself—especially since Lewis was holding her satchel. It also didn't hurt that her handsome landlord was wearing her favorite dark-blue shirt today. His dark hair was slicked back from his face, his black hat was pulled down a bit to block the sun, and he was wearing a gray hooded sweatshirt too.

"This is so nice of you to help me, Lewis. I was actually dreading my walk this morning."

"I'm not surprised. Your book bag is heavy. It must weigh twenty pounds."

"It felt like double that on my way home yesterday." Her shoulders had ached something awful when she woke up.

"Can't you take less home?"

"I could . . . if I didn't have to do so much work at night."

"How late were you up last night?"

"Midnight."

His green eyes clouded with concern. "Wendy, you should take care. As I've said before, I fear you're going to burn yourself out if you ain't careful."

Since she felt constantly exhausted these days, she knew he had a point. However, Wendy also knew the amount of work couldn't be helped. She needed to be outstanding so the school board would be pleased with her performance. "I hope I don't get burned out after just a few weeks of teaching! After all, my goal is to teach at the school again next year."

"Have you heard anything about that?"

"Not really. It's probably too soon for the school board to make a decision." She was afraid to tell Lewis she'd overheard two of her oldest students whispering that the school board members were actively trying to find someone else. Someone older with more experience.

As if Lewis sensed she wasn't giving him the whole truth, he looked at her with concern again. "We can talk about it, if you'd like. You know, if you just want to discuss what you think might happen. It's always helpful to share one's burdens."

"*Danke*, but that's not necessary." Especially since she was fairly certain neither the parents nor the students wanted her to return in the fall. No one had said anything specific, but she'd gotten the feeling more than once that everyone was simply biding their time until she went away.

If that was true, then she'd be back where she started, desperately hoping another school in the area would give her a chance.

After shifting her tote bag to his opposite shoulder, Lewis said, "I saw you got some letters yesterday."

"I did. They were from my family."

"All four of them?"

Lewis now knew that she was the youngest of five and the recipient of a lot of freely given advice. "*Jah.* Just because I'm in Charm and they're not doesn't change their need to share all their words of wisdom. Though I was thankful that *mei* sister Lena and *mei* brother J.B. elected to keep their opinions to themselves this week."

As she'd hoped, he laughed. "Every time you tell me stories about your family, I'm glad that I'm one of only two children. Plus, Judith Rose and I get along well."

"Being one of two sometimes sounds like heaven." She chuckled. "Though, to be honest, I like to laugh about their meddling, but I know it comes from love. They care about me, which I'm grateful for. Plus, every letter isn't just filled with advice. Sometimes, the notes are simply filled with stories about their days." Thinking about how much she looked forward to their letters, Wendy added, "I'd be lonely if I never heard from them."

"You've got friends here too."

Determined to lighten the mood, she grinned. "That is true. Fern speaks to me now. When I first got here two weeks ago, she wouldn't even look at me."

"Fern's not a big fan of change, I'm afraid."

Looking up at the school ahead, Wendy decided she was feeling vulnerable enough to let her guard down. "She's not the only one. I don't know if I'll ever win over my scholars. They really miss Mary Wagoner."

"Mary is a nice lady, but you are too. Just give it time, Wendy. And don't forget that you're in charge. Not the children. I believe in you."

Her insides melted. "*Danke*, Lewis. I not only appreciate you carrying my book bag, I enjoyed our talk. I've been a little blue of late. I guess I needed a pep talk."

Handing her the satchel, he tipped his hat. "In that case, I'm pleased I was able to give you one. Have a *gut* day, and I'll see you tonight."

Smiling at him, she waved goodbye. "Yes, see you then."

She turned—and ran into Beth Petersheim.

Mrs. Petersheim was in her early forties and was fourteen-year-old Marti's *mamm*. The first time Wendy had met the lady, she'd been grateful. Beth looked energetic and seemed to be very helpful. It was only later Wendy learned the woman was also judgmental, something of a gossip, and a fierce defender of her daughter. Wendy would've applauded that . . . if Marti didn't spend the majority of her days looking bored and acting disrespectful.

Wendy had started to give both mother and daughter a wide berth. She'd known a lot of girls like Marti when she'd been in eighth grade. All they'd wanted was to get through school so they could do what they wished. Marti was no different. And given that it was March, Wendy knew better than to try to convince Marti to suddenly start caring about school or her new teacher.

She just wished Marti's mother cared a little less about school as well.

Bracing herself for Mrs. Petersheim's latest complaint, Wendy forced herself to greet her politely. "Hello, Beth. How are you this morning?"

"Not as good as you, I gather, if you have Lewis Weaver walking you to school now."

She should have known his company would draw attention. "It was kind of him to offer to carry my book bag. I took home a lot of work last night."

There. Perhaps that comment would remind Beth how hard she was working.

"It's a shame you're still having a difficult time managing your schedule, dear. I don't remember Mary ever walking out the door with much. I guess your inexperience is hard to overcome."

Since her shoulder was already protesting the tote's weight, Wendy set it on the ground. "It is no secret that this is my first time to teach. But every teacher I've met has said they worked a lot of hours outside of the classroom their first few years. I guess it's to be expected."

"Perhaps. Perhaps not."

Precious minutes were ticking away. This impromptu meeting was creeping into her prep time and making her frustrated. "My students will start arriving soon. Is there something I may help you with?"

"Marti has shared with me how overwhelmed you've seemed at times. I came to offer my services."

"Your services?"

Mrs. Petersheim inclined her head as though she was bestowing a great honor on Wendy. "Although I am very busy, I decided that it was possible to rearrange my schedule to help you for a few hours every day."

A few hours with nosy Mrs. Petersheim? Wendy couldn't think of anything worse. Struggling to keep her expression serene, she said, "*Danke*, but I don't think that is necessary. I'll be fine."

"You are refusing my offer, Miss Schwartz? You're not even going to consider it?"

Wendy felt like she was being tested, and she wasn't even sure what the test was for. Though there was a small part of her that wanted to give in, her experience with her older siblings was coming in handy. Giving in without a fight was never a good idea.

Taking a deep breath, she said, "Mrs. Petersheim, what I'm attempting to tell you is that both your appearance and your offer have caught me off guard. I'll look at my schedule and get back to you." Thinking quickly, she added, "Would you like to meet me here tomorrow morning? Say, at eight? By then I'll have a better idea about what times of the day might be best for your help."

"Do you not realize that tomorrow is Saturday?"

Boy, Beth's opinion of her was mighty low. "I realize that. But I often come in on Saturday mornings to clean up the room and prepare for the following week." She smiled. "You could help me clean, if you'd like."

Mrs. Petersheim looked like she'd just swallowed a frog. "I don't believe I'm free on Saturday mornings. I spend that precious time with my daughter, you see."

"Oh?" Though she knew her mother would be shaking her head, Wendy continued. "How about Monday at four then?"

The other woman looked like she was tempted to refuse but stopped herself just in time. "*Jah.* I can do that."

Wendy smiled sweetly. "I'm so glad. I'll look forward to visiting with you then. Now, I really must get ready for the day. The eighth graders are presenting science projects, you know. I'm looking forward to seeing what Marti has been working on with you."

As Wendy turned to unlock the door, she could practically feel Beth Petersheim's gaze linger on her back. And because she wasn't near as good a person as her mother had cautioned her to be, Wendy smiled to herself.

She knew for a fact that Marti hadn't done much work on that project at all. It was going to be entertaining to see what her excuse was for not having it ready.

Walking into her classroom, confronted with that first whiff of chalk, glue, and children, Wendy felt a good dose of satisfaction. It was Friday, she was standing in her very own schoolhouse, and she'd just held her own with one of her most challenging parents.

It was going to be a great day.

CHAPTER 4

LEWIS HAD LONG BEEN used to his mother's penchant for community table conversations, but the habit was still new to Wendy. He hoped the good mood he'd left her in this morning had continued throughout the day. Otherwise, he was pretty sure Wendy would find *Mamm*'s "community conversation" extremely irritating.

They'd certainly strained his patience more than a time or two.

Lewis had meant to check on Wendy before suppertime, but Fern told him Wendy had gone to her rooms the moment she'd gotten home. Fern said she'd attempted to chat with Wendy about some of the baby lambs she'd watched during her walk, but Wendy hadn't smiled once at the lambs' antics. In fact, all she'd done was say she needed to take a shower and rest before joining everyone at supper.

However, just like always, she'd run into the house at five on the dot, greeted everyone like usual, and taken her place.

Now she ate spaghetti and seemed rather upbeat. She was chatting with Judith Rose. He'd even heard something about visiting the Berlin Bookmobile when it came to their area on Saturday afternoon.

All of that was why he felt a bit anxious to hear how Wendy would respond to his mother's chosen topic for the weekly Friday-night community conversation.

"Wendy," his mother began with a bright smile, "I thought you would go first this evening."

Setting her fork on the side of her plate, Wendy looked at his mother blankly. "You'd like me to be first for what?"

"Don't you remember, girly?" Mervin asked. "Every Friday we all have to go around the table and answer a question that Bonnie asks."

Wendy looked flustered, "Oh, of course. But I don't have to go first, do I?"

"We all have to go first at one time or another," said Mervin, sounding a bit like he was referring to some kind of awful chore.

"Come along, Wendy," Fern prodded. "The sooner you get going, the sooner we'll get this over with."

Lewis winced as he glanced at his mother. As he'd feared, she looked rather offended.

"No one has to answer or speak if they don't want to," *Mamm* said. "I thought it was an enjoyable tradition." Looking at them all intently, she raised an eyebrow. "Is it not enjoyable?"

"Oh, it's fine," said Fern quickly. "I've never minded it."

As compliments went, it was pretty weak. Though his stomach was growling, Lewis didn't have the heart to make things worse. "What's tonight's question, Mamm?"

"It's a *gut* one. Well, at least I thought it was." She cleared her throat. "Share a high and a low for the day."

"A high and a low," Wendy said.

"You know, like a good thing and a bad thing," Judith Rose added helpfully. "Surely you can come up with something for those things?"

To his dismay, Wendy looked a little pale. "Well, um, my bad thing is that one of my eighth graders brought in a volcano for his science experiment, and it exploded all over the classroom. And me." She took a deep breath. "I suppose my good thing is that I don't have to go back there until Monday."

Mervin sat up, his eyes bright with amusement. "What a time that must have been."

"That's one way of describing it, I suppose," Wendy responded. "It was also a big mess."

"Oh, dear," said *Mamm*.

Daed's lips twitched. "It might be wrong of me, but I would've liked to see that explosion. It sounds like it was quite a sight."

"It was, all right." A wrinkle formed between Wendy's brows. "It would have been more exciting if it hadn't exploded not just on me and Paul but also on little Miriam. She burst into tears."

"Poor Miriam," Judith Rose said. "She's a little thing, *jah*?"

"She's just six." Leaning back, Wendy continued. "Miriam might have gotten over it if her mother hadn't been quite so upset that the new dress she'd just made was likely ruined. Her *mamm* acted like Paul had done it on purpose or something."

"Surely he hadn't," said *Mamm*.

"I know he didn't," Wendy replied, sounding even more aggrieved. "But you see, the problem is that Paul had decided to color the, um, lava with beet juice. It was as red as, um . . . this spaghetti sauce."

"Beet juice does create quite a stain," Fern said. "It will likely never come out. I guess your dress now sports a stain, too, dear?"

"I'm afraid so." Wendy hung her head.

She looked so dejected, Lewis ached for her. Her attitude was a hundred and eighty degrees opposite of how she'd acted when she first arrived. It was hard to see how much her confidence and enthusiasm had fallen in ten days.

"Mamm, who should go next?" he asked.

"Hmm? Oh, um, how about you, Lewis?"

"My high for the day was that I finished the carving on the special-order front door I was working on."

"Congratulations," said *Daed*. "I'm sure it was impressive."

"It looked *gut*. Simon, my boss, seemed real pleased."

"What about your low for the day?" Mervin asked.

"Oh, that is easy. Someone ate my lunch, so I had to buy a sandwich at the café."

"That isn't necessarily a low, though, right?" Judith Rose asked. "I like the sandwiches at the Kinsinger Lumber cafe."

Thinking of how tasty his roast beef and white cheddar on rye had been, he smiled at his sister. "I canna deny that it was tasty. So, perhaps it wasn't exactly a low after all."

"My turn," said Mervin. "My high is that when I went for a little walk today I spied a hawk. *Mei* low is that I received a letter from my son John. His horse fell lame, so he won't be coming this way on Sunday."

"That's a shame," Judith Rose said. "I know you were looking forward to seeing him, Mervin."

And so it continued. As he periodically glanced at Wendy, Lewis noticed she had perked up a bit by the time they'd eaten the dessert Judith Rose had made—chocolate cheesecake.

He had to give credit to his mother. As much as he sometimes grew tired of her Friday discussions, they did bring everyone closer together. He felt sure that if it wasn't for his mother's prodding, Mervin never would've shared his disappointment about his son's missed trip. To Lewis, it seemed like a load had been pulled off Mervin's shoulders too. Mervin had needed to talk about his feelings instead of keeping everything all bottled up.

When they were all finished, Wendy got to her feet. "I'd like to help you ladies do the dishes tonight," she said.

"No need, Wendy," *Mamm* replied. "You pay for room and board. That includes dishes."

"That might be true, but I still think it would do me good to do something productive. I'm not quite ready to sit with my book just yet."

"Come along and help me, then," said *Mamm*. But along the way she nudged Lewis's father . . . who walked over to Lewis as soon as they were alone in the dining room.

"You need to do something with Wendy tonight," he said. "The poor girl can't spend the rest of her evening sitting by herself. She'll stew all night."

"It's dark and cold out. I think it's sleeting too."

"Play a game with her. Get some cards. Or Monopoly or something."

His father sounded extra enthusiastic. If Lewis didn't know better, he'd think his *daed* was playing matchmaker.

Though his first instinct was to leave poor Wendy alone, he realized he really did want to spend some time with her and attempt to cheer her up. "I'll go see what she says."

Two hours later, Wendy's mood was much improved, and Lewis was realizing he wasn't exactly a gracious loser.

"I had no idea you were so good at Monopoly," he said. And yes, he might have sounded disgruntled by it.

Wendy chuckled. "That's because you haven't seen what my family is like when games are involved. We're a crew of cutthroats."

He laughed at the image. "That sounds dangerous."

"It is. Every one of us is competitive and doesn't like to lose." She grinned. "No one takes into account a person's experience or age, either. That means even my grandfather never got any special treatment."

"Or, perhaps, not the youngest member of the family either?" he asked, trying to imagine what all that game playing must have been like for a little girl attempting to keep up with her older siblings.

She chuckled. "I most definitely did not receive special treatment. I had to learn at an early age not to give up. And to be devious."

"Devious, hmm?"

"Oh, I don't cheat or anything. I just learned to give whatever games we played my all."

"Did you ever win?"

"Oh, sure." Her eyes lit up, making her look happier than she'd appeared in days. "The first time I won Scrabble, I was thirteen, and I started jumping up and down like a child. It was a grand moment. Everyone looked just as pleased. My older brother twirled me around in a circle."

The image she spun was a good one. But the story helped him understand something even better. "I'm starting to understand why God put you in this school, Wendy. The average new teacher might just give up, but you are used to overcoming obstacles."

"You know, that's true. I . . . I never thought about it that way." Her eyes widened as she reached for his hand. "*Danke*, Lewis."

"For what?"

"For helping me out so much today. Actually, you've helped me all week, for that matter."

"I haven't done that much."

"You've done more than you know. I'm embarrassed, but I guess I've been feeling a bit sorry for myself these last couple of days. So much so, I had completely forgotten about all the times I lost those games—but how losing made me want to get better."

"Don't be so hard on yourself. I think anyone would've had a tough time in your situation."

"But my response hasn't been like me. Usually I can laugh off little things." She shook her head. "Boy, if my brothers had seen me get so upset about that volcano? Well, they would've told me to stop taking everything so seriously. I'm working with children, not trained pets. Mistakes happen, which is part of learning."

"I guess that's true."

"They would've wondered why I didn't start laughing, and they would've been right too. It was quite a sight, one I know I'll giggle about for years and years."

"So you feel a little better now?"

She nodded. Looking down at his hand that she was still clasping, she dropped it like a hot potato. "I'm sorry I grabbed ya. I . . . I don't know what came over me."

"I didn't mind it one bit," he said. And he surely didn't. The more time they spent together, the more he realized he wanted to get to know her. Wendy was a bright light, and he enjoyed her addition to his life.

She smiled at him, but her cheeks had turned pink. "I think I'm going to head up to my room. I have a new book, you know."

"See you tomorrow. I'm glad we played the game."

"I am too. *Gut naut*, Lewis."

"Good night." He watched her leave and walk down the lighted path to her room. Then, with some regret, he started putting the game pieces away.

Something had changed between them, and he was anxious to see where it led.

CHAPTER 5

THE INSIDE OF THE small wooden phone shanty was cold, especially since it was raining so hard. Though her feet were starting to feel frozen, Wendy did her best to ignore them—and the damp chill in the air.

She had something far better to concentrate on: her family's happy voices on the other end of the line. Everyone gathered around her parents' kitchen phone on Saturdays to check in with her. If she neglected to show up, everyone would worry. Not only did Wendy not want them to ever fret about her, she also needed this time with her parents and siblings. After a lifetime of basically taking them for granted, she treasured every moment with them, even when those moments happened over a phone line.

As she'd expected, her tale of Paul's red-beet volcano had brought roars of laughter.

"If only you could have gotten a picture, Win," her sister Lena said. "I would've loved to see you splatted with that mess."

"I daresay you looked like a crime scene," J.B., her second-oldest brother, joked.

Wendy giggled. "It wasn't quite that bad, but thank you for the description. Now I feel just a bit more exciting."

"I am sorry that Miriam's mother got mad at you, though," her *mamm* said. "If I had been there, I would've told her that new dresses weren't for school."

"It's probably good that you weren't there, then," Wendy said.

"How are all your students otherwise?" *Daed* asked.

"They're all right."

"It doesn't sound like that is true," Henry said. "What's wrong with them now?"

Tears pricked her eyes. That was her eldest brother. No matter how old she got, he would always be her protector. And ever since she'd shared that her students weren't as accepting as she'd hoped, Henry had worried. "Nothing is wrong. It's just that they miss their old teacher."

"And?"

She sighed. "Henry—"

"Tell us, Win," J.B. added. "Remember that part of our agreement with you? Everyone would let you go if you promised to tell us the truth?"

She'd had a lot to say about her family's group decision to "allow" her to go. No matter how many times she'd told them that she didn't need six parents—that two were more than enough, thank you—they'd overruled her.

"Fine," Wendy said at last. "The truth is I don't know if everyone trusts or respects me. Not all the parents and not all the *kinner*." When nobody said a word, she added in a small voice, "I think some of the older kids also don't think I'm old enough to listen to."

"But you are the teacher," *Mamm* pointed out.

"I'm also only five years older than some of the eighth graders." When she heard some of them scoff, Wendy added, "Come now. I'm sure all of you remember what that was like, being full of yourself in eighth grade."

"Perhaps you should come home. There's no need for you to be treated with disrespect," *Daed* said. "Even though you might be a bit on the young side to be in charge of a whole classroom."

"I am not too young," she said forcibly. Okay, she might have shouted it.

"Wendy, there's no need for that," *Mamm* chided.

"I'm sorry, everyone. I just don't want to defend my age anymore. I'm doing the best I can."

"Let's talk about something else," Chrissy interrupted. "How is being a boarder at the Weaver house?"

"It's *gut*." She smiled. "Mrs. Weaver does the funniest thing. She devises topics for conversations on Friday evenings. Everyone has to participate."

"And do you?"

"Oh, *jah*. We don't have a choice. What's funny is the

older boarders, Mervin and Fern, always act like they don't want to say anything, but they seem to like it most of all. Last night's topic was our highs and lows for the day."

"Maybe we should try that from time to time," *Mamm* said.

"No way," said Lena. "I've been enjoying our suppers the same way for twenty years. There's no need to change things now."

That was her sister to a *T*. She was as steady as a contented buggy horse. Lena was loyal and didn't make impulsive choices or decisions.

"Of course you're going to want things to stay the same, Lena," J.B. said. "You never have done well with change."

"Hey," Lena pouted.

"Oh, leave her alone," *Mamm* said. "Her loyalty is a good thing. I'm sure Eli is pleased about it."

"What?" Wendy asked. "Lena, is Eli finally courting you?"

"*Finally* is the key word, Win," said J.B.

"Come now. You must admit that it was likely hard for him to come calling when you boys always seem to be around."

"Hannah is one of seven children. All of them were watching when I called on her," Henry said. "It was about time for Eli to get a bit bolder. Our family is what it is—we're always going to be in each other's business. Besides, Lena isn't getting any younger, you know."

"You see what I have to put up with, Wendy?" Lena complained.

Wendy giggled. "Brothers can be a pain. That's true. Lena, write me all about what happened to make Eli start calling on you."

"I will."

"Now, I want to hear about everyone else."

Showing just why they were the best brothers and sisters, each sibling took a turn and filled in Wendy about their jobs and, in J.B.'s case, his new baby. As she listened, the rain turned to sleet. But inside the little phone shanty her heart felt as warm and cozy as if she were sitting on a comfy chair in front of the fire.

"Wendy, what is that racket?"

"Oh, it's started to sleet."

"You have to walk back in that?"

"Of course, Mamm." Peeking out the window of the shanty, she frowned. It was going to be a rather miserable trip back to her room.

"Do you have a coat?"

"*Jah,* Mamm. I've got an umbrella too. I'll be fine."

"I suppose we should let you go, then, so you can get home."

Knowing they'd been on the phone for almost an hour, Wendy murmured, "I suppose so."

"Would you like one of us to come out there for a few days?" Henry asked. "I could ask Hannah if she'd mind taking some time off."

As much as she knew Henry's steady presence would make her feel better, Wendy also knew she needed to do this herself. If she started leaning on her family too much, she'd have to admit she wasn't ready for a teaching job. And she really wanted to prove to them and herself that she was ready. "*Danke*, but I will be fine, Henry."

"Are you sure? It's no problem."

"Or we could come," *Daed* said. "*Mamm* and I could hire a driver and make a vacation of it."

"That's mighty nice of you, *Daed*. But I'm sure."

"We're proud of you, Wendy. Now go get home before you catch your death," *Mamm* said. "And don't forget to get some sleep."

"And wear socks!" Chrissy teased.

"I won't forget," Wendy said. "Bye, everyone."

After a chorus of goodbyes, she hung up the phone. Then she looked outside. The weather had turned fierce. The wind had picked up and now pelted tiny particles of snow and hail. Her skin was already sporting chill bumps at the thought of heading out into the storm.

After positioning her cloak more securely around her shoulders, she stepped out of the phone shanty and popped open her umbrella. With the way the wind was blowing, she wasn't sure if it would do much good. And indeed, as she walked home, the cold seeped into her clothes and skin and the rain made her mood sink. She felt all alone again and a little more unsure about her path forward.

At least she had the memory of a happy conversation to keep her warm.

CHAPTER 6

"YOU ATTENDING THE SINGING next Sunday night?" Chris asked as he unpacked his cooler.

Lewis always enjoyed watching his best friend at work pull out his dinner bounty. While most men made do with either a simple sandwich or leftovers from the previous night's supper, Chris Borntrager always took great care in what he packed. About two years ago he'd taken up cooking, saying that he saw no reason a bachelor like himself couldn't conquer a few simple recipes.

That first step eventually turned into what he was now—one of the best cooks in the area. He was so gifted, most everyone wondered why he hadn't decided to start working in one of the big restaurants in the area instead of in the lumberyard. But every time one of the men at the mill mentioned the idea, Chris shook his head at the suggestions. Cooking—and eating—were his hobbies, not his vocation.

Personally, Lewis was glad that his buddy intended to keep his position as a master carpenter at Kinsinger Lumber. The man was gifted at trim and in high demand for some of their bigger accounts.

He also brought more than enough food to share every day.

"What is that?" he asked as Chris poured some kind of stew out of his thermos.

"It's chicken-and-andouille-sausage gumbo." Pulling out a plastic container filled to the brim with cornbread, Chris added, "I'm not sharing my gumbo today, but you're welcome to have a piece of cornbread. It has fresh corn, jalapeños, and cheddar cheese baked into it."

Lewis didn't need to be asked twice. *"Danke."*

Chris shrugged like the offer was nothing. But he did raise his eyebrows. "So . . . the singing? Are you going?"

"I wasn't planning on it. What about you?"

"I might." He flashed a smile. "It all depends on if our new teacher is going. Do you know?"

The delicious, moist cornbread suddenly tasted like sawdust. He set it on his plate and took a gulp of Mountain Dew, his vice. After he pulled himself together, he answered Christopher at last. "Are you speaking of Wendy?"

"She's the only new schoolteacher I know of," Chris said as he took another spoonful of gumbo. "Do you know another?"

"Nee."

"And she does live with you. Ain't so?"

"She doesn't live with me. She lives in her furnished apartment on my family's farm."

Chris put his spoon down. "Settle down, Lewis. I realize that. I'm not questioning Wendy's virtue or anything." He smiled. "Just the opposite. I want to get to know her."

"You want to court her?" And yes, he sounded incredulous.

"Maybe, though since I haven't talked to her yet, I thought maybe we'd start off slow. You know, first have a conversation?"

Even though he was fighting off a wave of jealousy, Lewis couldn't help his smile. "That's usually a good first step."

"So, what's she like? She's adorable to look at."

"Wendy is a nice girl."

"She's hardly a girl, Lewis. She's in charge of a whole classroom of squirrelly students."

"She's only nineteen." He mentally cringed, since her young age hadn't done much to cool his own interest in her.

But instead of looking chagrinned, Chris just looked more interested. "That's it? Boy, she must be a mighty *gut* teacher if the school board hired her on."

A little dismayed that Wendy's age didn't seem to deter Chris's interest, he said, "I think she must be a good one. I don't know, though."

"I'll have to ask my aunt about what the board is thinking."

"I didn't know you had a connection with the school-board parents. Who is your aunt?"

"Beth Petersheim."

"I don't know her."

"Can't think why you would. She spends most of her time managing my cousins." He grunted. "They're a handful, Marti especially."

Seeing that their lunch hour was almost over, Lewis began cleaning up his area. But he couldn't leave without saying another word about Wendy—and his feelings for her. "Chris, I'm just gonna be honest. I'm interested in Wendy. I'd rather you didn't pursue her."

"Does she return your feelings?"

"I don't know. I haven't broached the subject."

Chris slowly smiled. "I reckon Wendy's feelings are up to her, then." Standing up, he added, "Encourage her to come to the singing, wouldja? She'll have an opportunity to meet a lot of folks. It will be good for her to make some new friends."

Watching him walk away, Lewis was struck dumb. Though he and Chris were close work friends, they didn't usually do a whole lot together socially. Lewis had thought it was simply because they hadn't had the opportunity, but now he was starting to wonder if it was more because they treated women so differently.

Honestly, he'd never imagined that Chris would ignore his warning like that. It made him a little angry too. His friend was basing a relationship with Wendy solely on her pretty appearance. He really didn't know a thing about her.

After putting his cooler back in his locker, Lewis walked back to his station. However, try as he might, he couldn't ignore that he now had competition for Wendy's interest—

and that Chris could well have the upper hand, since his aunt was probably already close to Wendy.

He was going to have to do some thinking and praying about what to do next.

CHAPTER 7

AS SHE WALKED BESIDE Judith Rose and Lewis on the way to the Lapps' barn, where the evening's singing was taking place, Wendy had the vague sense that Lewis was upset about her going.

So far, every time she'd asked him about the people who were supposed to be there or what some of the activities they usually did were, he'd responded with short, terse answers. It was getting annoying, especially considering the fact that she hadn't exactly wanted to go in the first place.

After her third attempt at conversation with him failed, she turned her attention to Judith Rose. At least *she* had no problems carrying a conversation.

"Tell me again about Marcus, Judith Rose. Did you like each other when you were still in school?"

"Not at all! Marcus wasn't interested in girls back then. Usually, the only time he ever talked to me was to see if I had an extra pencil."

Wendy giggled. "I'm guessing that you wished he had more to say?"

"I certainly did. I've liked him for ages now."

Ignoring Lewis's grunt, Wendy said, "Well, don't keep me in suspense. What changed?"

"I can't really point to one certain moment. All I remember is that one day Marcus only cared about school supplies, and then the next, he smiled at me and said *gut matin*."

"That's so sweet."

Judith Rose nodded. "After we graduated eighth grade, we both got jobs. He started working for his father at the blacksmith shop. I started helping my parents with our boarders and the cooking."

"And now he comes calling?" Wendy didn't recall seeing this mystery man, but that didn't mean much. There had been many days when she'd been in her rooms almost the entire evening.

"He doesn't come calling," Lewis interjected.

For the first time in the conversation, Judith Rose looked unsure. "Marcus hasn't come calling in a while. That's true. But at our last church meeting, he told me that he was looking forward to seeing me this evening."

There seemed to be something off about Judith Rose's story, but Wendy figured she was the last person to judge.

Back in her hometown, she'd been so focused on becoming a teacher she hadn't given any of the men who had shown interest the time of day.

"What my sister is trying to say is that Marcus has been something of a fair-weather suitor."

"That's not true, Lewis," Judith Rose said.

"Well, if he truly liked you, I think he would have shown more interest by now."

Seeing Judith Rose's expression falter, Wendy glared at him. "Lewis, that's rather rude to say, don't you think?"

"I'm her brother. Obviously, I'm going to be watching Marcus carefully. So far, he hasn't done much to lead me to think that she should settle for him."

"You don't know what Marcus thinks or wants," Judith Rose declared.

"I'm sorry, but I don't think you do either." Lifting his chin a bit, Lewis added, "And, before you get upset with me, I feel I should point out that I'm not being mean if I'm stating my opinion."

"Well, I should point out that it was an unasked for opinion."

Wendy covered her mouth to stifle the giggle that was escaping. Which, of course, earned dark looks from both siblings. "Sorry," she muttered. "It's just that you two bickering reminds me so much of me and my brothers and sisters."

Judith Rose looked appalled. "Truly? You all talk to each other like this?"

"Not exactly. We are much blunter."

"Lewis, at last!" a voice cried out. "We've been wondering when you all were going to get here."

Wendy craned her neck then saw a handsome, curly-haired man approaching. It was impossible to not stare at him in appreciation for a few seconds. His hair was dark, his eyes looked to be a light blue, and he was full of muscles. He was also smiling at her like there was no one else in the area.

"Hiya," he said as he stopped right in front of her. "I'm Chris Borntrager."

"Hi. I'm Wendy Schwartz."

"I was hoping you'd be here. I'm guessing Lewis told you that I asked about you at work."

"No. He didn't mention a thing." She glanced at Lewis in confusion.

"I figured it would be best if I didn't so you could come to your own conclusions," Lewis said.

"I see," Wendy said, though she didn't really.

Chris grinned. "That sounds about like Lewis. He's not one for conversation." He waved to the large barn in the distance. "Most everyone is there, and Ben Lapp is working on a bonfire. Will you let me show you around and introduce you to everyone?"

Just hours before, Wendy would have sworn she'd likely never leave Lewis's or Judith Rose's sides. But now she was thinking it might be a good idea to meet some other people. "I'd like that. *Danke*."

"I'll make sure we check in with you often, Lewis," Chris

said as he started to lead Wendy away. "I won't let you leave without her."

Lewis might have grumbled something behind them, but Wendy had no idea what it could have been. All she did know was that if Lewis had been excited to introduce her to other people, he would've.

Instead, he was simply standing in the middle of the lane and watching her walk away.

"Boy, you sure messed that up," Judith Rose said to Lewis after Wendy and Chris had walked out of sight.

Though Lewis reckoned his sister was exactly right, he didn't dare utter that out loud. "I didn't mess anything up. I had to let her go with him."

"Why?"

"Because Chris was anxious to meet her, and Wendy deserves to meet some other people in the community." He wasn't just saying those words either. He meant them. He wanted Wendy to be happy in Charm.

Judith Rose raised her eyebrows. "She's teaching in the school, Lewis. She's meeting lots of people already."

"You know what I mean."

"I suppose, but I think there's more to it. I think you secretly like Wendy Schwartz but are afraid to go after what you want. I think you're becoming mighty good at passing judgments about how other people are supposed to behave but got out of practice when it comes to looking in the mirror."

Again, he feared she might be right. But even if she was, it didn't exactly mean he was anxious to talk about it a couple of yards from all of their friends.

"Why don't you go on in? Marcus is probably waiting on ya."

"I hope so." She trotted inside, leaving him standing alone near the barn's entrance.

Looking around, he spied a couple of people his age. He realized with some dismay that they were there to chaperone the gathering. When he caught one fellow's eye, and the man cast him a knowing look, Lewis felt like he'd never been more embarrassed.

What was wrong with him? Why hadn't he already found someone special?

How come he couldn't seem to stop thinking about Wendy, even though she was one of their boarders? Or was he wrong about that? Did it even matter how they met?

Even though he knew his parents were expecting him to keep an eye on both Wendy and his sister, he felt suddenly tired of always doing what he was supposed to do.

Deciding he needed some time for himself, he strode out to Ben Lapp, who was standing next to the roaring fire and looking mighty pleased with himself.

When Ben spied him, he raised a hand. "Lewis, it's *gut* to see ya."

"*Danke*. Thanks for hosting too."

"It's the least I could do. *Mei frau*'s cousin is in town, and she ain't one for sitting around all weekend. I thought this would keep her occupied for a while. Plus, it gave me a chance to do this." With a proud expression, he pointed to the roaring fire. "It's a good one, ain't so?"

"One of the best I've seen in a while." Lewis wasn't lying. It was a right good bonfire. Everyone seemed to be enjoying it too. "You roasting hot dogs?"

"Hannah considered it, but we decided to stick with s'mores. It's easier that way."

"Want some help getting everything ready? I'd be happy to lend a hand."

"No need. We've got it handled. Besides, you should be enjoying yourself. Are you here for anyone special?"

Lewis felt like his whole face heated up. Was that what everyone was thinking? That he'd come in order to meet girls, just like the sixteen-year-old boys unabashedly flirting next to the barn? "I came here with Judith Rose and Wendy."

"Who's Wendy?"

"She's one of our new boarders. She's the new teacher."

"Ah. I heard she was a pretty thing. Spunky and determined too." Ben paused, as if he'd just noticed that Lewis was standing alone. "So, where is she?"

"I'm not sure. Chris Borntrager took it upon himself to walk her around." He tried to make his voice sound nonchalant, but the reality was he was jealous. Well, at least he had finally admitted it to himself.

"You all right with that?"

"Sure I am." He paused, caught off guard by Ben's look. "I mean, why wouldn't I be?"

Ben stuffed his hands in his pockets. "No reason."

"Are you sure?"

"It's only that Hannah has mentioned Chris has a bit of a reputation. Though I'm guessing you already knew about that."

"I really only know Chris from work. What kind of reputation are you talking about? Is it a bad one?" He was now actively looking through the crowd for them.

"*Nee*, not a bad one," Ben said quickly. "Chris is just a flirt."

"Ah."

"If Wendy is a schoolteacher, I'm sure she can hold her own. Sorry I brought it up."

"No, I'm glad you did."

Looking uncomfortable now, Ben gestured to Judith Rose and Marcus, who had come outside. "At least you don't have to keep too long an eye on your sister. Those two are a match for sure."

"They've been seeing each other a long time."

"And growing closer. I betcha Marcus will be paying a call to your *haus* before too long."

"I hope so. That would relieve my mother's mind, I think."

"Ah, don't be too hard on him. It's a tricky thing, making that visit to a girl's father. *Mei* hands were practically shaking." Ben chuckled. "I tell ya, I was half embarrassed to shake Jonas's hand. I feared he'd discover it sopping wet." Slapping Lewis's shoulder, he said, "Don't worry, buddy. You'll be paying one of those calls before you know it . . . if you can ever decide on the right woman." He chuckled.

"*Jah.*" Lewis smiled uncomfortably.

"Well, I'll leave you to it. I'd best go check on those teens over by my barn." He winked as he wandered off.

Lewis watched him go, stopping to chat with a couple of teenagers along the way. Suddenly, he felt like he'd swum across a creek, and it had turned into a raging river, and he was stuck on the wrong side. Somehow, while he'd been going about his business, working at the lumberyard and helping his parents with the boarders, all of his friends had moved on.

Now he was starting to feel as if he had nothing in common with them anymore. They'd entered the world of wives and pregnancies and homeownership and chaperoning.

He, on the other hand, was settled firmly in the past.

To make matters worse, it looked as if his little sister was going to beat him into that world as well.

"Hiya, Lewis."

He turned to the voice. Maryanne Lapp, Ben's younger sister, smiling up at him. "Evening, Maryanne."

"Ben told me to come over to where everyone else is." She looked up at him with a pretty smile. "Want to join me?"

Good manners meant there was only one acceptable response. "Of course. *Danke.*"

As they started walking, she said, "I was surprised to see you here."

"Oh?"

"I guess I'd thought you'd given up on dating."

"I'm only twenty-five. I'm not an old man."

"No, you aren't. Not even close." She looked down at her feet. "I'm sorry. I didn't mean to offend."

Now he felt even worse—and like a bit of a jerk too. "I'm sorry, Maryanne. Please don't apologize." Realizing that he needed to try harder—Ben was a good friend of his, and Maryanne was a nice woman and easy to be around—he added, "It's been a while since we've spent any time together. Tell me what you've been doing."

She lit up again and proceeded to talk a mile a minute about the toddlers she watched several times a week. Maryanne was entertaining, as well. He found himself chuckling at some of the antics she described. So, all in all, he was glad she'd sought him out.

It was only when he spied Wendy laughing at something Chris said that Lewis realized there was a reason he hadn't already taken a wife. It was because no other woman had grabbed his attention like Wendy. No other woman's laughter sounded as vibrant or companionship seemed as fulfilling. All this time, he'd just been waiting for Wendy to come into his life.

Now all he had to do was figure out how to make sure she didn't leave.

CHAPTER 8

THE HOUR HAD GROWN late, and Wendy was starting to feel uncomfortable. At first, she'd been flattered by Chris's attention and obvious interest. But after the first hour in his company, she'd begun to feel stuck.

To make matters worse, Lewis had never returned to her side. She'd been forced to come to terms with the fact that Lewis had set something up with his friend. He'd brought her there to spend time with Chris, which made her feel slightly sick.

It wasn't that she didn't enjoy Chris's company. It was the fact that he and Lewis had planned it without any thought to her feelings. Lewis hadn't even informed her about it! The more she thought about it, the more she stewed.

Which meant she was becoming increasingly irritated.

"Would you like another s'more?" Chris asked. "I'd be happy to roast a marshmallow for ya. It's no trouble."

"I've already had two, and I fear there's still chocolate on my face."

"There isn't. I would've noticed if there was."

"*Jah*, but would you have told me?" she teased lightly. After all, her irritation wasn't so much with Chris as with Lewis.

He leaned a little closer. "I guess it depends on if I thought you'd let me take care of the mess."

Her eyes widened as she realized what he meant. She wasn't exactly a prude and had let a boy kiss her before. But she certainly wasn't going to allow Chris to kiss her— especially not on the first night they'd met!

Deciding she'd had more than enough of his company, she stood up. "Chris, I'm sorry, but I'm getting tired. Would you help me find Lewis?"

Chris got to his feet as well but looked uneasy. "Lewis? He . . . Well, last time I saw him, he was sitting over with Maryanne and her brother. Do you need something?"

"*Jah*. I need to go home."

"Oh." After a second's pause, he smiled again. "Well, I'd be happy to take you home. Let me just go tell Lewis what we're going to do."

"No offense, but I'd like to talk to Lewis myself, please." When Chris looked like he was going to try to convince her otherwise, she folded her arms over her chest. "Now, where is he?"

Chris pointed toward the cement patio. "He's over there."

"Danke."

As she started walking, she realized Chris wasn't going to accompany her. He was also looking annoyed—rather like a child who hadn't gotten his way. Wendy mentally rolled her eyes. She dealt with children all week; it didn't seem right that she had to put up with such childish behavior the first time she went out too.

Though the idea of simply walking away without another word was tempting, she forced herself to remember her manners and try to end things on a better note. She stopped and turned. "Chris, it was kind of you to spend so much time with me this evening. I really enjoyed it."

"I did, too, Wendy." Thawing slightly, he walked to her side and held out his arm. "Come on. I'll take you over to Lewis."

Feeling better about the situation, she wrapped her fingers around his proffered arm and walked by his side. Noticing how comfortable Lewis looked with his friends and Maryanne, however, she felt her mood shift yet again. She'd been so hopeful this evening would be the start of a romance between them. Now she realized that had been a foolish assumption. One game of Monopoly was not the start of a relationship.

When they were only a few steps away, Lewis raised his head and looked directly at her. She smiled.

He stood up and walked toward them without a single glance back at Maryanne. "Hiya." Looking between her and Chris, he added, "What's going on?"

"Lewis, do you know how much longer you're planning to be here?" she asked.

"Why?"

"She's tired and ready to go home," Chris said.

"Oh." After glancing at Chris again, Lewis offered, "I'll be happy to take you home now if you'd like, Wendy."

"Are you sure?" Realizing that a few other people were actively listening, Wendy felt more like her siblings' pesky little sister than Lewis's boarder and a grown, competent teacher. "I don't want to spoil your evening." She felt her cheeks heat in embarrassment, since it was obvious she was doing just that.

But what else could she say or do? Honestly, she probably wouldn't mind staying longer if she didn't have to be paired with Chris for another two hours.

"You won't spoil it at all," said Lewis easily. "Hey, have you met Ben, Hannah, and Maryann?"

"I don't know." Looking up at Chris, she attempted to joke. "Have I? I feel like you've introduced me to most everyone."

"I think you met everyone but them," Chris said. "But that can be fixed. Ben—"

"I'll do the honors," Lewis interrupted as he took her hand and pulled her closer. "Wendy, please meet Hannah and Ben Lapp. This is their home. And this is Maryanne, Ben's younger sister."

All three of them stood up. Wendy let go of Lewis's hand and stepped nearer. "I'm Wendy Schwartz. Thank you for allowing a stranger into your midst."

"You won't be a stranger for long," said Hannah. "We're happy to have you here. I hear you're doing great things at school."

"I'm trying my best."

"I understand it's your first teaching job. Are you enjoying it?" Ben asked kindly.

"For the most part, I am," she answered honestly. "It's been a bit of a challenge to step into Mrs. Wagoner's shoes. The children liked her very much."

"My aunt said she was a really good teacher but that you are doing all right," Chris said.

She looked at him curiously. "Who is your aunt?"

"Beth Petersheim."

It took just about everything she had to keep a straight face. "*She* is your aunt?"

"*Jah.* Beth is my mother's younger sister." A bit of his confident smile faded. "Do you know her?"

"*Jah.*" Hoping to temper her reaction, she added, "Beth has been to the school many times." Mrs. Petersheim had followed through on her offer to "volunteer" for an hour or two on some days.

"That sounds like her. She likes being involved."

"I've noticed that." Wendy pursed her lips, trying her best to keep a pleasant expression on her face when all she wanted was to say how she really felt about the interfering woman.

Stepping closer, Lewis said, "I'll see you all later. I'm going to take Wendy home."

"Will Marcus be taking Judith Rose home?" Chris asked. "If not, I can walk her for you."

"*Danke*, but she's fine. Judith Rose has already made plans with Marcus." Looking down at Wendy, Lewis smiled. "Shall we get on our way?"

"Yes, please."

After saying their goodbyes again, Wendy followed Lewis through the dwindling crowd. When they finally stepped off the Lapps' lawn and onto the street, she let out a sigh of relief.

Lewis laughed. "Boy, you must have been really tired."

Though it would be easiest to let Lewis think that, she felt compelled to tell him the truth. The last thing she wanted to happen was to be put in that position again. "I am tired, but to be honest, I needed a break from Chris," she explained.

His footsteps slowed. "Why? Did something happen? Was he disrespectful?"

"He was fine, but we didn't really suit." There was no way she was going to share that Chris had been too flirty with her. "Lewis, I . . . Well, I don't like how you just left me with him."

"I didn't just leave you. Every time I looked for you in the crowd, you were smiling. You seemed happy to be by Chris's side."

She wasn't going to let him believe that. "Did it seem that way to you? How did you even know how I was doing, Lewis? You never came over to check on me. You and Judith Rose were the only people I knew. I felt pretty abandoned."

"I . . . I'm sorry. I guess I misinterpreted your happy smiles."

Happy smiles? What in the world? "Lewis, if I was smiling, it was because Chris was amusing and it would've been rude to act otherwise. Besides, I didn't have a choice, did I? I mean, it wasn't like I had anywhere else to go."

He stopped and faced her. "Wendy, you're right. I . . . I wasn't thinking about how my distance would seem to you. I'm sorry."

"I started wondering if the two of you had planned something and neglected to tell me."

"I didn't," he said quickly before shaking his head. "I mean, not really."

"Perhaps you could explain yourself?"

"At work, Chris was talking about you. He'd seen you from a distance and thought you were pretty. I guess he knew a lot about you because of his aunt as well. He begged me to take you to the bonfire so he could meet you. So, in a way, that was why I brought you. But I had intended to stay by your side. I promise you that."

"I really wish you would've done that."

Even in the dark, she could see his frown. "I wish I would have too."

Looking up into Lewis's face, she gathered her courage. "You might think this is bold of me to say, but I'd hoped *you* would be the one to take me around and introduce me to all of your friends."

"Why, Wendy?"

"Because you mean something to me, Lewis, and I hoped I meant something to you too." Mentally cringing, she added, "I mean, I hoped that I meant something more to you than just being one of your boarders."

He chuckled. "You are not just another boarder. I can promise you that."

She gazed into his eyes and leaned forward slightly. She was so ready for him to share what he was thinking as well.

A moment passed before he murmured, "I was jealous of Chris." When she smiled up at him, he reached for her hand, linked his fingers with hers, and they continued their walk.

He might never have noticed in the dark, but she was wearing a very pleased smile the whole rest of the way.

CHAPTER 9

IT WAS MONDAY AGAIN. On Mondays, Wendy assigned spelling words, checked reading logs, and ate lunch with her fifth- and sixth-grade students. She'd learned that half the day seemed to be spent getting her scholars back on track after their busy weekends. However, this Monday was special because it marked her fourth week as a teacher. March had given way to April. She'd now been teaching her students for one whole month.

As she stood in the front of the room and watched them arrive and take care of their backpacks and lunch pails and pull out their supplies, Wendy realized that she'd made great strides. They all called her Miss Schwartz or Miss Wendy now. And she couldn't remember the last time one of the children had begun a sentence with "But Mrs. Wagoner did it this way." Almost all of the students had become helpful and tried hard.

There were two exceptions. The first was Paul, and the second was Marti Petersheim. Maybe it was because they were the two oldest students . . . Or maybe it was because Mrs. Petersheim now visited three afternoons a week and seemed determined to point out every one of Wendy's faults to the whole class.

Whatever the reason, they were very difficult and sometimes even acted as if that was their goal all along.

At first Wendy had felt very discouraged, but both Lewis and her mother had given her the same advice, which was that some children simply weren't going to try to make Wendy's day easier. She could either dwell on the two troublesome teens or focus on the eighteen other children in the building who were becoming so dear to her heart.

"*Gut matin*, scholars," she said with a smile. "I'm glad to see all of you. I trust you had a nice weekend?"

"I did," Jonas said. "But you know that because I saw you yesterday."

"That is true. I saw you as well, Violet," Wendy said.

"I wish I saw you at church," one of her tiny first graders said.

Her school was made up of children from three church districts. "We are all different. That's what makes each of us special, ain't so?" She clapped her hands. "Now, today I am going to work with the older scholars first. Sixth, seventh, and eighth graders, meet me at the circle table in the back. Everyone else may either work on their spelling or read until I get to you."

She picked up her math book, pencil, and chalkboard and headed to the back of the room. Three minutes later, six of the oldest students were sitting with her. One was missing: Marti.

"Marti, please join us now," she said.

"I'm looking for something. You go on ahead."

Wendy had quickly learned that giving Marti an inch meant giving her a mile. "*Nee*, that's not how this works. Please join us now."

Marti rolled her eyes but still didn't seem to be moving any quicker.

"Marti, quit being such a pain and get over here," Jack called out. When Marti froze and glared at him, he shook his head. "Come on. Everyone knows you're just upset that Robbie likes Anna and not you."

Inwardly Wendy winced.

"Shut up, Jack," Marti spat out. Though Wendy noted she had finally taken her seat and actually had her work out.

"Marti, don't say *shut up*," Wendy said.

"That's all you have to say? What about him embarrassing me in front of the whole classroom?"

Before Wendy could say a word, Paul groaned. "Oh, stop, Marti. It ain't like Jack said anything we all didn't already know. Plus, if you would've just come over here, we would've probably already gotten our assignment. You might not care about lugging it all home, but I've got stuff to do when I get home besides homework."

When Marti looked like she was about to start arguing,

Wendy opened the math book. "Everyone, let's review what you remember about fractions from Friday. Who remembers how to get a common denominator?"

Luckily, Autumn, her star pupil, raised her hand and used the chalkboard to explain the steps.

"Very good, Autumn. Now, if you all would switch papers, we'll review your homework, and then I'll give you your assignment. Paul, it's a short assignment today." She smiled. "Hopefully you won't have too much to take home."

For the first time, he smiled right back. "*Danke*, Miss Wendy."

She sailed through the rest of the day. Maybe she'd finally progressed with her class, she thought. That gave her so much hope. She'd learned a lot of things during this first month of teaching. One was that the job was much harder than she'd imagined. She'd been prepared to teach subjects, but she hadn't counted on the amount of time she'd spent as a counselor, moderator, and part-time enforcer. But she'd done those things, and she was still standing. She'd made so much progress that she felt certain by the time Memorial Day arrived at the end of May she'd be looking forward to returning after Labor Day.

Deciding to celebrate by not taking twenty pounds of work back to her rooms, Wendy organized her desk. She'd just put her empty lunch pail in her tote bag when Mrs. Petersheim and Mrs. Beachy, the mother of one of her sixth-grade boys, appeared at her door.

Surprised, she stood up. "Good afternoon. May I help you with something?"

"I'm sure you're ready to go home to relax, but we'd like to speak with you for a few moments," Beth Petersheim said as she walked in. Emma Beachy walked in as well, though she looked a little embarrassed to be there.

"Won't you two sit down?" Wendy's mind started to spin as she watched them each take a chair and bring it to the back table. She couldn't imagine why they had come. It obviously wasn't about Marti.

Then she remembered Emma Beachy was also on the governing council for the school. Her pulse started to race. Maybe they had news about next year?

Taking a seat across from them, she smiled. "I hope you both had a nice Monday?"

"I did," Emma said. "And from what Johnny told me before he ran out to do chores, you had a nice day too."

"I did. It's taken me a little while, but I feel like the children and I have settled into our new routine."

Beth, who sat very primly with her hands folded on her lap, cleared her throat. "Yes, well, that is what we came here to speak to you about."

"Yes?"

"As you know, we are nearing the end of the school year. The last day will be the Friday right after Memorial Day."

They were here to discuss next year! Wendy sat up straighter too. "*Jah*. I had planned on that."

After sharing a look with Emma, Beth cleared her throat again. "Emma and I were the ones chosen to inform you that you will not be asked to return after Labor Day."

Wendy felt like her heart had just free-fallen into her stomach. "Pardon me?"

"I'm sorry, Wendy, but we—I mean, the majority of the parents—have decided to hire someone else for next year."

"Why?" she blurted. "What did I do wrong?"

Looking even more pained, Emma said, "You didn't do anything wrong, dear. It's just . . ." Her voice drifted off.

"While you have been an acceptable substitute, it's become obvious that the children need someone older and with more experience."

"But things have gotten much better. Why, I believe all of the children would tell you the classroom is running smoothly now. They seem happy too." Looking at Emma, Wendy added, "I'm surprised Johnny told you differently."

"He has not had any complaints, but that isn't his way either. He's a good student and gets along well with most people," Emma said. After a pause, she added quietly, "Unfortunately, that doesn't seem to be the case with all the students."

"I see," she said.

Beth stood up. "I'm sorry this isn't the news you had hoped to hear, but I can't imagine you are surprised, Miss Schwartz. We made it quite clear that you were given this temporary position because we simply couldn't find anyone else. We're going to be starting our search for the new teacher very soon. I expect you to help us as much as possible."

Everything in Wendy wanted to shake her head. She didn't want to assist them in their search, and she certainly didn't like how Beth was giving her directions like she had the right to do so.

But of course there was only one thing to say. "I'm always happy to do whatever I can to help the children." She stood up. "Now, if you will excuse me, I'd like to go home."

Looking far too satisfied with the conversation's outcome, Beth inclined her head before walking right out. Emma paused, then put up both her chair and Beth's. Just as she walked out, she turned to face Wendy. "I regret that we had to tell you this news."

"It was hard news to hear. I had hoped things would turn out differently."

A faint flush colored Emma's cheeks before she turned and walked out the door.

Wendy felt frozen as the women's footsteps faded away. She was not going to be asked back. She was so very disappointed, and more than a little surprised. And hurt.

Nee, she was worse than simply hurt. She felt like all the confidence that had taken a month to build up had vanished in a heartbeat.

She felt like such a failure!

Quickly, she gathered her purse and tote bag and rushed out of the room, locking the door behind her as quickly as possible. As she started home, all of the ramifications hit her even harder. She was not only losing her job and dream, she'd have to go back to her family and hear all the reasons why this hadn't been a good idea in the first place.

And she'd also have to leave her cute little room at the Weavers'. And the Friday-night community conversations. And Lewis.

Lewis!

She was going to have to leave Lewis just as she was sure something wonderful was about to happen between them.

She was going to have to leave it all.

CHAPTER 10

LEWIS WAS IN THE living room with his parents about an hour before supper when there came a knock at the door. "I'll get it," he said, thinking that maybe it was Marcus calling for Judith Rose. His sister's beau had taken to stopping by almost every evening since the singing.

"Tell Marcus I made a roast beef and there's plenty for him," *Mamm* called out.

"Will do." Thinking about how his mother was plying Judith Rose's suitor with beef, Lewis was grinning when he opened the door.

But the visitor was a stranger about his age, with brown hair and brown eyes. "Hi, there," he said, feeling foolish. "I'm sorry. I thought you might be someone else. May I help you?"

"I hope so. My name is Henry Schwartz. I'm Wendy's brother. Is she here?"

Ushering him in, Lewis nodded. "*Jah*. I mean, she's in her

rooms over by the barn." He held out his hand. "I'm Lewis Weaver. It's nice to meet you."

Henry's expression softened slightly, but he still looked a bit formidable. "Ah, yes. She's mentioned you. *Gut* to meet you as well," he replied as they shook hands.

Lewis led Henry into the living room. "Mamm, Daed, Wendy's brother Henry is here."

Both of Lewis's parents approached, his father looking concerned, his mother all smiles.

After introductions, *Mamm* said, "Henry, I'm mighty pleased to meet you, but I'm afraid you've caught me off guard. I guess Wendy forgot to tell me that you were going to be paying her a visit."

"I'm sorry I arrived unannounced," Henry murmured. "I thought I would only bother my sister, not the whole household." Looking solemn, he added, "Wendy doesn't know I'm here. I came as a surprise."

Mamm smiled graciously. "Well, now, isn't this the best sort of surprise? I'm sure Wendy will be so happy to see you. Would you like to stay for supper? We eat at five o'clock around here. We're having roast beef."

"*Danke.*" Henry sighed, as if he was frustrated with himself. "I mean, I think that would be nice, but I should probably see what Wendy wants to do first. Maybe she'll want me to take her out to supper so we can talk."

Henry's voice was so somber, Lewis couldn't help but grow concerned. "I'm sorry, but is something the matter? Would you like me to take you to her right away?"

"You know, if you don't mind, it might be best if we talk for a minute or two first. I'd like to know how she's doing."

"Please, come sit down," *Mamm* said. "May I get you some coffee or a glass of water?"

"Actually, I'm more worried than anything. Is she doing all right?"

Henry's expression was somber, his voice thick with tension. It was becoming more and more apparent that he wasn't there just to check on his sister. "What is wrong?" Lewis blurted.

Henry looked from one to the other of them. "Wendy called us on Monday afternoon crying about the news she received at school."

"What news?" *Daed* asked.

Henry looked taken aback. "Wendy didn't speak with you about it?"

"*Nee*," Lewis said, getting impatient now. "What news are ya referring to?"

"That Wendy's teaching contract wasn't renewed." When they all stared at Henry, he added, "It seems that two of her students' mothers showed up on Monday afternoon and told Wendy that the parents' board already decided they don't want her to return next year."

"I canna believe they already made a decision," *Daed* said. "She's only been there for a month."

Henry looked even more irritated. "One of the mothers has been bothering her a lot, apparently. From what Wendy has been relaying, I wouldn't put it past this woman to have forced the board to make a decision. But in any case, they told Wendy the news without any warning. She was blindsided."

"This is awful. Poor little thing." *Mamm* shook her head. "I bet she was heartbroken."

Lewis feared she was. He also thought they had gotten close and was surprised Wendy hadn't confided in him. He wondered why not. Did she not trust him? "I wish she would have shared her news," he said quietly. "I don't know why she didn't."

"I do," Henry responded. "Wendy keeps things to herself. Bad news, anyway. I guess it's the product of being the youngest in the family. We all gather around her and try to fix things."

"Is that why you're here today?" *Daed* asked.

Henry nodded. "All of us have been up in arms from the moment my sister Chrissy heard her crying." He lowered his voice. "I'm afraid we're all pretty hopeless around her. We love her dearly." He sighed. "Since I elected not to join the church, I have a car. So, I volunteered to come check on her."

"She's blessed to have you all," *Daed* said.

"*Danke*, Frank, but at the moment it's all I can do not to march over to those women's doors and give them a piece of my mind. Wendy really loves being a teacher, and this news has crushed her heart."

"She works hard too," said Lewis.

At that moment they all heard footsteps. Familiar footsteps. Getting to his feet, Lewis walked into the hall to meet Wendy. "Hiya. You're early today."

She smiled. "I know! Are you surprised to see me?" she asked. "I decided to get here fifteen minutes early today."

"I have a surprise for you too," Lewis said. "Your brother is here."

"*Mei bruder*? You mean . . ." She moved past Lewis. "Henry?"

Henry was standing tall and still, almost as if he had every right to show up unannounced. But then, as he met Wendy's bewildered expression, he smiled slowly. "Hiya, Wendy."

Wendy looked nervously over at Lewis and his parents before facing her brother again. "Why have you come?"

"Why do you think? You know not a one of us can ever handle you crying. Plus, what happened to you just ain't right. We feel terrible for you. I had to come. Now, get over here and give your big brother a hug."

And just like that, Wendy ran into his awaiting arms. "Oh, Henry, it's been so horrible," she moaned as tears filled her eyes.

He pulled her into another hug and looked at Lewis, who stood helplessly watching them. Lewis wasn't sure if he and his parents should give them some privacy and go to another room or simply stand there in case Wendy finally decided to speak to them.

The decision was made when both Fern and Mervin walked in.

"What on earth has happened?" Fern asked.

Wendy broke apart from her brother. "Mervin and Fern, this is my brother Henry. He came to visit."

"Is he staying for supper?" Mervin asked. "Because it's almost five, you know."

And just like that, they all started laughing. Wendy looked up at Henry. "Would you like to stay for supper or no? Bonnie is a great cook."

"That depends," Henry said. "Is it community conversation night?"

"It's not," *Mamm* answered. "But for you we might make an exception."

"I'll stay, then, but I'll need to clean up first."

"I'll show you where the washroom is," said Judith Rose, who had just walked out of the kitchen.

"*Danke.*" Henry smiled.

While his mother rushed off to fix another place setting and his father walked into the dining room with Mervin and Fern, Lewis stood by Wendy's side.

"Did Henry already tell you why he came?" Wendy asked.

"He did. I'm pretty shocked."

"I've been shocked too."

"I hate the thought of you bearing this burden on your own, Wendy."

"I'm sorry I didn't tell you," she said softly. "But . . . Well, I wasn't ready to talk about it."

"It's okay. Henry relayed that you tend to keep bad news to yourself."

"That's true. I do have that tendency. However, in this case, I think it's simply been that I haven't known what to say. Realizing that everything I've been hoping and praying for is about to slip from my grasp? Well, it's been really hard. I still can't believe it." She straightened her shoulders. "But I'm going to be okay. At the end of the day, I know the Lord will show me the right path. I just have to believe that and be patient."

Lewis was proud of her strength—and felt that her words had a lot of truth to them too. The Lord really was in charge and knew best. Wendy coming into his life was proof of that.

When Wendy noticed Henry walking down the hall, she reached for her brother's hand and escorted him into the dining room. Watching the way she smiled up at her brother, Lewis felt his admiration for Wendy grow. She might be young, but she was as bright as a penny and strong beyond those years. He knew he'd be lost if she wasn't in his life anymore.

Caught up in that thought, Lewis was the last person to the table, but no one appeared to mind. It seemed everyone had something to think about.

CHAPTER 11

AS MUCH AS HENRY'S visit brightened her spirits, the next two days were difficult for Wendy. She felt as if a dark cloud was now hanging over her, and she was besieged by regrets and worries. She found herself doubting everything she did and wished she could go back in time and start over. If such a thing were possible, why, she'd be more confident with her lessons, firmer with the students who didn't mind her, and try harder to win over all the parents.

She'd be a better teacher.

"Miss Wendy?"

Realizing she'd been lost in her thoughts while Becca read next to her, Wendy blinked. "I'm sorry, Becca. Yes?"

The girl pointed out the window. "Have you seen all the snow?"

It had been lightly snowing outside when the children

arrived, but since then she hadn't paid more than scant attention to it. "It is a snowy day, isn't it?"

Looking concerned, little Becca nodded. "Paul said the wind picked up too."

"Don't worry, dear. We're snug in here." By now, she'd learned how to work the kerosene heater and had made the schoolhouse pleasant. So pleasant she'd almost forgotten that it had been snowing at all.

When Becca's worry didn't seem to ease, Wendy smiled more brightly. "Just think of all the snow angels our class will be able to make at recess. That will be a sight to see, ain't so?"

"*Jah*, Miss Schwartz."

After she sent Becca back to her seat, Wendy opened the front door and peeked outside. To her shock, the wind was howling, the snow was practically falling in sheets, and the sky had darkened. It was only eleven o'clock too.

Realizing that several of the *kinner* had gotten to their feet and were staring with wide-eyed wonder at the blizzard, she closed the door securely. "Scholars, I think we'll eat our lunches inside today."

A couple of the children giggled and returned to their desks.

But Paul was still standing next to her. "It's gotten a lot worse, Miss Schwartz."

"It does seem like it, Paul," she murmured.

"I don't know how everyone is going to get home."

She'd thought about that as well. "We'll have to tackle

that problem at three o'clock, Paul. The good news is that we're all safe inside, and the heater is working."

Though he looked skeptical, Paul nodded before going back to sit next to Marti. Wendy noticed that Marti looked worried too. As difficult as the past week had been, both Paul and Marti had been a source of surprise. Their attitudes had greatly improved. They acted more respectful, and they even seemed to like her now. Wendy wasn't sure if their change in demeanor was because they knew she was leaving or because they'd at last decided to stop fighting her so much. Whatever the reason, she was glad of the change.

Feeling the tension in the air, Wendy clapped to get everyone's attention. "Scholars, I know the storm is worrying some of you, but there's nothing we can do about it at the moment. However, I thought I'd read aloud from our book for a little longer than usual today. Each of you may sit quietly and listen or draw at your seats. After that, we'll eat lunch."

Looking pleased about the change in routine, some of the *kinner* pulled out carpet squares and sat near her chair. Others stayed at their seats but pulled out crayons and paper.

When Wendy was satisfied everyone was settled, she opened the library book she'd checked out from the bookmobile: *Dangers in Rocky Hill*.

"Now, where were we?"

"Emmitt had just gotten lost, and the bad guys were nearby!" Jonas said.

"Ah, yes. I've been worrying about them all morning," Wendy exclaimed.

Several of the younger *kinner* giggled while the older students exchanged amused glances. But overriding the laughter and amusement lay a new sense of community. Wendy had been told about that from older, more experienced teachers. There was a moment in every school year that the classroom became like a family. A noisy, sometimes discordant family, to be sure, but a family all the same.

Sitting in front of the students, holding the library book in her hands, Wendy realized that was what had happened for all of them. For better or worse, they'd at last bonded. She knew she needed to thank the Lord for that gift. He'd given her many trials, but He had also given her this success too. No matter what happened in the future, she would always be able to treasure the memory and savor it.

Returning to the moment, she cleared her throat. "Chapter twelve."

As she read the first page—which really was rather exciting—Wendy became lost in the story. Soon, most of the students had stopped drawing. All of them were on the run with the ten-year-old hero of the book.

Then, just as she flipped the page and Emmitt seemed seconds from falling off the edge of a dangerous cliff, the school door opened.

Well, rather, it flew open with a bang.

Wendy felt like she jumped a good foot in the air. A few of the children gasped.

"Sorry if I scared ya," Lewis said as he strode in along with a burst of snow.

Wendy rushed over to him as he slammed the door. "Lewis, what are you doing here? Is everything all right?"

"Hold on, Wendy. Let me thaw out for a minute." Standing next to the heater, he pulled off his gloves and unbuttoned his coat, which she now noticed was covered in snow.

"Miss Wendy?" Becca looked up at her with big eyes. "I'm scared."

She wrapped her arms around the little girl and gave her a hug. "I know, but as I said before, we're snug inside here, and that's what counts."

By the time Becca went to sit by the others, most of the children were either sitting at their desks or standing quietly while Lewis thawed out.

When he turned around to face them all at last, his expression was grave. "Everyone, I spoke with the bishop and stopped by several of your parents' homes. Because the roads are already bad and the storm is supposed to get even worse, it's been decided that everyone should stay put and not go out in this storm."

"But how are we going to get home?" Becca asked.

"No one is going anywhere today or tonight," Lewis said in a firm tone. "All of you are going to have to stay here."

Noticing Becca's bottom lip tremble, Wendy stepped closer to him and lowered her voice. "Lewis, are you sure about this?"

"I'm sorry, but I'm positive. It's as bad a storm as I've ever seen. Everyone has agreed that it's not safe to have anyone out in it. We even discussed the possibility of hiring a driver to come and deliver the children to their homes. But even if we could find someone to do that, it's simply far too dangerous."

"What about you? How will you get home?"

His voice softened. "Oh, Win. I'd never leave you alone. I volunteered to come here to tell you the news and to help." While she digested that information—and the fact that he'd just called her by her nickname—he grinned at the class. "Scholars, it looks like it's back to school for me. I'll be staying with all of ya until morning."

The room erupted into chaos. Children started calling out questions, at least four of them were tugging on her arm for attention, and several began to cry.

Realizing that all of their responses were very normal, Wendy let the chaos reign for five minutes before getting down to business.

"Scholars, I want to talk to all of you. It is time for you to sit down." While they were getting back to their seats, she said a quick, hasty prayer. She also forced herself to relax and to think clearly.

Both the prayer and the mental pep talk helped. She realized all that really mattered was the welfare of the children. She no longer cared about doing the "right" thing in order to gain the board's approval. She'd already lost that battle. Ironically, that knowledge actually made the situation easier to handle. She was going to concentrate on making her students feel cared for and healthy and secure.

When the class quieted, she took a deep breath and began.

"Everyone, I know you are worried and that this is most unusual. However, I agree this decision is for the best. I would be so upset if something happened to one of you—or if one of your parents got sick or hurt trying to come get you.

"The fact of the matter is that you are all wonderful-*gut* students, and smart too. We are also a family of sorts. Together, we'll show everyone in the community that we can handle a little thing like a snowstorm just fine." Looking into each of the twenty shining faces before her, she said, "It is now lunchtime. We're going to have a picnic in the room! Everyone go get your lunch boxes and pails and find a place to sit and enjoy your meal. While you do that, I'll speak with Mr. Lewis and make plans for the rest of our day."

Amazingly, everyone followed her directions without any fuss at all. She noticed some of the older students helping the younger ones, just as they likely did in their homes.

When she was satisfied that she wasn't needed, she walked to Lewis's side. "I'm not sure what will happen next, but I think we'll just take things a minute at a time."

Lewis reached for her hands and squeezed before releasing them again. "Wendy, you are incredible. I'm so glad I'm getting the chance to see you in action."

"Well, I'm mighty grateful that you were the one to come with the news and that you're going to stay with us until the morning."

"I volunteered. I didn't want to be anywhere else but by your side." Suddenly brightening, he said, "I almost forgot—I left a large duffel bag outside on the porch. It's filled with blankets and some hastily packed snacks and sandwiches."

She beamed at him. They had blankets, food, heat, and each other. The next twenty-four hours might not be easy, but they had everything they needed. The Lord really did provide.

CHAPTER 12

IT WAS SIX IN the morning when Lewis realized he and Wendy were the only two people awake in the entire schoolhouse. It had finally stopped snowing about three hours before. Praise God, the wind had died down soon after.

Now, as the first rays of sunlight appeared on the horizon, the weather remained peaceful and still . . . much like the atmosphere in the room where they were all gathered. Wendy sat next to him, the two of them leaning up against the wall. They were close enough for their red plaid blanket to cover both sets of legs. About an hour ago, as she'd lightly dozed, he'd wrapped a comforting arm around her shoulders. Now that she'd sat up, Wendy was using her black cloak as an additional covering over the rest of her body.

Lewis was exhausted but felt surprisingly relaxed too. Glancing at Wendy, he noticed her eyes were at half-mast and she looked at peace.

"Sun's coming up," he whispered.

"That's *gut*." She smiled. "It always does, doesn't it?"

He couldn't help but smile at her—or hide the love he had grown to feel for her. "You look pretty, Win."

Surprise flared in her eyes before she glanced away. "Surely not."

"I wouldn't lie about that." Actually, he didn't know if he'd ever seen a lovelier sight than the morning light shining on her. Not wanting to embarrass her further, he said, "Now that the weather is cleared, I reckon help will be here soon. You, Miss Schwartz, have almost survived your first teacher-led sleepover."

She chuckled. "Indeed I have. But let us hope and pray it's my last teacher-led sleepover too."

Stretching a bit, he looked at her in concern. "How are you feeling?" Yes, her blue dress was wrinkled and wisps of hair had escaped from her white *kapp*, but her eyes appeared bright.

"It's been a long night but . . . not terrible," she whispered. "I can honestly say I've had worse nights than this one."

"I thought the same thing." He would have never guessed that yesterday afternoon and evening would've gone so well or so smoothly. Maybe it was because the children were Amish and not used to a lot of creature comforts. Or because many were treating the experience like a grand adventure. But Lewis believed much of the credit went to Wendy.

She'd been amazing. While the students ate their lunches, she'd gotten out a tablet and quickly written down a schedule—

thinking of activities all the way until eleven that night. After sharing with Lewis that she wasn't even going to attempt to teach math that afternoon, Wendy played games with the kids. Before long, they were immersed in Seven-Up, Duck-Duck-Goose, and Hangman.

She'd also supervised bathroom and water breaks, journal writing, and giving out graham crackers as snacks, and had finally had all the children help her rearrange the room so there would be plenty of places for each child to spread out when it was time to sleep.

Lewis had been wowed by Wendy's seemingly never-ending supply of ideas, treats, and limitless hugs.

"You've made a scary situation feel like an adventure," he said.

"Hardly that. I just have a lot of experience playing with other children. Like I told you, my brothers and sisters and I were a rambunctious lot. We played lots and lots of games when we were little."

"Well, whatever the reason, I feel sure each child will always remember this night fondly. I bet they'll tell their parents that you took good care of them too."

"I didn't do it alone. You helped, Lewis."

"I did what I could, but you were the person they trusted." Feeling like it needed to be said, he added, "I really am sorry that you won't be returning. You should. You're a wonderful-*gut* teacher."

She shrugged. "I'm sure whoever they hire for next year will do just fine. After a lot of prayer, I decided to let my disappointment go. After all, my *mamm* always says that dwelling on things that I canna change doesn't made things better. All it does is foster regret."

While he agreed with the sentiment, Lewis couldn't help but bring up what he'd been thinking and praying about over the last few days. "Wendy, I'm sorry you won't be teaching, but even if you're not, I don't want you to leave Charm. Would you consider staying no matter what?"

"I can't stay and rent a room at your place without a job, Lewis." Even in the dim light, he could see the regret on her features.

He made sure all of the children were still sound asleep before he spoke again. "I know this is a poor time to discuss it . . . but maybe you could stay if you had a better reason."

"Such as?"

"Such as becoming my wife."

She gaped at him. "Are you seriously mentioning marriage right now, right here?" she whispered.

He shrugged. "I guess I am."

"I . . . I don't even know what to say."

"Then how about I do the talking?" Taking care to keep his voice down, he said, "I've fallen in love with you, Wendy. I hate the idea of you leaving. I can't bear the thought of being without you."

Her eyes filled with tears. "Oh, Lewis."

"You don't have to love me back yet." Reaching for her hands, he added, "I don't want to push you . . . but please think about a future with me."

Just as she was about to answer, they heard the unmistakable sound of sleigh bells approaching. Wendy jumped to her feet, glanced out the window, and gasped. "Oh, my word! Lewis! Children, come look!"

One by one, each sleepy child climbed to his or her feet and padded to the window. Almost immediately, cheers rang up around the room.

It was certainly a sight to see too. Seven sleighs were now lined up outside the schoolhouse, each led by horses wearing blankets. Each sleigh held two adults and many more blankets. And the sky! With the clouds gone, the sun was rising over a clear-blue sky. It was beautiful.

Stretching out her arms, Wendy beamed at them all. "Children, let's open the door and welcome everyone in!"

That was all the prompting they needed. Paul, who had been standing next to the door, opened it and peeked out. "Hiya," he said simply to the crowd that stood outside.

Next thing Lewis knew, the room was flooded with parents, promises that more parents were waiting at home, and lots of exclamations and hugs. Children talked excitedly, sharing stories about their adventures and pointing out their makeshift beds.

Emma Beachy walked right up to Wendy and gave her a hug. "*Danke* for taking such good care of the children."

Startled by the hug as much as the kind words, Wendy nodded. "You're welcome, but they took care of me too."

"I won't forget this," said Emma. "None of us will. You took care of our *kinner* when we couldn't."

"I'm glad I was here."

"And still in one piece too," teased a father of one of the children.

Looking at all the children fondly, Wendy smiled. "I have a feeling, years from now, after I've taught many, many children, lots of those days will meld together. But I can be fairly certain I'll never forget the last twenty hours."

"You know, you're right," said Emma. "It's always the burnt dinners, messed-up plans, and broken bones that one talks about, isn't it?"

And with that, Emma and two other parents proceeded to help Wendy, Lewis, and the other adults gather up the children, fold blankets, throw away trash, and begin bundling students and taking them out to the sleighs. In the midst of it all, there were lots of hugs and jokes between Wendy and her twenty students.

Finally, there was only one sleigh left. "This one is for you," Jonas's father said. Grinning, he added, "It's also my pleasure to inform you that there will be no school today or tomorrow. We'll see you on Monday."

"*Danke*," said Wendy, her voice subdued. Lewis figured she was exhausted. He knew he was, and he hadn't been feeling the weight of responsibility she had.

"Hand me the key, and I'll lock the door, Win," he said as she stepped out into the cold.

"What about the blankets and such? I'll need to sort them and—"

"And there will be plenty of time this weekend. Not

today." He waggled his fingers. "The key, if you please?" After she handed it to him, he locked the door and took her elbow to help her down the steps and into the sleigh.

"Here's a good blanket," Emma said. "It was the warmest one we had at the house."

"It's cozy, *danke*," Wendy said.

Lewis got in beside her and wrapped his arm around her shoulders. Minutes later they were off. The horse practically pranced and danced in the snow as he led the sleigh down the snowy road. Jingle bells rang through the air, making the moment magical.

On another day, at another time, Lewis knew it would feel incredible to be sitting in a sleigh with his arm around Wendy. However, at the moment, all he felt was relief that they'd made it through the day and night.

"Wendy, isn't it pretty out?"

It was a shame she was already asleep.

Smiling to himself, he realized Wendy had been wrong. It wasn't just the bad moments that were memorable. Sometimes, it was a perfect instant like this.

CHAPTER 13

WENDY COULDN'T RECALL IF she'd ever felt so motivated to go to church. After their return home on Thursday, she'd eaten a hot breakfast, taken a long bath, then fallen into bed. She'd slept most of the day. Bonnie had even delivered some soup and a grilled cheese sandwich to her room on Thursday evening. After Wendy ate, she again fell into an exhausted slumber.

On Friday, she'd finally walked down to the phone shanty to tell her whole family about her week. Then she'd hung around the main house with Lewis and his family. They seemed content to play cards and games with her and Lewis. Mervin and Fern even spent time with them. Fern, especially, loved hearing all of their middle-of-the-night stories.

By Saturday, Wendy felt a lot more like herself and was ready to put her classroom back to rights. All of Lewis's family—and Mervin and Fern—came to the schoolhouse and helped. The men shoveled, Fern and Judith Rose cleaned the bathroom and swept the floor, and Bonnie and Lewis helped Wendy wash the blackboard, rearrange the desks, and generally put everything back into place. Frank even made sure the heater was filled with kerosene and working properly.

By the time they left, feeling worn out but exhilarated, Wendy was ready to face another week.

Sunday, however, was a day to be spent giving thanks, and Wendy didn't know if she'd ever feel as thankful as she did that day. By the time the service was over, she'd expressed her gratitude to the Lord and also praised Him for the blessings He'd bestowed.

They stayed quite a while at the hosts' house for the luncheon. It was midafternoon when they finally headed back home.

But when the buggy arrived at the Weavers' property, Wendy was shocked to see a big group there. All her students—and all their parents. When Frank parked his buggy, the crowd cheered.

"What is going on?" she asked Bonnie. When Bonnie just smiled, Wendy realized she was the only person who'd been in the dark. "You knew about this?"

"Well, of course! Why do you think we stayed at the luncheon so long?"

Judith Rose nodded. "We all kept whispering to each other to make up more excuses to stay."

"Miss Schwartz!" several children called out to her.

Turning to them, Wendy felt her heart fill. She'd actually missed them!

After she'd greeted all the children—each of whom seemed determined to tell her how they'd been—five parents approached. Wendy knew they were the school board. Mrs. Petersheim was in the middle, and Emma Beachy stood right by her side.

Sounding rather imperious, Beth said, "Wendy, we came over not only to thank you for the care of our children but to tell you how impressed we were with how you handled the whole day's and evening's events during the snowstorm. It couldn't have been easy, but from everything we've heard, you made the children feel secure, safe, and even happy."

"*Danke.* I canna take all the credit, though. Lewis was there with blankets and food. He also helped in many ways." Looking out at the twenty faces she knew she was going to miss so much, Wendy added, "Plus, your children are wonderful. They were helpful and kind to each other. Anyone would have done well with them."

Beth cleared her throat. "Actually, we don't think that is true. Marti made a point to inform me she didn't think any teacher but *you* could have taken care of the class as well. She—and most every other one of the students—can't praise you enough. Marti has even shared that she thinks I've been far too judgmental and hard on you." After taking a breath, Mrs. Petersheim nodded. "I think she is probably correct. I am sorry that I doubted you so much, Miss Schwartz."

"I . . . *danke*, Mrs. Petersheim."

"I hope you will forgive my initial lack of support."

"There is nothing to forgive. I promise." Not knowing what else to say, Wendy turned to Lewis for help.

He moved closer to her side. Smiling down at her, he said, "Well, now. It seems our Wendy is at a loss for words. Maybe you should tell her the other reason you came, Beth."

With a happy smile, Mrs. Petersheim continued. "I'll be glad to do that." She took a deep breath. "Wendy, we took a vote, and it's unanimous. We'd like you to return next year."

Wendy froze. "I'm sorry?"

One of the gentlemen came forward. "We can discuss this later, but we're also giving you a raise. This week's adventure made us all realize—especially after speaking with Lewis here—that we expect a great deal from you. You should be compensated."

Wendy turned to Lewis in shock. "What did you say?"

"I'll tell you later."

Emma Beachy reached out and clasped Wendy's hand. "Please say you'll think about it. We want you to be our children's teacher next year and maybe even longer. Why, even if you marry, we'd like you to stay at the school."

Frank Weaver laughed. "It sounds like you had quite a talk with the school board, Lewis."

He inclined his head. "I did have quite a bit to say."

"Now, let's have cake!" Becca said. "*Mei mamm* made a big one!"

Realizing there would be plenty of time to contemplate

everything the school board members had said, Wendy laughed and smiled at Becca. "Yes, by all means. Let's have cake. It seems we have much to celebrate."

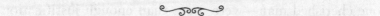

Later that night, long after they'd eaten lots of cake and a light supper, and after everyone else had gone to bed, Lewis held Wendy close on the sofa in the living room. Two vanilla-scented candles burned nearby, and the fireplace still glowed with the last of the embers.

Soon, there wouldn't be any more surprise bursts of snow, and they'd only be looking forward to warm sunny days and maybe the chance of rain.

Wendy couldn't remember when she'd ever been so happy. She'd loved seeing the children earlier and had been so touched by all of the parents' compliments and gratitude.

"So, what do you want to do? Have you given it some thought?"

"I have." She smiled. "What do you think I should do?"

"You know what I think. I want you to marry me, be my wife, and teach children to your heart's content."

She raised her eyebrows. "Do you really think I can do all that?"

"Of course I do. After all, I think you already have. And if you have any doubts, I can name twenty reasons why you need to stay. No, make that twenty-one," he said as he kissed her.

Wendy kissed him back, loving the way he held her so close and whispered promises every time they paused for breath. Lewis was right, she realized.

Twenty-one reasons—twenty bright young students and one cherished man—were more than enough justification to say yes.

Especially because all she'd really needed was one reason: Lewis's love.

ACKNOWLEDGMENTS

ONCE AGAIN, I'M HONORED for the opportunity to work with the team at HarperCollins Christian Publishing. I'm so grateful to the many people who work so hard to make these collections come to life. I'm in awe of your hard work, expertise, and dedication.

DISCUSSION QUESTIONS

1. Wendy is close to her family and both enjoys and dreads their attempts to offer advice. Who in your family dispenses the most advice? What is some of the best advice you've been given?

2. Wendy's first "real" teaching job is filled with a lot of mistakes and rewards. How does that compare to your first "real" job?

3. What did you think about Lewis? Why was he such a good match for Wendy?

4. How would you have handled the storm? Have you ever been forced to change your plans or make sacrifices because of bad weather? What did you learn from that experience?

5. The following verse from Proverbs guided the writing of this story. What does it mean to you? "Joyful is the person who finds wisdom, the one who gains understanding" (Proverbs 3:13).

6. I thought the following Amish proverb fit Wendy's story well. How might it apply to something that's happened in your life? *"We make our decisions, and then our decisions turn around and make us."*

Cozy up with three charming stories of quilting circles and budding romances.

COMING DECEMBER 2021

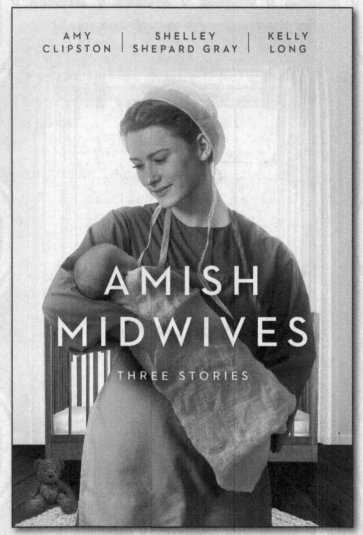

ABOUT THE AUTHORS

AMY CLIPSTON

Amy Clipston is the award-winning and bestselling author of the Kauffman Amish Bakery, Hearts of Lancaster Grand Hotel, Amish Heirloom, Amish Homestead, and Amish Marketplace series. Her novels have hit multiple bestseller lists including CBD, CBA, and ECPA. Amy holds a degree in communication from Virginia Wesleyan University and works full-time for the City of Charlotte, NC. Amy lives in North Carolina with her husband, two sons, and five spoiled rotten cats.

Photo by Dan Davis Photography

Visit her online at AmyClipston.com
Facebook: @AmyClipstonBooks
Twitter: @AmyClipston
Instagram: @amy_clipston
Bookbub: bookbub.com/profile/amy-clipston

KATHLEEN FULLER

With over a million copies sold, Kathleen Fuller is the author of several bestselling novels, including the Hearts of Middlefield novels, the Middlefield Family novels, the Amish of Birch Creek series, and the Amish Letters series as well as a middle-grade Amish series, the Mysteries of Middlefield.

❧

Visit her online at KathleenFuller.com
Facebook: @WriterKathleenFuller
Twitter: @TheKatJam
Instagram: @kf_booksandhooks